THE VANCOUVER STORIES

West Coast Fiction from Canada's Best Writers

INTRODUCTION BY DOUGLAS COUPLAND

RAINCOAST BOOKS
Vancouver

Raincoast Books gratefully acknowledges The Listel Hotel for inspiring and helping conceive this collection. Their ongoing support of the arts in Vancouver is admirable.

Editor: Derek Fairbridge
Text design and typesetting: Tannice Goddard

LIBRARY AND ARCHIVES CANADA CATALOGUING IN PUBLICATION

The Vancouver stories: West Coast fiction from Canada's best writers.

ISBN 13: 978-1-55192-795-4
ISBN 10: 1-55192-795-0

1. Vancouver (B.C.) — Fiction. 2. Short stories, Canadian (English)
3. Canadian fiction (English) — 20th century.

PS8323.V35V36 2005   C813'.01083271133   C2004-906938-1

Raincoast Books
9050 Shaughnessy Street
Vancouver, British Columbia
Canada V6P 6E5
www.raincoast.com

At Raincoast Books we are committed to protecting the environment and to the responsible use of natural resources. We are acting on this commitment by working with suppliers and printers to phase out our use of paper produced from ancient forests. This book is one step towards that goal. It is printed on 100% ancient-forest-free paper (100% post-consumer recycled), processed chlorine- and acid-free, and supplied by New Leaf paper. It is printed with vegetable-based inks. For further information, visit our website at www.raincoast.com. We are working with Markets Initiative (www.oldgrowthfree.com) on this project.

Printed in Canada
10 9 8 7 6 5 4 3 2

FOREWORD

Our dream for this book is that it will give our guests an experience of Vancouver beyond the typical tourist fare, beyond the stuff of oceans and mountain vistas. We want our guests to get a taste of our city's diversity, from the village of Lee Maracle's Downtown Eastside, through the multi-generational homes of Wayson Choy's Chinatown, to Shani Mootoo's sugar-laden Main Street. This collection will also give a sense of this city's history, from the legends of Pauline Johnson, to Ethel Wilson's evocation of the early 1900s, through to Stephen Osborne's present day and on to William Gibson's future. And we want our guests to have this experience simply by rolling over in bed and fishing through the drawer of their bedside table!

We also wish for travellers to Vancouver to hear the city's finest jazz, taste the Okanagan's finest wines, view the works of our country's most extraordinary artists, all without leaving our hotel. Art critic Robin Laurence once called us "Vancouver's

Most Art-Full" hotel. We are very proud of this epithet, and we're determined to remain worthy of it for years to come.

For their enthusiasm and professionalism, we thank Derek Fairbridge, Michelle Benjamin and Lynn Henry of Raincoast Books. For their continued support in our vision of a symbiotic partnership with the visual, performing and written arts, we must thank our indulgent owners, the Suzuki family.

We dedicate this book to the curious traveller.

— *The Listel Hotel*

CONTENTS

INTRODUCTION

Douglas Coupland

I was late for a one o'clock lunch meeting with the editor of this book you hold in your hands. I needed to drive from downtown Vancouver to the North Shore, and what ought to have taken fifteen minutes took forty-five — forty-five *lonnngggg* minutes. A simple drive across town assumed the look and feel of a military driving-simulator test with the dial marked "VANCOUVER" cranked to its highest level.

For starters, most of the three-lane one-way streets downtown were pared down to one lane to make way for two film shoots and the construction of dozens of condominium towers. Protesters outside the Vancouver Art Gallery's back steps shut down the corners of Hornby, Georgia and Howe. And it was American Thanksgiving, so the roads were packed with dawdling tourists from California, Oregon and Washington. Exiting downtown and headed on to the Stanley Park causeway, a Rolls-Royce had stalled just past Lost Lagoon, forcing cranky drivers to cut through the park, where a conga line of hissing Canada geese waddled across Park Drive, letting everybody in their cars know just who held the power here. Once on Lions Gate Bridge, traffic flew into West Vancouver and I showed up about a half-hour late, just in time to see municipal workers finish installing white Christmas lights on the palm trees at Dundarave Pier. After lunch I drove home to find that in my absence, two bear cubs had made piñatas of my trashcans and had converted the garage into a customized private landfill.

The whole episode reminded me of a visit a few years back from an American friend. As I was driving her out to the Museum of Anthropology at UBC, she kept on saying, "Doug, take the faster way! Take the faster way!" I assured her there was no such thing in Vancouver, but she didn't believe me. I said, "They were going to build a freeway from downtown out to the Trans-Canada in the late sixties and early seventies, but it got killed by green politics."

"Doug, even Honolulu has a freeway."

"You have to trust me. There is no faster way."

She moved to Vancouver shortly thereafter, and years later at a dinner she laughed about her impatience. "Okay, I crumble on this issue. There really *is* no faster way in Vancouver."

Quickly, what makes Vancouver, Vancouver? Here's a crash course outline (in no particular order):

Bridge traffic; mountains; tall trees; outdoor sports; the bodies to match those sports; outdoor clothing to cover those bodies; nude sunbathing; pot; sushi; dim sum; Chinatown; Sikh temples; multiethnic couples; First Nations culture; wildlife (especially whales); hostility toward smokers; ferries; a really good airport; cruise ships in summer; the film industry; green politics; empty glass towers; rhododendrons; Japanese maples; hydroponic agriculture; appalling real estate prices; interesting architecture from 1946 to 1970; vague earthquake jitters; a sense of disconnection from the rest of Canada; the US is close (but somehow far away, too); people from elsewhere who want to vanish; people from elsewhere who want the city to fix them; harbours, inlets and bridges; log booms, wheat pools and rail cars ...

Some of these items are cliché yet they remain integral to the city's character. Many of these traits are also shared by other cities, but with Vancouver it's the amount and combination that make the place what it is.

January 01, 2005. It's a month after my lunch meeting. I'm returning from New York City on Cathay Airlines flight 889, the first leg of the New York-Hong Kong milk run. This flight and its sister flight, 888, are yet two more things that makes Vancouver, Vancouver. For those who commute between Vancouver and the US regularly, this flight is as commonplace as a ride on an elevator. Seated a few rows up is Vancouver's local-boy-made-good, actor Michael J. Fox. About half of the passengers are watching programs on video screens in Cantonese, the other half in English. Two films on the video menu were made in Vancouver.

I'm still looking for an easy answer to the question that came up at that lunch meeting: what makes Vancouver the place it is? But I doubt there is an easy answer. Part of living in Vancouver is dealing with people from elsewhere making too many dorky oversimplifications about this city — often made after a failed attempt to localize themselves. Many of the characters in the stories in this book confront both their expectations of Vancouver and the realities they eventually encounter here.

But here's an idea: maybe Vancouver is simply a nice place to live. It has warts and inconsistencies and flaws, too, all of which are chronicled herein, but on the whole Vancouver is simply nice. Maybe it's *too* nice?

A few minutes later, just before landing:

Earlier on I listed some traits that define Vancouver, but ultimately it's stories like the ones in this book that define a place. To read these stories feels like an adventure in time travel. From Pauline Johnson onward to Bill Gibson, we blast across a century and watch the city morph not only in shape but in emotional texture, and dream life as well. And at the end of this collection, the reader will be left with a sense of momentum that might gently nudge them into guessing where the city is headed next.

We're losing altitude, so I have to be quick: Above all, remember that the one thing that defines Vancouver more than any other trait is that it's a young place — one of the youngest cities on earth — and as such it's very much a work in progress. It's one of the few remaining cities in North America that has yet to become what it will finally be. There is joy to be found in being young. There is joy to be found in not being fully formed. And there is joy to be found in this book's stories.

THE TWO SISTERS

Pauline Johnson

You can see them as you look towards the north and the west, where the dream-hills swim into the sky amid their ever-drifting clouds of pearl and grey. They catch the earliest hint of sunrise, they hold the last colour of sunset. Twin mountains they are, lifting their twin peaks above the fairest city in all Canada, and known throughout the British Empire as "The Lions of Vancouver."

Sometimes the smoke of forest fires blurs them until they gleam like opals in a purple atmosphere, too beautiful for words to paint. Sometimes the slanting rains festoon scarves of mist about their crests, and the peaks fade into shadowy outlines, melting, melting, forever melting into the distances. But for most days in the year the sun circles the twin glories with a sweep of gold. The moon washes them with a torrent of silver.

Oftentimes, when the city is shrouded in rain, the sun yellows their snows to a deep orange; but through sun and shadow they stand immovable, smiling westward above the waters of the restless Pacific, eastward above the superb beauty of the Capilano Canyon. But the Indian tribes do not know these peaks as "The Lions." Even the chief whose feet have so recently wandered to the Happy Hunting Grounds never heard the name given them until I mentioned it to him one dreamy August day, as together we followed the trail leading to the canyon. He seemed so surprised at the name that I mentioned the reason it had been applied to them, asking him if he recalled the Landseer Lions in Trafalgar Square. Yes, he remembered those splendid sculptures, and his quick eye saw the resemblance instantly. It appeared to please him, and his fine face expressed the haunting memories of the faraway roar of Old London. But the "call of the blood" was stronger, and presently he referred to the Indian legend of those peaks — a legend that I have reason to believe is absolutely unknown to thousands of Pale-faces who look upon "The Lions" daily, without the love for them that is in the Indian heart, without knowledge of the secret of "The Two Sisters." The legend was intensely fascinating as it left his lips in the quaint broken English that is never so dulcet as when it slips from an Indian tongue. His inimitable gestures, strong, graceful, comprehensive, were like a perfectly chosen frame embracing a delicate painting, and his brooding eyes were as the light in which the picture hung.

"Many thousands of years ago," he began, "there were no twin peaks like sentinels guarding the outposts of this sunset coast. They were placed there long after the first creation, when the Sagalie Tyee moulded the mountains, and patterned the mighty rivers where the salmon run, because of His love for His Indian children, and His wisdom for their necessities. In those times there were many and mighty Indian tribes along the Pacific — in the mountain ranges, at the shores and sources of the great Fraser River. Indian Law ruled the land. Indian customs prevailed. Indian beliefs were regarded. Those were the legend-making ages when great things occurred to make the traditions we repeat to our children today. Perhaps the greatest of these traditions is the story of 'The Two Sisters,' for they are known to us as 'The Chief's Daughters,' and to them we owe the Great Peace in which we live, and have lived for many countless moons.

"There is an ancient custom amongst the coast tribes that, when our daughters step from childhood into the great world of womanhood, the occasion must be made one of extreme rejoicing. The being who possesses the possibility of some day mothering a man-child, a warrior, a brave, receives much consideration in most nations; but to us, the Sunset tribes, she is honoured above all people. The parents usually give a great potlatch, and a feast that lasts many days. The entire tribe and the surrounding tribes are bidden to this festival. More than that, sometimes when a great Tyee celebrates for his daughter, the tribes from far up the coast, from the distant north, from inland, from the island, from the Cariboo country, are gathered as guests to the feast. During these days of rejoicing the girl is placed in a high seat, an exalted position, for is she not marriageable? And does not marriage mean motherhood? And does not motherhood mean a vaster nation of brave sons and of gentle daughters, who, in their turn, will give us sons and daughters of their own?

"But it was many thousands of years ago that a great Tyee had two daughters that grew to womanhood at the same springtime, when the first great run of salmon thronged the rivers, and the ollallie bushes were heavy with blossoms. These two daughters were young, lovable and oh! very beautiful. Their father, the great Tyee, prepared to make a feast such as the coast had never seen. There were to be days and days of rejoicing, the people were to come for many leagues, were to bring gifts to the girls and to receive gifts of great value from the chief, and hospitality was to reign as long as pleasuring feet could dance, and enjoying lips could laugh, and mouths partake of the excellence of the chief's fish, game and ollallies.

"The only shadow on the joy of it all was war, for the tribe of the great Tyee was at war with the Upper Coast Indians, those who lived north, near what is named by the Pale-face as the port of Prince Rupert. Giant war-canoes slipped along the entire coast, war-parties paddled up and down, war-songs broke the silences of the nights, hatred, vengeance, strife, horror festered everywhere like sores on the surface of the earth. But the great Tyee, after warring for weeks, turned and laughed at the battled and the bloodshed, for he had been victor in every encounter, and he could well afford to leave the strife for a brief week and feast in his daughters' honour, not permit any mere enemy to come between him and the traditions of his race and household. So he turned insultingly deaf ears to their war-cries; he ignored with arrogant indifference their paddle-dips that encroached within his own coast water; and he prepared, as a great Tyee should, to royally entertain his tribesmen in honour of his daughters.

"But seven suns before the great feast, these two maidens came before him, hand clasped in hand.

"'Oh! our father,' they said, 'may we speak?'

"'Speak, my daughters, my girls with the eyes of April, the hearts of June' (early spring and early summer would be the more accurate Indian phrasing).

"'Some day, oh! our father, we may mother a man-child, who may grow to be just such a powerful Tyee as you are, and for this honour that may some day be ours we have come to crave a favour of you — you, oh! our father.'

"'It is your privilege at this celebration to receive any favour your hearts may wish,' he replied graciously, placing his fingers beneath their girlish chins. 'The favour is yours before you ask it, my daughters.'

"'Will you, for our sakes, invite the great northern hostile tribe — the tribe you war upon — to this, our feast?' they asked fearlessly.

"'To a peaceful feast, a feast in the honour of women?' he exclaimed incredulously.

"'So we desire it,' they answered.

"'And so shall it be,' he declared. 'I can deny you nothing this day, and some time you may bear sons to bless this peace you have asked, and to bless their mother's sire for granting it.' Then he turned to all the young men of the tribe and commanded: 'Build fires at sunset on all the coast headlands — fires of welcome. Man your canoes and face the north, greet the enemy, and tell them that I, the Tyee of the Capilanos, ask — no, command — that they join me for a great feast in honour of my two daughters.'

"And when the northern tribe got this invitation they flocked down the coast to this feast of a Great Peace. They brought their women and their children; they brought game and fish, gold and white stone beads, baskets and carven ladles, and wonderful woven blankets to lay at the feet of their now acknowledged ruler, the great Tyee. And he, in turn, gave such a potlatch that nothing but tradition can vie with it. There were long, glad days of joyousness, long, pleasurable nights of dancing and campfires, and vast quantities of food. The war-canoes were emptied of their deadly weapons and filled with the daily catch of salmon. The hostile war-songs ceased, and in their place was heard the soft shuffle of dancing feet, the singing voices of women, the play-games of the children of two powerful tribes which had been until now ancient enemies, for a great and lasting brotherhood was sealed between them — their war-songs were ended forever.

"Then the Sagalie Tyee smiled on His Indian children: 'I will make these young-eyed maidens immortal,' He said. In the cup of His hands He lifted the chief's two daughters and set them for ever in a high place, for they had borne two offspring —

Peace and Brotherhood — each of which is now a great Tyee ruling this land.

"And on the mountain crest the chief's daughters can be seen wrapped in the suns, the snows, the stars of all seasons, for they have stood in this high place for thousands of years, and will stand for thousands of years to come, guarding the peace of the Pacific Coast and the quiet of the Capilano Canyon."

This is the Indian legend of "The Lions of Vancouver" as I had it from one who will tell me no more the traditions of his people.

DOWN AT ENGLISH BAY

Ethel Wilson

Once upon a time there was a Negro who lived in Vancouver and his name was Joe Fortes. He lived in a small house by the beach at English Bay and there is now a little bronze plaque to his honour and memory nearby, and he taught hundreds of little boys and girls how to swim. First of all he taught them for the love of it and after that he was paid a small salary by the City Council or the Parks Board, but he taught for love just the same. And so it is that now there are Judges, and Aldermen, and Cabinet Ministers, and lawyers, and doctors, and magnates, and ordinary business men, and grandmothers, and prostitutes, and burglars, and Sunday School superintendents, and drycleaners, and so on whom Joe Fortes taught to swim, and they will be the first to admit it. And Joe Fortes saved several people from drowning; some of them were worth saving and some were not worth saving in the slightest — take the man who was hanged in Kingston jail; but Joe Fortes could not be expected to know this, so he saved everyone regardless. He was greatly beloved and he was respected.

Joe Fortes was always surrounded by little boys and girls in queer bathing suits in the summertime. The little boys' bathing suits had arms and legs, not to speak of bodies and almost skirts on them; and the little girls were covered from neck to calf in blue serge or alpaca with white braid — rows of it — round the sailor collar and the full skirt, and a good pair of black wool stockings. This all helped to weigh them down when they tried to learn to swim, and to drown the little girls, in particular, when possible.

Joe had a nice round brown face and a beautiful brown body and arms and legs as he waded majestically in the waves of English Bay amongst all the little white lawyers and doctors and trained nurses and seamstresses who jumped up and down and splashed around him. "Joe," they called, and "Look at me, Joe! Is this the way?" and they splashed and swallowed and Joe supported them under their chins and by their behinds and said in his rich slow fruity voice, "Kick out, naow! Thassa-way. Kick right out!" And sometimes he supported them, swimming like frogs, to the raft, and when they had clambered onto the raft they were afraid to jump off and Joe Fortes became impatient and terrible and said in a very large voice, "Jump now! I'll catch you! You jump off that raff or I'll leave you here all night!" And that was how they learned to swim.

Rose was one of the children who learned to swim with Joe

Fortes, and she was one of the cowardly ones who shivered on the raft while Joe roared, "You jump off of that raff this minute, or I'll leave you there all night!" So she jumped because the prospect was so terrible and so real, and how threatening the wet sea by night, and who knows what creatures will come to this dark raft alone. So she jumped.

Aunt Rachel did not let Rose go swimming in her good blue serge bathing costume with white braid and black wool stockings unless some grownup was there. Aunts and guardians feel much more responsible for children than parents do, and so they are overanxious and they age faster. Aunt Topaz was not very much good as a guardian because she did not bathe, could not swim, was irresponsible, and usually met friends on the beach with whom she entered into conversation and then forgot about Rose.

One day, however, Rose persuaded her Aunt Rachel to let her go to the beach with Aunt Topaz who was quite ready for an outing, and in any case wanted to take her bicycle for a walk. So Rose and her Great-Aunt started off down Barclay Street in very good spirits on a sunny July afternoon. Tra-la-la, how happy they were! They talked separately and together. Aunt Topaz wheeled her bicycle, which gave her a very sporting appearance, and she wore her hat which looked like a rowboat. She carried some biscuits in the string bag which was attached to the shining handlebars of her noble English bicycle. Rose carried a huge parcel in a towel and swung it by a strap. She further complicated her walk by taking her hoop and stick. So Great-Aunt and Great-Niece proceeded down Barclay Street towards English Bay, Rose bowling her hoop whenever she felt like it.

When they arrived at English Bay Rose rushed into the bath-house with five cents, and Aunt Topaz got into conversation with a young man called Eustace Flowerdew, with whose mother she was acquainted. Eustace Flowerdew wore a stiff straw hat attached to him somewhere by a black cord, so that if in his progress along the sands the hat should blow off, it would still remain attached to the person of Eustace. He wore pince-nez which made him look very refined. His collar was so high and stiff that it hurt him, and his tie was a chaste and severe four-in-hand. He collected tie-pins which were called stick-pins. Today he wore a stick-pin with the head of a horse.

"Oh, good afternoon, Eustace," said Aunt Topaz, "how nice you do look to be sure. How is your mother? What a nice horse!"

After taking off his hat and putting it on again, Eustace hitched up each of his trouser legs and sat down beside Aunt Topaz, and looked over the top of his collar. In so doing he jiggled the bicycle which was unusually heavy and was inexpertly propped against the log on which he and Aunt Topaz were sitting. The bicycle intentionally fell on them both and knocked them down. This bicycle was very ill-tempered and ingenious, and was given to doing this kind of thing when possible on purpose. Aunt Topaz lay prone, and Eustace Flowerdew crawled out and lifted the bicycle off her and led it away to a tree where it could not touch them any more. Aunt Topaz exclaimed a great deal, got up, dusted the sand off herself, and Rose was as forgotten as though she had never existed.

"What are you doing on the beach at this time of the after-noon, Eustace?" asked Aunt Topaz.

Eustace did not want to tell Aunt Topaz the truth, which was that he hoped to meet a girl called Mary Evans in whom he had become interested, so he told her a lie.

"I have come here to forget, Miss Edgeworth," he said, looking at the ocean over his collar.

"And what do you want to forget? ... Oh, I suppose I shouldn't ask you if you want to forget it! How very interesting!"

The young man took his hat off and passed his hand over his forehead wearily. "He is good-looking, but he looks rather silly," thought Topaz.

"The fact is that I am writing a play," he said at last.

Topaz was frightfully excited. She had never before sat on a log with someone who was writing a play. Memories of Sir Henry Irving, Ellen Terry and the Lyceum Theatre in general romped through her mind and she did not know where to begin. She bubbled a little but the young man did not seem to hear. He was still looking out to sea. How beautiful it was, beyond the cries and splashings of children who crowded round Joe Fortes. There is a serenity and a symmetry about English Bay. It is framed by two harmonious landfalls. Out stretches Point Grey sloping to the southwest. Undulations of mountain, mainland and island come to a poetic termination on the northwest. Straight ahead to the westward sparkles the ocean as far as the dim white peaks of Vancouver Island. Seagulls flash and fly and cry in the wide summer air. Sitters on the beach regarded this beauty idly.

"What are you calling your play, Eustace?" asked Aunty when she had recovered.

"Break, Break, Break," said the young man. "Who is this uncommonly plain little girl standing in front of us? How very wet she is!"

"That?" said Aunt Topaz, suddenly seeing Rose. "Oh, there you are. How do you do, Rose? That is my great-niece. Yes, she is plain, isn't she? When wet. When dry she looks better, because her hair curls. Now run away and enjoy yourself and make sure you don't drown. Well, what is it?"

"May I get a biscuit?" asked Rose, who had come up full of rapture and talk now quenched.

"Yes, yes. Get a biscuit but be careful of the bicycle. It's against that tree."

Rose looked hatingly at Eustace Flowerdew and went over to the bicycle, dripping as she went. No sooner did she touch the heavy bicycle than it rushed violently away from her down the beach and hurled itself into the sand where it lay with its pedals quivering. Rose looked, but the two had not seen this. So she went and pulled up the bicycle and led it over to the tree again. She propped it up against the tree as best she could, dusted some of the sand off the biscuits, ate them grit and all, and ran off again to the heavenly waves and children surrounding Joe Fortes.

"What does your mother say about your writing a play? I should think she would feel very nervous. Are you introducing the sex element at all ... illicit love, so to speak ... or are you, if I may say so, keeping it thoroughly wholesome?" asked Topaz.

"My dear Miss Edgeworth," answered the young man pityingly, "I trust that you do not still regard Art as being in any way connected with morality!" He saw in the distance a figure that looked like Mary Evans, and his muscles were already flexing to rise. A shadow fell across Aunty and Eustace.

"Well, I do declare!" exclaimed Aunty joyously. "If this isn't Mrs. Hamilton Coffin! Mrs. Coffin, let me present to you a rising young ..." but the rising young playwright was no longer there. He was striding away down the beach.

"Do sit down, Mrs. Coffin!" said Topaz. "This is nice! How very athletic you do look!" She was filled with admiration. Mrs. Coffin was tall and the black serge bathing suit which she wore did not become her. On this fine summer day Mrs. Coffin, warmly dressed for swimming, displayed no part of her body except her face and ears and her arms as far up as her elbows. "How delightful!" exclaimed Topaz sincerely.

"I have lately, Miss Edgeworth," said Mrs. Coffin, who was a serious woman, "come under the influence of Ralston's Health Foods, and so has my husband. We are making a careful study of physical health and exercise and right thinking. We eat Ralston's Health Foods and a new food called Grape Nuts" ("'Grape Nuts!' That sounds delicious!" said Topaz) "twice a day. Already complexion is brighter, our whole mental attitude is improved, and I may say," she lowered her voice, "that faulty elimination is corrected."

"Faulty elimination! Well, well! Fancy that!" echoed Aunt Topaz, and wondered, "What on earth is she talking about?"

"I have also made an appointment with Mr. Fortes for a swimming lesson and I hope very soon to have mastered the art. This is my third lesson."

"Never too old to learn! Never too old to learn!" said Topaz merrily but without tact. She had no intention of taking swimming lessons herself. "I will come down to the water's edge and cheer you on." "I wonder if it's her costume or her name that makes me think of the tomb," she thought cheerfully.

Mrs. Coffin and Aunt Topaz went down to the water's edge. Joe Fortes disentangled himself from the swimming, bobbing, prancing, screaming children, and came out of the ocean to speak to Mrs. Coffin. He looked very fine, beautiful brown seal that he was, with the clear sparkling water streaming off him.

Mrs. Coffin advanced into the sea, and unhesitatingly dipped herself. "How brave! How brave! Bravo!" cried Topaz from the brink, clapping. Joe Fortes discussed the motions of swimming with Mrs. Coffin, doing so with his arms, and then so with his big legs like flexible pillars, and Mrs. Coffin took the first position. Joe Fortes respectfully supported her chin with the tips of his strong brown fingers. He dexterously and modestly raised her rear, and held it raised by a bit of bathing suit. "How politely he does it!" thought Topaz, admiring Joe Fortes and Mrs. Coffin as they proceeded up and down the ocean. When Mrs. Coffin had proceeded up and down supported and exhorted by Joe Fortes for twenty minutes or so, with Topaz addressing them from the brink, she tried swimming alone. She went under several times dragged down by her bathing suit but emerged full of hope. She dressed, and came and sat with Aunt Topaz.

"I understand, Miss Edgeworth," said Mrs. Coffin, "that you are the President of the Minerva Club!"

"I! President! Oh dear no!" said Topaz laughing merrily. "Never again will I be President of anything as long as I live! I was for a year President of our Ladies' Aid, and the worry nearly killed me! I'd as soon be hanged as be President of anything — much sooner, I assure you! No, Mrs. Coffin, I am the Secretary of the Minerva Club — Honorary you understand — and Mrs. Aked, the President, promises that I can toss it up! toss it up! at any moment that I wish!"

Mrs. Coffin seemed to be about to say something further when a miserable-looking object appeared in front of them. It was Rose, blue and dripping.

"J-Joe F-F-Fortes s-s-says that I'm b-b-b-blue and I must g-g-go home," stuttered Rose shivering. "I d-d-d-don't want to. D-D-Do I have to?

"Oh dear me, what a sight!" said Aunt Topaz who had forgotten Rose again. "Certainly, certainly! Rush into your clothes and we'll walk home briskly and have some tea! What a delightful afternoon!"

On the way home the two pushed their impedimenta. Rose took the superfluous hoop, and Aunt Topaz wheeled her bicycle. The bicycle kicked her with its large protruding pedals as often as possible, and became entangled in her long skirt from time to time, so she often had to stop. When she was disentangled they went on. The bicycle bided its time, and then it kicked her again. Their minds were full of their own affairs, of which they talked regardless.

"A very silly young man, I'm afraid, but he may grow out of it. It is possible, however, that he has talent ..."

"I swam six strokes alone. I swam six strokes alone ..."

"I'm sure Mrs. Hamilton Coffin deserves a great deal of credit at her age ..."

"Joe Fortes says that if I can just master the ..."

"But what she meant by 'faulty elimination' I cannot imagine. It may have something to do with the Mosaic Law ..."

"Joe Fortes can swim across English Bay easy-weasy. A big boy said that Joe Fortes could swim across the English Channel easy-weasy ..."

"I do wish you'd stop saying 'easy-weasy' ... oh ..." The bicycle, behaving coarsely, swerved, turned and tried to run Aunt Topaz down.

"And Geraldine has been swimming longer than me and she can't swim as good as me ..."

"As well as I. 'Grape Nuts' sound delicious! A combination of grapes and nuts no doubt ..."

This kind of conversation went on all the way home, and after they reached home too, until Rose went to bed. It was plain to Rachel and her mother that Aunty and Rose had enjoyed going down to English Bay, and Rachel was greatly relieved that Rose had not been drowned.

On the next afternoon Aunt Topaz prepared to go to the meeting of the Minerva Club. She dressed very prettily, and wore a feather boa. Her success in dress was a matter of luck rather than taste, but today she looked uncommonly well. "How nice you look, Aunty!" said Rachel admiringly. Aunty was very happy. She pranced up Barclay Street, carrying her Minutes of the previous meeting — which were brief — in her hand.

There were nine ladies gathered at Mrs. Aked's house for the meeting of the Minerva Club. Tap, tap went Mrs. Aked on a little table. "We will now call the meeting to order, and our Honorary Secretary will read the Minutes of the previous meeting — Miss Edgeworth."

Everybody admired the experience and aplomb of Mrs. Aked.

Topaz arose and smiled at the ladies. Nine of them. When it came to reading aloud, even Minutes, she enjoyed herself thoroughly. But if she had to utter a single impromptu word in public, on her feet, she suffered more than tongue could tell. Therefore she was careful never to place herself in a position where she might have to make a speech. Considering that she spent her whole life in speaking, this was strange. But human beings are very strange, and there you are.

Topaz reported, smiling over her Minutes, that at the previous meeting the Minerva Club had listened to a paper on Robert Browning and that selections from that great man's less obscure poems had been read aloud. It had been decided that today's meeting should include a brief comprehensive paper on "Poets of the Elizabethan Era" by Mrs. Howard Henchcliffe who certainly had her work cut out, and that selections from the verses of Elizabethan poets would be read by Mrs. Isaacs, Mrs. Simpson, and — modestly — Miss Edgeworth. Then Aunt Topaz sat down. How she enjoyed this!

"Any business, ladies?" inquired Mrs. Aked. "Ah, yes, one vacancy in the Club. The name of Mrs. Hamilton Coffin is up for election. Any discussion before we vote Mrs. Hamilton Coffin into the Club? I think not."

But a rather pudding-faced lady raised a tentative hand. She cleared her throat. "Pardon me," she said. "I hope we are all friends here, and that discussion may be without prejudice?"

Mrs. Aked nodded, and the ladies murmured and rustled and adjusted their boas.

"Before voting on the name of Mrs. Hamilton Coffin," said the pudding-faced lady, "may I remind ladies present that the reputation of our members has always been beyond reproach?"

"I'm sure Mrs. Hamilton Coffin ..." began a small lady with sparkling eyes, in outraged tones. "Whatever can this be?" wondered Topaz.

The pudding-faced lady again held up her hand. "Pardon me," she said, "I have nothing at all to say against the personal reputation of Mrs. Hamilton Coffin. But do the Ladies of the Minerva Club know that Mrs. Hamilton Coffin has been seen more than once in a public place, bathing in the arms of a black man."

A rustle of indignation ran through the room, whether at the pudding-faced lady or at Mrs. Hamilton Coffin it was impossible to say.

Suddenly in that inward part of her that Topaz had not known to exist, arose a fury. She who did not know of the existence of private life because she had no private life of her own, she who feared so greatly to speak in public, she who was never roused to anger, rose to her feet, trembling and angry. She was angry for Joe Fortes; and for Mrs. Hamilton Coffin; and for herself, a spectator on that innocent blue day. She was aware of something evil and stupid in the room.

"Ladies," she said, shaking, "I shall now count ten because I think I shall then be better able to say what I want to say and because I am very frightened. Excuse me just a minute." And Topaz was silent, and they could see her counting ten. All the ladies waited; emotions were held in check. Then the plain and interesting face of Topaz lighted with its usual friendly smile.

"Ladies," she said, "I was present yesterday when that admirable woman Mrs. Hamilton Coffin had her swimming lesson from our respected fellow-citizen Joe Fortes. I know that the lady who has just spoken," and Aunty smiled winningly upon the pudding-faced lady, "will be quite properly relieved to hear that so far from swimming in the arms of Mr. Fortes, which any of us who were drowning would be grateful to do, Mrs. Hamilton Coffin was swimming in his fingertips. I feel that we should be honoured to have as a fellow member so active, progressive and irreproachable a lady as Mrs. Hamilton Coffin. I therefore beg to propose the name of Mrs. Hamilton Coffin as the tenth member of the Minerva Club." And she sat down scarlet-cheeked, shaking violently.

"Hear-hear, hear-hear," said all the ladies — including the pudding-faced lady — with one accord and very loud, clapping. "Order, order," cried the President, enjoying herself im-mensely. "I hereby declare Mrs. Hamilton Coffin a member of the Minerva Club, and I instruct our Honorary Secretary to write a letter of invitation. I will now call upon Miss Topaz Edgeworth to read the introductory selection from one of the poets of the Elizabethan Era."

The ladies slipped back their boas and emitted releasing

breaths of warm air (the room had become close), adjusted their positions and adopted postures suitable to those about to listen to the poets.

Aunt Topaz stood and read. This was her great day. How beautifully she read! Her chattering tones were modulated and musical. The training of the classical Mrs. Porter had made Aunty a reader in the classical style. She was correct, deliberate, flowing, unemotional, natural. She was very happy, reading aloud slowly to the Minerva Club. She read clearly —

> *"Even such is Time, that takes in trust*
> *Our youth, our joys, our all we have,*
> *And pays us but with earth and dust;*
> *Who, in the dark and silent grave,*
> *When we have wandered all our ways,*
> *Shuts up the story of our days.*
> *But from this earth, this grave, this dust,*
> *My God shall raise me up, I trust."*

Everybody clapped.

Aunty went home disturbed and happy; and that evening she told her sister and Rachel about the meeting, and her indignation rose and fell and was satisfied. She told it several times.

The Grandmother said, "I am glad you spoke as you did, my dear sister. You were right."

Rachel put down her work. She thought, "How often I am angry with Aunty! How often I scold her! She is aggravating, but just see this!" Rachel looked across at Aunt Topaz with eyes at once sombre and bright that were Rachel's only beauty. "Yes, Aunty," she said, "that's true. I have never heard you say an unkind thing about anyone. I have never heard you cast an aspersion on anyone. I really believe that you are one of the few people who think no evil."

Aunty was amazed! Rachel, who seldom praised, had praised her. She —Topaz — who was never humble and embarrassed became humble and embarrassed. What could she say. "I think," she said, "that I will go to bed. I will take the newspaper." And she stumbled upstairs in her hasty way.

Above, in her bedroom, they heard her singing in that funny little flute voice of hers.

THE BRAVEST BOAT

Malcolm Lowry

It was a day of spindrift and blowing sea-foam, with black clouds presaging rain driven over the mountains from the sea by a wild March wind.

But a clean silver sea light came from along the horizon where the sky itself was like glowing silver. And far away over in America the snowy volcanic peak of Mount Hood stood on high, disembodied, cut off from earth, yet much too close, which was an even surer presage of rain, as though the mountains had advanced, or were advancing.

In the park of the seaport the giant trees swayed, and taller than any were the tragic Seven Sisters, a constellation of seven noble red cedars that had grown there for hundreds of years, but were now dying, blasted, with bare peeled tops and stricken boughs. (They were dying rather than live longer near civilization. Yet though everyone had forgotten they were called after the Pleiades and thought they were named with civic pride after the seven daughters of a butcher, who seventy years before when the growing city was named Gaspool had all danced together in a shop window, nobody had the heart to cut them down.)

The angelic wings of the seagulls circling over the tree tops shone very white against the black sky. Fresh snow from the night before lay far down the slopes of the Canadian mountains, whose freezing summits, massed peak behind spire, jaggedly traversed the country northward as far as the eye could reach. And highest of all an eagle, with the poise of a skier, shot endlessly down the world.

In the mirror, reflecting this and much besides, of an old weighing machine with the legend YOUR WEIGHT AND YOUR DESTINY encircling its forehead and which stood on the embankment between the streetcar terminus and a hamburger stall, in this mirror along the reedy edge of the stretch of water below known as Lost Lagoon two figures in mackintoshes were approaching, a man and a beautiful passionate-looking girl, both bare-headed, and both extremely fair, and hand-in-hand, so that you would have taken them for young lovers, but that they were alike as brother and sister, and the man, although he walked with youthful nervous speed, now seemed older than the girl.

The man, fine-looking, tall, yet thick-set, very bronzed, and on approaching still closer obviously a good deal older than the girl, and wearing one of those blue-belted trenchcoats favoured by merchant marine officers of any country, though without any corresponding cap — moreover the trenchcoat was rather too short in the sleeve so that you could see some tattooing on his wrist, as he approached nearer still it seemed to be an anchor — whereas the girl's raincoat was of some sort of entrancing forest-green corduroy — the man paused every now and then to gaze into the lovely laughing face of his girl, and once or twice they both stopped, gulping in great draughts of salty clean sea and mountain air. A child smiled at them, and they smiled back. But the child belonged elsewhere, and the couple were unaccompanied.

In the lagoon swam wild swans, and many wild ducks: mallards and buffleheads and scaups, golden eyes and cackling black coots with carved ivory bills. The little buffleheads often took flight from the water and some of them blew about like doves among the smaller trees. Under these trees lining the bank other ducks were sitting meekly on the sloping lawn, their beaks tucked into their plumage rumpled by the wind. The smaller trees were apples and hawthorns, some just opening into bloom even before they had foliage, and weeping willows, from whose branches small showers from the night's rain were scattered on the two figures as they passed.

A red-breasted merganser cruised in the lagoon, and at this swift and angry sea bird, with his proud disordered crest, the two were now gazing with a special sympathy, perhaps because he looked lonely without his mate. Ah, they were wrong. The red-breasted merganser was now joined by his wife and on a sudden duck's impulse and with immense fuss the two wild creatures flew off to settle on another part of the lagoon. And for some reason this simple fact appeared to make these two good people

— for nearly all people are good who walk in parks — very happy again.

Now at a distance they saw a small boy, accompanied by his father who was kneeling on the bank, trying to sail a toy boat in the lagoon. But the blustery March wind soon slanted the tiny yacht into trouble and the father hauled it back, reaching out with his curved stick, and set it on an upright keel again for his son.

YOUR WEIGHT AND YOUR DESTINY.

Suddenly the girl's face, at close quarters in the weighing machine's mirror, seemed struggling with tears: she unbuttoned the top button of her coat to readjust her scarf, revealing, attached to a gold chain around her neck, a small gold cross. They were quite alone now, standing on top of the embankment by the machine, save for a few old men feeding the ducks below, and the father and his son with the toy yacht, all of whom had their backs turned, while an empty tram abruptly city-bound trundled around the minute terminus square; and the man, who had been trying to light his pipe, took her in his arms and tenderly kissed her, and then pressing his face against her cheek, held her a moment closely.

The couple, having gone down obliquely to the lagoon once more, had now passed the boy with his boat and his father. They were smiling again. Or as much as they could while eating hamburgers. And they were smiling still as they passed the slender reeds where a northwestern redwing was trying to pretend he had no notion of nesting, the northwestern redwing who like all birds in these parts may feel superior to man in that he is his own customs official, and can cross the wild border without let.

Along the far side of Lost Lagoon the green dragons grew thickly, their sheathed and cowled leaves giving off their peculiar animal-like odour. The two lovers were approaching the forest in which, ahead, several footpaths threaded the ancient trees. The park, seagirt, was very large, and like many parks throughout the Pacific Northwest, wisely left in places to the original wilderness. In fact, though its beauty was probably unique, it was quite like some American parks, you might have thought, save for the Union Jack that galloped evermore by a pavilion, and but for the apparition, at this moment, passing by on the carefully landscaped road slightly above, which led with its tunnels and detours to a suspension bridge, of a posse of Royal Canadian Mounted Policemen mounted royally upon the cushions of an American Chevrolet.

Nearer the forest were gardens with sheltered beds of snowdrops and here and there a few crocuses lifting their sweet chalices. The man and his girl now seemed lost in thought, breasting the buffeting wind that blew the girl's scarf out behind her like a pennant and blew the man's thick fair hair about his head.

A loudspeaker, enthroned on a wagon, barked from the city of Enochvilleport composed of dilapidated half-skyscrapers, at different levels, some with all kinds of scrap iron, even broken airplanes, on their roofs, others being mouldy stock exchange buildings, new beer parlours crawling with verminous light even in mid-afternoon and resembling gigantic emerald-lit public lavatories for both sexes, masonries containing English tea-shoppes where your fortune could be told by a female relative of Maximilian of Mexico, totem pole factories, drapers' shops with the best Scotch tweed and opium dens in the basement (though no bars, as if, like some hideous old roué shuddering with every unmentionable secret vice this city without gaiety had cackled "No, I draw the line at that. What would our wee laddies come to then?"), cerise conflagrations of cinemas, modern apartment buildings, and other soulless behemoths, housing, it might be, noble invisible struggles, of literature, the drama, art or music, the student's lamp and the rejected manuscript; or indescribable poverty and degradation, between which civic attractions were squeezed occasional lovely dark ivy-clad old houses that seemed weeping, cut off from all light, on their knees, and elsewhere bankrupt hospitals, and one or two solid-stoned old banks, held up that afternoon; and among which appeared too, at infrequent intervals, beyond a melancholy never-striking black and white clock that said three, dwarfed spires belonging to frame façades with blackened rose windows, queer grimed onion-shaped domes, and even Chinese pagodas, so that first you thought you were in the Orient, then Turkey or Russia, though finally, but for the fact that some of these were churches, you would be sure you were in hell: despite that anyone who had ever really been in hell must have given Enochvilleport a nod of recognition, further affirmed by the spectacle, at first not unpicturesque, of the numerous sawmills relentlessly smoking and champing away like demons, Molochs fed by whole mountainsides of forests that never grew again, or by trees that made way for grinning regiments of villas in the background of "our expanding and fair

city," mills that shook the very earth with their tumult, filling
the windy air with their sound as of a wailing and gnashing of
teeth: all these curious achievements of man, together creating as
we say "the jewel of the Pacific," went as though down a great
incline to a harbour more spectacular than Rio de Janeiro and
San Francisco put together, with deep sea freighters moored
at every angle for miles in the roadstead, but to whose heroic
prospect nearly the only human dwellings visible on this side
of the water that had any air of belonging, or in which their
inhabitants could be said any longer to participate, were,
paradoxically, a few lowly little self-built shacks and floathouses,
that might have been driven out of the city altogether, down to
the water's edge into the sea itself, where they stood on piles, like
fishermen's huts (which several of them apparently were), or on
rollers, some dark and tumbledown, others freshly and prettily
painted, these last quite evidently built or placed with some
human need for beauty in mind, even if under the permanent
threat of eviction, and all standing, even the most sombre, with
their fluted tin chimneys smoking here and there like toy tramp
steamers, as though in defiance of the town, before eternity.
In Enochvilleport itself some ghastly-coloured neon signs had
long since been going through their unctuous twitchings and
gesticulations that nostalgia and love transform into a poetry
of longing: more happily one began to flicker: PALOMAR, LOUIS
ARMSTRONG AND HIS ORCHESTRA. A huge new grey dead hotel
that at sea might be a landmark of romance, belched smoke out
of its turreted haunted-looking roof, as if it had caught fire,
and beyond that all the lamps were blazing within the grim

courtyard of the law courts, equally at sea a trysting place of the heart, outside which one of the stone lions, having recently been blown up, was covered reverently with a white cloth, and inside which for a month a group of stainless citizens had been trying a sixteen-year-old boy for murder.

Nearer the park the apron lights appeared on a sort of pebble-dashed YMCA-Hall-cum-variety-theatre saying TAMMUZ THE MASTER HYPNOTIST, TONITE 8:30, and running past this the tram-lines, down which another parkwise streetcar was approaching, could be seen extending almost to the department store in whose show window Tammuz' subject, perhaps a somnolent descendant of the seven sisters whose fame had eclipsed even that of the Pleiades, but whose announced ambition was to become a female psychiatrist, had been sleeping happily and publicly in a double bed for the last three days as an advance publicity stunt for tonight's performance.

Above Lost Lagoon on the road now mounting toward the suspension bridge in the distance much as a piece of jazz music mounts toward a break, a newsboy cried: "LASH ORDERED FOR SAINT PIERRE! SIXTEEN-YEAR-OLD BOY, CHILD-SLAYER, TO HANG! Read all about it!"

The weather too was forboding. Yet, seeing the wandering lovers, the other passers-by on this side of the lagoon, a wounded soldier lying on a bench smoking a cigarette, and one or two of those destitute souls, the very old who haunt parks — since, faced with a choice, the very old will sometimes prefer, rather than to keep a room and starve, at least in such a city as this, somehow to eat and live outdoors — smiled too.

For as the girl walked along beside the man with her arm through his and as they smiled together and their eyes met with love, or they paused, watching the blowing seagulls, or the ever-changing scale of the snow-freaked Canadian mountains with their fleecy indigo chasms, or to listen to the deep-tongued majesty of a merchantman's echoing roar (these things that made Enochvilleport's ferocious aldermen imagine that it was the city itself that was beautiful, and maybe they were half right), the whistle of a ferryboat as it sidled across the inlet northward, what memories might not be evoked in a poor soldier, in the breasts of the bereaved, the old, even, who knows, in the mounted policemen, not merely of young love, but of lovers, as they seemed to be, so much in love that they were afraid to lose a moment of their time together?

Yet only a guardian angel of these two would have known — and surely they must have possessed a guardian angel — the strangest of all strange things of which they were thinking, save that, since they had spoken of it so often before, and especially, when they had opportunity, on this day of the year, each knew of course that the other was thinking about it, to such an extent indeed that it was no surprise, it only resembled the beginning of a ritual when the man said, as they entered the main path of the forest, through whose branches that shielded them from the wind could be made out, from time to time, suggesting a fragment of music manuscript, a bit of the suspension bridge itself:

"It was a day just like this that I set the boat adrift. It was twenty-nine years ago in June."

"It was twenty-nine years ago in June, darling. And it was June twenty-seventh."

"It was five years before you were born, Astrid, and I was ten years old and I came down to the bay with my father."

"It was five years before I was born, you were ten years old, and you came down to the wharf with your father. Your father and grandfather had made you the boat between them and it was a fine one, ten inches long, smoothly varnished and made of wood from your model airplane box, with a new strong white sail."

"Yes, it was balsa wood from my model airplane box and my father sat beside me, telling me what to write for a note to put in it."

"Your father sat beside you, telling you what to write," Astrid laughed, "and you wrote:

'Hello.

'My name is Sigurd Storlesen. I am ten years old. Right now I am sitting on the wharf at Fearnought Bay, Clallam County, State of Washington, U.S.A., five miles south of Cape Flattery on the Pacific side, and my Dad is beside me telling me what to write. Today is June 27, 1922. My Dad is a forest warden in the Olympic National Forest but my Granddad is the lighthouse keeper at Cape Flattery. Beside me is a small shiny canoe which you now hold in your hand. It is a windy day and my Dad said to put the canoe in the water when I have put this in and glued down the lid which is a piece of balsa wood from my model airplane box.

'Well must close this note now, but first I will ask you to tell the Seattle Star that you have found it, because I am going to start reading the paper from today and looking for a piece that says, who when and where it was found.

'Thanks. Sigurd Storlesen.'"

"Yes, then my father and I put the note inside, and we glued down the lid and sealed it and put the boat on the water."

"You put the boat on the water and the tide was going out and away it went. The current caught it right off and carried it out and you watched it till it was out of sight!"

The two had now reached a clearing in the forest where a few grey squirrels were scampering about on the grass. A dark-browed Indian in a windbreaker, utterly absorbed by his friendly task, stood with a sleek black squirrel sitting on his shoulder nibbling popcorn he was giving it from a bag. This reminded them to get some peanuts to feed the bears, whose cages were over the way.

Ursus Horribilis: and now they tossed peanuts to the sad lumbering sleep-heavy creatures — though at least these two grizzlies were together, they even had a home — maybe still too sleepy to know where they were, still wrapped in a dream of their timberfalls and wild blueberries in the Cordilleras Sigurd and Astrid could see again, straight ahead of them, between the trees, beyond a bay.

But how should they stop thinking of the little boat?

Twelve years it had wandered. Through the tempests of winter, over sunny summer seas, what tide rips had caught it, what wild sea birds, shearwaters, storm petrels, jaegers, that follow the thrashing propellers, the dark albatross of these northern waters, swooped upon it, or warm currents edged it lazily toward land — and blue-water currents sailed it after the albacore, with fishing boats like white giraffes — or glacial drifts tossed it about fuming Cape Flattery itself. Perhaps it had rested, floating in a sheltered cove, where the killer whale smote, lashed, the deep clear water; the eagle and the salmon had seen it, a baby seal stared with her wondering eyes, only for the little boat to be thrown aground, catching the rainy afternoon sun, on cruel barnacled rocks by the waves, lying aground knocked from side to side in an inch of water like a live thing, or a poor old tin can, pushed, pounded ashore, and swung around, reversed again, left high and dry, and then swept another yard up the beach, or carried under a lonely salt-grey shack, to drive a seine fisherman crazy all night with its faint plaintive knocking, before it ebbed out in the dark autumn dawn, and found its way afresh, over the deep, coming through thunder, to who will ever know what fierce and desolate uninhabited shore, known only to the dread Wendigo, where not even an Indian could have found it, unfriended there, lost, until it was borne out to sea once more by the great brimming black tides of January, or the huge calm tides of the midsummer moon, to start its journey all over again —

Astrid and Sigurd came to a large enclosure, set back from a walk, with two vine-leaved maple trees (their scarlet tassels, delicate precursors of their leaves, already visible) growing through the top, a sheltered cavernous part to one side for a lair, and the whole, save for the barred front, covered with stout large-meshed wire — considered sufficient protection for one of the most Satanic beasts left living on earth.

Two animals inhabited the cage, spotted like deceitful pastel leopards, and in appearance like decorated, maniacal-looking cats: their ears were provided with huge tassels and, as if this were in savage parody of the vine-leaved maples, from the brute's chin tassels also depended. Their legs were as long as a man's arm, and their paws, clothed in grey fur out of which shot claws curved like scimitars, were as big as a man's clenched fist.

And the two beautiful demonic creatures prowled and paced endlessly, searching the base of their cage, between whose bars there was just room to slip a murderous paw — always a hop out of reach an almost invisible sparrow went pecking away in the dust — searching with eternal voraciousness, yet seeking in desperation also some way out, passing and repassing each other rhythmically, as though truly damned and under some compelling enchantment.

And yet as they watched the terrifying Canadian lynx, in which seemed to be embodied in animal form all the pure ferocity of nature, as they watched, crunching peanuts themselves now and passing the bag between them, before the lovers' eyes still sailed that tiny boat, battling with the seas, at the mercy of a wilder ferocity yet, all those years before Astrid was born.

Ah, its absolute loneliness amid those wastes, those wildernesses of rough rainy seas bereft even of sea birds, between contrary winds, or in the great dead windless swell that comes following a gale; and then with the wind springing up and blowing the spray across the sea like rain, like a vision of creation, blowing the lithe boat as it climbed the highland into the skies, from which sizzled cobalt lightnings, and then sank down into the abyss, but already was climbing again, while the whole sea crested with foam like lambs' wool went furling off to leeward, the whole vast moon-driven expanse like the pastures and valleys and snow-capped ranges of a Sierra Madre in delirium, in ceaseless motion, rising and hilling, and the little boat rising, and hilling into a paralyzing sea of white drifting fire and smoking spume by which it seemed overwhelmed: and all this time a sound, like a high sound of singing, yet as sustained in harmony as telegraph wires, or like the unbelievably high perpetual sound of the wind where there is nobody to listen, which perhaps does not exist, or the ghost of the wind in the rigging of ships long lost, and perhaps it was the sound of the wind in its toy rigging, as again the boat slanted onward: but even then what further unfathomed deeps had it oversailed, until what birds of ill omen turned heavenly for it at last, what iron birds with sabre wings skimming forever through the murk above the grey immeasurable swells, imparted mysteriously their own homing knowledge to it, the lonely buoyant little craft, nudging it with their beaks under golden sunsets in a blue sky, as it sailed close in to mountainous coasts of clouds with stars over them, or burning coasts at sunset once more, as it rounded not only the terrible spume-drenched rocks, like incinerators in sawmills, of Flattery, but other capes unknown, those twelve years, of giant pinnacles, images of barrenness and desolation, upon which the heart is thrown and impaled eternally! — And strangest of all how many ships themselves had threatened it, during that voyage of only some three score miles as the crow flies from its launching to its final port, looming out of the fog and passing by harmlessly all those years — those years too of the last sailing ships, rigged to the moonsail, sweeping by into their own oblivion — but ships cargoed with guns or iron for impending wars, what freighters now at the bottom of the sea he, Sigurd, had voyaged in for that matter, freighted with old marble and wine and cherries-in-brine, or whose engines even now were still somewhere murmuring: *Frère* Jacques! *Frère* Jacques!

What strange poem of God's mercy was this?

Suddenly across their vision a squirrel ran up a tree beside the cage and then, chattering shrilly, leaped from a branch and darted across the top of the wire mesh. Instantly, swift and deadly as lightning, one of the lynx sprang twenty feet into the air, hurtling straight to the top of the cage toward the squirrel, hitting the wire with a twang like a mammoth guitar, and simultaneously flashing through the wire its scimitar claws: Astrid cried out and covered her face.

But the squirrel, unhurt, untouched, was already running lightly along another branch, down to the tree, and away, while the infuriated lynx sprang straight up, sprang again, and again and again and again, as his mate crouched spitting and snarling below.

Sigurd and Astrid began to laugh. Then this seemed obscurely unfair to the lynx, now solemnly washing his mate's face. The innocent squirrel, for whom they felt such relief, might almost have been showing off, almost, unlike the oblivious sparrow, have been taunting the caged animal. The squirrel's hairbreadth escape — the thousand-to-one chance — that on second thought must take place every day, seemed meaningless. But all at once it did not seem meaningless that they had been there to see it.

"You know how I watched the paper and waited," Sigurd was saying, stopping to relight his pipe, as they walked on.

"The Seattle *Star*," Astrid said.

"The Seattle *Star* ... It was the first newspaper I ever read. Father always declared the boat had gone south — maybe to Mexico, and I seem to remember Granddad saying no, if it didn't break up on Tatoosh, the tide would take it right down Juan de Fuca Strait, maybe into Puget Sound itself. Well, I watched and waited for a long time and finally, as kids will, I stopped looking."

"And the years went on —"

"And I grew up. Granddad was dead by then. And the old man, you know about him. Well, he's dead too now. But I never forgot. Twelve years! Think of it —! Why, it voyaged around longer than we've been married."

"And we've been married seven years."

"Seven years today —"

"It seems like a miracle!"

But their words fell like spent arrows before the target of this fact.

They were walking, as they left the forest, between two long rows of Japanese cherry trees, next month to be an airy avenue of celestial bloom. The cherry trees behind, the forest reappeared, to left and right of the wide clearing, and skirting two arms of the bay. As they approached the Pacific, down the gradual incline, on this side remote from the harbour the wind grew more boisterous: gulls, glaucous and raucous, wheeled and sailed overhead, yelling, and were suddenly far out to sea.

And it was the sea that lay before them, at the end of the slope that changed into the steep beach, the naked sea, running deeply below, without embankment or promenade, or any friendly shacks, though some prettily built homes showed to the left, with one light in a window, glowing warmly through the trees on the edge of the forest itself, as of some stalwart Columbian Adam, who had calmly stolen back with his Eve into Paradise, under the flaming sword of the civic cherubim.

The tide was low. Offshore, white horses were running around a point. The headlong onrush of the tide of beaten silver flashing over its cross-flowing underset was so fast the very surface of the sea seemed racing away.

Their path gave place to a cinder track in the familiar lee of an old frame pavilion, a deserted tea house boarded up since last summer. Dead leaves were slithering across the porch, past which on the slope to the right picnic benches, tables, a derelict swing, lay overturned, under a tempestuous grove of birches. It seemed cold, sad, inhuman there, and beyond, with the roar of that deep low tide. Yet there was that between the lovers which moved like a warmth, and might have thrown open the shutters, set the benches and tables aright, and filled the whole grove with the voices and children's laughter of summer. Astrid paused for a moment with a hand on Sigurd's arm while they were sheltered by the pavilion, and said, what she too had often said before, so that they always repeated these things almost like an incantation:

"I'll never forget it. That day when I was seven years old, coming to the park here on a picnic with my father and mother and brother. After lunch my brother and I came down to the beach to play. It was a fine summer day, and the tide was out, but there'd been this very high tide in the night, and you could see the lines of driftwood and seaweed where it had ebbed ... was playing on the beach, and I found your boat!"

"You were playing on the beach and you found my boat. And the mast was broken."

"The mast was broken and shreds of sail hung dirty and limp. But your boat was still whole and unhurt, though it was scratched and weather-beaten and the varnish was gone. I ran to my mother, and she saw the sealing wax over the cockpit, and, darling, I found your note!"

"You found our note, my darling."

Astrid drew from her pocket a scrap of paper and holding it between them they bent over (though it was hardly legible by now and they knew it off by heart) and read:

Hello.

My name is Sigurd Storlesen. I am ten years old. Right now I am sitting on the wharf at Fearnought Bay, Clallam County, State of Washington, U.S.A., five miles south of Cape Flattery on the Pacific side, and my Dad is beside me telling me what to write. Today is June 27, 1922. My Dad is a forest warden in the Olympic National Forest but my Granddad is the lighthouse keeper at Cape Flattery. Beside me is a small shiny canoe which you now hold in your hand. It is a windy day and my Dad said to put the canoe in the water when I have put this in and glued down the lid which is a piece of balsa wood from my model airplane box.

Well must close this note now, but first I will ask you to tell the Seattle Star that you have found it, because I am going to start reading the paper from today and looking for a piece that says, who when and where it was found.

Thanks.
Sigurd Storlesen.

They came to the desolate beach strewn with driftwood, sculptured, whorled, silvered, piled everywhere by tides so immense there was a tideline of seaweed and detritus on the grass behind them, and great logs and shingle-bolts and writhing snags, crucificial, or frozen in a fiery rage — or better, a few bits of lumber almost ready to burn, for someone to take home, and automatically they threw them up beyond the sea's reach for some passing soul, remembering their own winters of need — and more snags there at the foot of the grove and visible high on the sea-scythed forest banks on either side, in which riven trees were growing, yearning over the shore. And everywhere they looked was wreckage, the toll of winter's wrath: wrecked hencoops, wrecked floats, the wrecked side of a fisherman's hut, its boards once hammered together, with its wrenched shiplap and extruding nails. The fury had extended even to the beach itself, formed in hummocks and waves and barriers of shingle and shells they had to climb up in places. And everywhere too was the grotesque macabre fruit of the sea, with its exhilarating iodine smell, nightmarish bulbs of kelp like antiquated motor horns, trailing brown satin streamers twenty feet long, sea wrack like demons, or the discarded casements of evil spirits that had been cleansed. Then more wreckage: boots, a clock, torn fishing nets, a demolished wheelhouse, a smashed wheel lying in the sand.

Nor was it possible to grasp for more than a moment that all this with its feeling of death and destruction and barrenness was only an appearance, that beneath the flotsam, under the very shells they crunched, within the trickling overflows of winter-bournes they jumped over, down at the tide margin, existed, just as in the forest, a stirring and stretching of life, a seething of spring.

When Astrid and Sigurd were almost sheltered by an uprooted tree on one of these lower billows of beach they noticed that the clouds had lifted over the sea, though the sky was not blue but still that intense silver, so that they could see right across the Gulf and make out, or thought they could, the line of some Gulf Islands. A lone freighter with upraised derricks shipped seas on the horizon. A hint of the summit of Mount Hood remained, or it might have been clouds. They remarked too, in the southeast, on the sloping base of a hill, a triangle of storm-washed green, as if cut out of the overhanging murk there, in which were four pines, five telegraph posts and a clearing resembling a cemetery. Behind them the icy mountains of Canada hid their savage peaks and snowfalls under still more savage clouds. And they saw that the sea was grey with whitecaps and currents charging offshore and spray blowing backwards from the rocks.

But when the full force of the wind caught them, looking from the shore, it was like gazing into chaos. The wind blew away their thoughts, their voices, almost their very senses, as they walked, crunching the shells, laughing and stumbling. Nor could they tell whether it was spume or rain that smote and stung their faces, whether spindrift from the sea or rain from which the sea was born, as now finally they were forced to a halt, standing there arm in arm ... And it was to this shore, through that chaos, by those currents, that their little boat with its innocent message had been brought out of the past finally to safety and a home.

But ah, the storms they had come through!

WHAT IS REMEMBERED

Alice Munro

In a hotel room in Vancouver, Meriel as a young woman is putting on her short white summer gloves. She wears a beige linen dress and a flimsy white scarf over her hair. Dark hair, at that time. She smiles because she has remembered something that Queen Sirikit of Thailand said, or was quoted as saying, in a magazine. A quote within a quote — something Queen Sirikit said that Balmain had said.

"Balmain taught me everything. He said, 'Always wear white gloves. It's best.'"

It's best. Why is she smiling at that? It seems so soft a whisper of advice, such absurd and final wisdom. Her gloved hands are formal, but tender-looking as a kitten's paws.

Pierre asks why she's smiling and she says, "Nothing," then tells him.

He says, "Who is Balmain?"

They were getting ready to go to a funeral. They had come over on the ferry last night from their home on Vancouver Island to be sure of being on time for the morning ceremony. It was the first time they'd stayed in a hotel since their wedding night. When they went on a holiday now it was always with their two children, and they looked for inexpensive motels that catered to families.

This was only the second funeral they had been to as a married couple. Pierre's father was dead, and Meriel's mother was dead, but these deaths had happened before Pierre and Meriel met. Last year a teacher at Pierre's school died suddenly, and there was a fine service, with the schoolboy choir and the sixteenth-century words for the Burial of the Dead. The man had been in his mid-sixties, and his death seemed to Meriel and Pierre only a little surprising and hardly sad. It did not make much difference, as they saw it, whether you died at sixty-five or seventy-five or eighty-five.

The funeral today was another matter. It was Jonas who was being buried. Pierre's best friend for years and Pierre's age — twenty-nine. Pierre and Jonas had grown up together in West Vancouver — they could remember it before the Lions Gate Bridge was built, when it seemed like a small town. Their parents were friends. When they were eleven or twelve years old they had built a rowboat and launched it at Dundarave Pier. At the university they had parted company for a while — Jonas was studying to be an engineer, while Pierre was enrolled in Classics, and the Arts and Engineering students traditionally despised each other. But in the years since then the friendship had to some extent been revived. Jonas, who was not married, came to visit Pierre and Meriel, and sometimes stayed with them for a week at a time.

Both of these young men were surprised by what had happened in their lives, and they would joke about it. Jonas was the one whose choice of profession had seemed so reassuring to his parents, and had roused a muted envy in Pierre's parents, yet it was Pierre who had married and got a teaching job and taken on ordinary responsibilities, while Jonas, after university, had never settled down with a girl or a job. He was always on a sort of probation that did not end up in a firm attachment to any company, and the girls — at least to hear him tell it — were always on a sort of probation with him. His last engineering job was in the northern part of the province, and he stayed on there after he either quit or was fired. "Employment terminated by mutual consent," he wrote to Pierre, adding that he was living at the hotel, where all the high-class people lived, and might get a job on a logging crew. He was also learning to fly a plane, and thinking of becoming a bush pilot. He promised to come down for a visit when present financial complications were worked out.

Meriel had hoped that wouldn't happen. Jonas slept on the living room couch and in the morning threw the covers on the floor for her to pick up. He kept Pierre awake half the night talking about things that had happened when they were teenagers, or even younger. His name for Pierre was Piss-hair, a nickname from those years, and he referred to other old friends as Stinkpool or Doc or Buster, never by the names Meriel had always heard — Stan or Don or Rick. He recalled with a gruff pedantry the details of incidents that Meriel did not think so remarkable or funny (the bag of dog shit set on fire on the teacher's front steps, the badgering of the old man who offered boys a nickel to pull down their pants), and grew irritated if the conversation turned to the present.

When she had to tell Pierre that Jonas was dead she was apologetic, shaken. Apologetic because she hadn't liked Jonas and shaken because he was the first person they knew well, in their own age group, to have died. But Pierre did not seem to be surprised or particularly stricken.

"Suicide," he said.

She said no, an accident. He was riding a motorcycle, after dark, on gravel, and he went off the road. Somebody found him, or was with him, help was at hand, but he died within an hour. His injuries were mortal.

That was what his mother had said, on the phone. *His injuries were mortal.* She had sounded so quickly resigned, so unsurprised. As Pierre did when he said, "Suicide."

After that Pierre and Meriel had hardly spoken about the death itself, just about the funeral, the hotel room, the need for an all-night sitter. His suit to be cleaned, a white shirt obtained. It was Meriel who made the arrangements, and Pierre kept checking up on her in a husbandly way. She understood that he wished her to be controlled and matter-of-fact, as he was, and not to lay claim to any sorrow which — he would be sure

— she could not really feel. She had asked him why he had said, "Suicide," and he had told her, "That's just what came into my head." She felt his evasion to be some sort of warning or even a rebuke. As if he suspected her of deriving from this death — or from their proximity to this death — a feeling that was discreditable and self-centred. A morbid, preening excitement.

Young husbands were stern, in those days. Just a short time before, they had been suitors, almost figures of fun, knock-kneed and desperate in their sexual agonies. Now, bedded down, they turned resolute and disapproving. Off to work every morning, clean-shaven, youthful necks in knotted ties, days spent in unknown labours, home again at suppertime to take a critical glance at the evening meal and to shake out the newspaper, hold it up between themselves and the muddle of the kitchen, the ailments and emotions, the babies. What a lot they had to learn, so quickly. How to kowtow to bosses and how to manage wives. How to be authoritative about mortgages, retaining walls, lawn grass, drains, politics, as well as about the jobs that had to maintain their families for the next quarter of a century. It was the women, then, who could slip back — during the daytime hours, and always allowing for the stunning responsibility that had been landed on them, in the matter of the children — into a kind of second adolescence. A lightening of spirits when the husbands departed. Dreamy rebellion, subversive get-togethers, laughing fits that were a throwback to high school, mushrooming between the walls that the husband was paying for, in the hours when he wasn't there.

After the funeral some people had been invited back to Jonas's parents' house in Dundarave. The rhododendron hedge was in bloom, all red and pink and purple. Jonas's father was complimented on the garden.

"Well, I don't know," he said. "We had to get it in shape in a bit of a hurry."

Jonas's mother said, "This isn't a real lunch, I'm afraid. Just a pickup." Most people were drinking sherry, though some of the men had whisky. Food was set out on the extended dining room table — salmon mousse and crackers, mushroom tarts, sausage rolls, a light lemon cake and cut-up fruit and pressed-almond cookies, as well as shrimp and ham and cucumber-and-avocado sandwiches. Pierre heaped everything onto his small china plate, and Meriel heard his mother say to him, "You know, you could always come back for a second helping."

His mother didn't live in West Vancouver any more but had come in from White Rock for the funeral. And she wasn't quite confident about a direct reprimand, now that Pierre was a teacher and a married man.

"Or didn't you think there'd be any left?" she said.

Pierre said carelessly, "Maybe not of what I wanted."

His mother spoke to Meriel. "What a nice dress."

"Yes, but look," said Meriel, smoothing down the wrinkles that had formed while she sat through the service.

"That's the trouble," Pierre's mother said.

"What's the trouble?" said Jonas's mother brightly, sliding some tarts onto the warming-dish.

"That's the trouble with linen," said Pierre's mother. "Meriel was just saying how her dress had wrinkled up" — she did not say, "during the funeral service" — "and I was saying that's the trouble with linen."

Jonas's mother might not have been listening. Looking across the room, she said, "That's the doctor who looked after him. He flew down from Smithers in his own plane. Really, we thought that was so good of him."

Pierre's mother said, "That's quite a venture."

"Yes. Well. I suppose he gets around that way, to attend people in the bush."

The man they were talking about was speaking to Pierre. He was not wearing a suit, though he had a decent jacket on, over a turtlenecked sweater.

"I suppose he would," said Pierre's mother, and Jonas's mother said, "Yes," and Meriel felt as if something — about the way he was dressed? — had been explained and settled, between them.

She looked down at the table napkins, which were folded in quarters. They were not as big as dinner napkins or as small as cocktail napkins. They were set in overlapping rows so that a corner of each napkin (the corner embroidered with a tiny blue or pink or yellow flower) overlapped the folded corner of its neighbour. No two napkins embroidered with the same colour of flower were touching each other. Nobody had disturbed them, or if they had — for she did see a few people around the room holding napkins — they had picked up napkins from the end of the row in a careful way and this order had been maintained.

At the funeral service, the minister had compared Jonas's life on earth to the life of a baby in the womb. The baby, he said, knows nothing of any other existence and inhabits its warm, dark, watery cave with not an inkling of the great bright world it will soon be thrust into. And we on earth have an inkling, but are really quite unable to imagine the light that we will enter after we have survived the travail of death. If the baby could somehow be informed of what would happen to it in the near future, would it not be incredulous, as well as afraid? And so are we, most of the time, but we should not be, for we have been given assurance. Even so, our blind brains cannot imagine, cannot conceive of, what we will pass into. The baby is lapped in its ignorance, in the faith of its dumb, helpless being. And we who are not entirely ignorant or entirely knowing must take care to wrap ourselves in our faith, in the word of our Lord.

Meriel looked at the minister, who stood in the hall doorway with a glass of sherry in his hand, listening to a vivacious woman with blond puffed hair. It didn't seem to her that they were talking about the pangs of death and the light ahead. What would he do if she walked over and tackled him on that subject?

Nobody would have the heart to. Or the bad manners.

Instead she looked at Pierre and the bush doctor. Pierre was talking with a boyish liveliness not often seen in him these days. Or not often seen by Meriel. She occupied herself by pretending that she was seeing him for the first time, now. His curly, short-cropped, very dark hair receding at the temples, baring the smooth, gold-tinged ivory skin. His wide, sharp shoulders and long, fine limbs and nicely shaped rather small skull. He smiled enchantingly but never strategically and seemed to distrust smiling altogether since he had become a teacher of boys. Faint lines of permanent fret were set in his forehead.

She thought of a teachers' party — more than a year ago — when she and he had found themselves, at opposite sides of the room, left out of the nearby conversations. She had circled the room and got close to him without his noticing, and then she had begun to talk to him as if she were a discreetly flirtatious stranger. He smiled as he was smiling now — but with a difference, as was natural when talking to an ensnaring woman — and he took up the charade. They exchanged charged looks and vapid speeches until they both broke down laughing. Someone came up to them and told them that married jokes were not allowed.

"What makes you think we're really married?" said Pierre, whose behaviour at such parties was usually so circumspect.

She crossed the room to him now with no such foolishness in mind. She had to remind him that they must soon go their separate ways. He was driving to Horseshoe Bay to catch the next ferry, and she would have to get across the North Shore to Lynn Valley by bus. She had arranged to take this chance to visit a woman her dead mother had loved and admired, and in fact had named her daughter for, and whom Meriel had always called Aunt, though they were not related by blood. Aunt Muriel. (It was when she went away to college that Meriel had changed the spelling.) This old woman was living in a nursing home in Lynn Valley, and Meriel had not visited her for over a year. It took too much time to get there, on their infrequent family trips to Vancouver, and the children were upset by the atmosphere of the nursing home and the looks of the people who lived there. So was Pierre, though he did not like to say so. Instead, he asked what relation this person was to Meriel, anyway.

It's not as if she was a real aunt.

So now Meriel was going to see her by herself. She had said that she would feel guilty if she didn't go when she had the chance. Also, though she didn't say so, she was looking forward to the time that this would give her to be away from her family.

"Maybe I could drive you," Pierre said. "God knows how long you'll have to wait for the bus."

"You can't," she said. "You'd miss the ferry." She reminded him of their arrangement with the sitter.

He said, "You're right."

The man he'd been talking to — the doctor — had not had any choice but to listen to this conversation, and he said unexpectedly, "Let me drive you."

"I thought you came here in an airplane," said Meriel, just as Pierre said, "This is my wife, excuse me. Meriel."

The doctor told her a name which she hardly heard.

"It's not so easy landing a plane on Hollyburn Mountain," he said. "So I left it at the airport and rented a car."

Some slight forcing of courtesy, on his part, made Meriel think that she had sounded obnoxious. She was either too bold or too shy, much of the time.

"Would that really be okay?" Pierre said. "Do you have time?"

The doctor looked directly at Meriel. This was not a disagreeable look — it was not bold or sly, it was not appraising. But it was not socially deferential, either.

He said, "Of course."

So it was agreed that this was how it would be. They would start saying their goodbyes now and Pierre would leave for the ferry and Asher, as his name was — or Dr. Asher — would drive Meriel to Lynn Valley.

What Meriel planned to do, after that, was to visit with Aunt Muriel — possibly even sitting through supper with her, then catch the bus from Lynn Valley to the downtown bus depot (buses to "town" were relatively frequent) and board the late-evening bus which would take her on to the ferry, and home.

The nursing home was called Princess Manor. It was a one-storey building with extended wings, covered in pinkish-brown stucco. The street was busy, and there were no grounds to speak of, no hedges or screen-fences to shut out noise or protect the scraps of lawn. On one side there was a Gospel Hall with a joke of a steeple, on the other a gas station.

"The word 'Manor' doesn't mean anything at all any more, does it?" said Meriel. "It doesn't even mean there's an upstairs. It just means that you're supposed to think that a place is something it doesn't even pretend to be."

The doctor said nothing — perhaps what she had said didn't make any sense to him. Or just wasn't worth saying even if it was true. All the way from Dundarave she had listened to herself talking and she had been dismayed. It wasn't so much that she was prattling — saying just anything that came into her head — rather that she was trying to express things which seemed to her interesting, or that might have been interesting if she could get them into shape. But these ideas probably sounded pretentious if not insane, raffled off in the way she was doing. She must seem like one of those women who were determined not to have an ordinary conversation but a *real* one. And even though she knew nothing was working, that her talk must seem to him an imposition, she was unable to stop herself.

She didn't know what had started this. Unease, simply because she so seldom talked to a stranger nowadays. The oddity of riding alone in a car with a man who wasn't her husband.

She had even asked, rashly, what he thought of Pierre's notion that the motorcycle accident was suicide.

"You could float that idea around about any number of violent accidents," he had said.

"Don't bother pulling into the drive," she said. "I can get out here." So embarrassed, so eager she was to get away from him and his barely polite indifference, that she put her hand on the door handle as if to open it while they were still moving along the street.

"I was planning to park," he said, turning in anyway. "I wasn't going to leave you stranded."

She said, "I might be quite a while."

"That's all right. I can wait. Or I could come in and look around. If you wouldn't mind that."

She was about to say that nursing homes can be dreary and unnerving. Then she remembered that he was a doctor and would see nothing here that he had not seen before. And something in the way he said "if you wouldn't mind that" — some formality, but also an uncertainty in his voice — surprised her. It seemed that he was making an offering of his time and his presence that had little to do with courtesy, but rather something to do with herself. It was an offer made with a touch of frank humility, but it was not a plea. If she had said that she would really rather not take up any more of his time, he would not have tried any further persuasion, he would have said goodbye with an even courtesy and driven away.

As it was, they got out of the car and walked side by side across the parking lot, toward the front entrance.

Several old or disabled people were sitting out on a square of pavement that had a few furry-looking shrubs and pots of petunias around it, to suggest a garden patio. Aunt Muriel was not among them, but Meriel found herself bestowing glad greetings. Something had happened to her. She had a sudden mysterious sense of power and delight, as if with every step she took, a bright message was travelling from her heels to the top of her skull.

When she asked him later, "Why did you come in there with me?" he said, "Because I didn't want to lose sight of you."

Aunt Muriel was sitting by herself, in a wheelchair, in the dim corridor just outside her own bedroom door. She was swollen and glimmering — but that was because of being swathed in an asbestos apron so she could smoke a cigarette. Meriel believed that when she had said goodbye to her, months and seasons ago, she had been sitting in the same chair in the same spot — though without the asbestos apron, which must accord with some new rule, or reflect some further decline. Very likely she sat here every day beside the fixed ashtray filled with sand, looking at the liverish painted wall — it was painted pink or mauve but it looked liverish, the corridor being so dim — with the bracket shelf on it supporting a spill of fake ivy.

"Meriel? I thought it was you," she said. "I could tell by your steps. I could tell by your breathing. My cataracts have got to be bloody hell. All I can see is blobs."

"It's me, all right, how are you?" Meriel kissed her temple. "Why aren't you out in the sunshine?"

"I'm not fond of sunshine," the old woman said. "I have to think of my complexion."

She might have been joking, but it was perhaps the truth. Her pale face and hands were covered with large spots — dead-white spots that caught what light there was here, turning silvery. She had been a true blond, pink-faced, lean, with straight well-cut hair that had gone white in her thirties. Now the hair was ragged, mussed from being rubbed into pillows, and the lobes of her ears hung out of it like flat teats. She used to wear little diamonds in her ears — where had they gone? Diamonds in her ears, real gold chains, real pearls, silk shirts of unusual colours — amber, aubergine — and beautiful narrow shoes.

She smelled of hospital powder and the licorice drops she sucked all day between the rationed cigarettes.

"We need some chairs," she said. She leaned forward, waved the cigarette hand in the air, tried to whistle. "Service, please. Chairs."

The doctor said, "I'll find some."

The old Muriel and the young one were left alone.

"What's your husband's name?"

"Pierre."

"And you have the two children, don't you? Jane and David?"

"That's right. But the man who's with me —"

"Ah, no," the old Muriel said. "That's not your husband."

Aunt Muriel belonged to Meriel's grandmother's generation, rather than her mother's. She had been Meriel's mother's art teacher at school. First an inspiration, then an ally, then a friend. She had painted large abstract pictures, one of which — a present to Meriel's mother — had hung in the back hall of the house where Meriel grew up and had been moved to the dining room whenever the artist came to visit. Its colours were murky — dark reds and browns (Meriel's father called it "Manure Pile on Fire") — but Aunt Muriel's spirit seemed always bright and dauntless. She had lived in Vancouver when she was young, before she came to teach in this town in the Interior. She had been friends with artists whose names were now in the papers. She longed to go back there and eventually did, to live with and manage the affairs of a rich old couple who were friends and patrons of artists. She seemed to have lots of money while she lived with them, but she was left out in the cold when they died. She lived on her pension, took up watercolours because she could not afford oils, starved herself (Meriel's mother suspected) so that she could take Meriel out to lunch — Meriel being then a university student. On these occasions she talked in a rush of jokes and judgements, mostly pointing out how works and ideas that people raved about were rubbish, but how here and there — in the output of some obscure contemporary or half-forgotten figure from another century — there was something extraordinary. That was her stalwart word of praise — "extraordinary." A hush in her voice, as if there and then and rather to her own surprise she had come upon a quality in the world that was still to be absolutely honoured.

The doctor returned with two chairs and introduced himself, quite naturally, as if there'd been no chance to do it till now.

"Eric Asher."

"He's a doctor," said Meriel. She was about to start explaining about the funeral, the accident, the flight down from Smithers, but the conversation was taken away from her.

"But I'm not here officially, don't worry," the doctor said.

"Oh, no," said Aunt Muriel. "You're here with her."

"Yes," he said.

At this moment he reached across the space between their two chairs and picked up Meriel's hand, holding it for a moment in a hard grip, then letting it go. And he said to Aunt Muriel, "How could you tell that? By my breathing?"

"I could tell," she said with some impatience. "I used to be a devil myself."

Her voice — the quaver or titter in it — was not like any voice of hers that Meriel remembered. She felt as if there was some betrayal stirring, in this suddenly strange old woman. A betrayal of the past, perhaps of Meriel's mother and the friendship she had treasured with a superior person. Or of those lunches with Meriel herself the rarefied conversations. Some degradation was in the offing. Meriel was upset by this, remotely excited.

"Oh, I used to have friends," Aunt Muriel said, and Meriel said, "You had lots of friends." She mentioned a couple of names.

"Dead," Aunt Muriel said.

Meriel said no, she had seen something just recently in the paper, a retrospective show or an award.

"Oh? I thought he was dead. Maybe I'm thinking of somebody else — Did you know the Delaneys?"

She spoke directly to the man, not to Meriel.

"I don't think so," he said. "No."

"Some people who had a place where we all used to go, on Bowen Island. The Delaneys. I thought you might have heard of them. Well. There were various goings-on. That's what I meant when I said I used to be a devil. Adventures. Well. It looked like adventures, but it was all according to script, if you know what I mean. So not so much of an adventure, actually. We all got drunk as skunks, of course. But they always had to have the candles lit in a circle and the music on, of course — more like a ritual. But not altogether. It didn't mean you mightn't meet somebody new and let the script go all to hell. Just meet for the first time and start kissing like mad and run off into the forest. In the dark. You couldn't get very far. Never mind. Struck down."

She had started to cough, tried speaking through the cough, gave up and hacked violently. The doctor got up and struck her expertly a couple of times, on her bent back. The coughing ended with a groan.

"Better," she said. "Oh, you knew what you were doing, but you pretended not to. One time they had a blindfold on me. Not out in the woods, this was inside. It was all right, I consented. It didn't work so well, though — I mean, I did know. There probably wasn't anybody there that I wouldn't have recognized, anyway."

She coughed again, though not so desperately as before. Then she raised her head, breathed deeply and noisily for a few minutes, holding up her hands to stall the conversation, as if she would soon have something more, something important, to say. But all she did, finally, was laugh and say, "Now I've got a permanent blindfold. Cataracts. Doesn't get me taken advantage of now, not in any debauch that I know about."

"How long have they been growing?" the doctor said with a respectful interest, and to Meriel's great relief there began an absorbed conversation, an informed discussion about the ripening of cataracts, their removal, the pros and cons of this operation, and Aunt Muriel's distrust of the eye doctor who was shunted off — as she said — to look after the people in here. Salacious fantasy — that was what Meriel now decided it had been — slid without the smallest difficulty into a medical chat, agreeably pessimistic on Aunt Muriel's side and carefully reassuring on the doctor's. The sort of conversation that must take place regularly within these walls.

In a little while there was a glance exchanged between Meriel and the doctor, asking whether the visit had lasted long enough. A stealthy, considering, almost married glance, its masquerade and its bland intimacy arousing to those who were after all not married.

Soon.

Aunt Muriel took the initiative herself. She said, "I'm sorry, it's rude of me, I have to tell you, I get tired." No hint in her manner, now, of the person who had launched the first part of the conversation. Distracted, play-acting, and with a vague sense of shame, Meriel bent over and kissed her goodbye. She had a feeling that she would never see Aunt Muriel again, and she never did.

Around a corner, with doors open on rooms where people lay asleep or perhaps watching from their beds, the doctor touched her between her shoulder blades and moved his hand down her back to her waist. She realized that he was picking at the cloth of her dress, which had stuck to her damp skin when she sat pressed against the chair back. The dress was also damp under her arms.

And she had to go to the bathroom. She kept looking for the Visitors' Washrooms, which she thought she had spotted when they were on their way in.

There. She was right. A relief, but also a difficulty, because she had to move suddenly out of his range and to say, "Just a moment," in a voice that sounded to herself distant and irritated. He said, "Yes," and briskly headed for the Men's, and the delicacy of the moment was lost.

When she went out into the hot sunlight she saw him pacing by the car, smoking. He hadn't smoked before — not in Jonas's parents' house or on the way here or with Aunt Muriel. The act seemed to isolate him, to show some impatience, perhaps an impatience to be done with one thing and get on to the next. She was not so sure now, whether she was the next thing or the thing to be done with.

"Where to?" he said, when they were driving. Then, as if he thought he had spoken too brusquely, "Where would you like to go?" It was almost as if he was speaking to a child, or to Aunt

Muriel — somebody he was bound to entertain for the afternoon. And Meriel said, "I don't know," as if she had no choice but to let herself become that burdensome child. She was holding in a wail of disappointment, a clamour of desire. Desire that had seemed to be shy and sporadic but inevitable, yet was now all of a sudden declared inappropriate, one-sided. His hands on the wheel were all his own, reclaimed as if he had never touched her.

"How about Stanley Park?" he said. "Would you like to go for a walk in Stanley Park?"

She said, "Oh, Stanley Park. I haven't been there for ages," as if the idea had perked her up and she could imagine nothing better. And she made things worse by adding, "It's such a gorgeous day."

"It is. It is indeed."

They spoke like caricatures, it was unbearable.

"They don't give you a radio in these rented cars. Well, sometimes they do. Sometimes not."

She wound her window down as they crossed the Lions Gate Bridge. She asked him if he minded.

"No. Not at all."

"It always means summer to me. To have the window down and your elbow out and the breeze coming in — I don't think I could ever get used to air-conditioning."

"Certain temperatures, you might."

She willed herself to silence, till the forest of the park received them, and the high, thick trees could perhaps swallow witlessness and shame. Then she spoiled everything by her too appreciative sigh.

"Prospect Point." He read the sign aloud.

There were plenty of people around, even though it was a weekday afternoon in May, with vacations not yet started. In a moment they might remark on that. There were cars parked all along the drive up to the restaurant, and line-ups on the viewing platform for the coin-use binoculars.

"Aha." He had spotted a car pulling out of its place. A reprieve for a moment from any need for speech, while he idled, backed to give it room, then manoeuvred into the fairly narrow spot. They got out at the same time, walked around to meet on the sidewalk. He turned this way and that, as if deciding where they were to walk. Walkers coming and going on any path you could see.

Her legs were shaking, she could not put up with this any longer.

"Take me somewhere else," she said.

He looked her in the face. He said, "Yes."

There on the sidewalk in the world's view. Kissing like mad.

Take me, was what she had said. *Take me somewhere else*, not *Let's go somewhere else.* That is important to her. The risk, the transfer of power. Complete risk and transfer. *Let's go* — that would have the risk, but not the abdication, which is the start for her — in all her reliving of this moment — of the erotic slide. And what if he had abdicated in his turn? *Where* else? That would not have done, either. He has to say just what he did say. He has to say, *Yes*.

He took her to the apartment where he was staying, in Kitsilano. It belonged to a friend of his who was away on a fish boat, somewhere off the west coast of Vancouver Island. It was in a small, decent building, three or four storeys high. All that she would remember about it would be the glass bricks around the front entrance and the elaborate, heavy hi-fi equipment of that time, which seemed to be the only furniture in the living room.

She would have preferred another scene, and that was the one she substituted, in her memory. A narrow six- or seven-storey hotel, once a fashionable place of residence, in the West End of Vancouver. Curtains of yellowed lace, high ceilings, perhaps an iron grille over part of the window, a fake balcony. Nothing actually dirty or disreputable, just an atmosphere of long accommodation of private woes and sins. There she would have to cross the little lobby with head bowed and arms clinging to her sides, her whole body permeated by exquisite shame. And he would speak to the desk clerk in a low voice that did not advertise, but did not conceal or apologize for, their purpose.

Then the ride in the old-fashioned cage of the elevator, run by an old man — or perhaps an old woman, perhaps a cripple, a sly servant of vice.

Why did she conjure up, why did she add that scene? It was for the moment of exposure, the piercing sense of shame and pride that took over her body as she walked through the (pretend) lobby, and for the sound of his voice, its discretion and authority speaking to the clerk the words that she could not quite make out.

That might have been his tone in the drugstore a few blocks away from the apartment, after he had parked the car and said, "Just a moment in here." The practical arrangements which seemed heavy-hearted and discouraging in married life could in these different circumstances provoke a subtle heat in her, a novel lethargy and submission.

After dark she was carried back again, driven through the park and across the bridge and through West Vancouver, passing only a short distance from the house of Jonas's parents. She arrived at Horseshoe Bay at almost the very last moment, and walked onto the ferry. The last days of May are among the longest of the year, and in spite of the ferry-dock lights and the lights of the cars streaming into the belly of the boat, she could see some glow in the western sky and against it the black mound of an island — not Bowen but one whose name she did not know — tidy as a pudding set in the mouth of the bay.

She had to join the crowd of jostling bodies making their way up the stairs, and when the passenger deck was reached she sat in the first seat she saw. She did not even bother as she usually did to look for a seat next to a window. She had an hour and a half before the boat docked on the other side of the strait, and during this time she had a great deal of work to do.

No sooner had the boat started to move than the people beside her began to talk. They were not casual talkers who had met on the ferry but friends or family who knew each other well and would find plenty to say for the entire crossing. So she got up and went out on deck, climbed to the top deck, where there were always fewer people, and sat on one of the bins that contained life preservers. She ached in expected and unexpected places.

The job she had to do, as she saw it, was to remember everything — and by "remember" she meant experience it in her mind, one more time — then store it away forever. This day's experience set in order, none of it left ragged or lying about, all of it gathered in like treasure and finished with, set aside.

She held on to two predictions, the first one comfortable, and the second easy enough to accept at present, though no doubt it would become harder for her, later on.

Her marriage with Pierre would continue, it would last.

She would never see Asher again.

Both of these turned out to be right.

Her marriage did last — for more than thirty years after that, until Pierre died. During an early and fairly easy stage of his illness, she read aloud to him, getting through a few books that they had both read years ago and meant to go back to. One of these was *Fathers and Sons*. After she had read the scene in which Bazarov declares his violent love for Anna Sergeyevna, and Anna is horrified, they broke off for a discussion. (Not an argument — they had grown too tender for that.)

Meriel wanted the scene to go differently. She believed that Anna would not react in that way.

"It's the writer," she said. "I don't usually ever feel that with Turgenev, but here I feel it's just Turgenev coming and yanking them apart and he's doing it for some purpose of his own."

Pierre smiled faintly. All his expressions had become sketchy. "You think she'd succumb?"

"No. Not succumb. I don't believe her, I think she's as driven as he is. They'd do it."

"That's romantic. You're wrenching things around to make a happy ending."

"I didn't say anything about the ending."

"Listen," said Pierre patiently. He enjoyed this sort of conversation, but it was hard on him, he had to take little rests to collect his strength. "If Anna gave in, it'd be because she loved him. When it was over she'd love him all the more. Isn't that what women are like? I mean if they're in love? And what he'd do — he'd take off the next morning maybe without even speaking to her. That's his nature. He *hates* loving her. So how would that be any better?"

"They'd have something. Their experience."

"He would pretty well forget it and she'd die of shame and rejection. She's intelligent. She knows that."

"Well," said Meriel, pausing for a bit because she felt cornered. "Well, Turgenev doesn't say that. He says she's totally taken aback. He says she's cold."

"Intelligence makes her cold. Intelligent means cold, for a woman."

"No."

"I mean in the nineteenth century. In the nineteenth century, it does."

That night on the ferry, during the time when she thought she was going to get everything straightened away, Meriel did nothing of the kind. What she had to go through was wave after wave of intense recollection. And this was what she would continue to go through — at gradually lengthening intervals — for years to come. She would keep picking up things she'd missed, and these would still jolt her. She would hear or see something again — a sound they made together, the sort of look that passed between them, of recognition and encouragement. A look that was in its way quite cold, yet deeply respectful and more intimate than any look that would pass between married people, or people who owed each other anything.

She remembered his hazel-grey eyes, the close-up view of his coarse skin, a circle like an old scar beside his nose, the slick breadth of his chest as he reared up from her. But she could not have given a useful description of what he looked like. She believed that she had felt his presence so strongly, from the very beginning, that ordinary observation was not possible. Sudden recollection of even their early, unsure, and tentative moments could still make her fold in on herself, as if to protect the raw surprise of her own body, the racketing of desire. *My-love-my-love*, she would mutter in a harsh, mechanical way, the words a secret poultice.

When she saw his picture in the paper, no immediate pangs struck her. The clipping had been sent by Jonas's mother, who as long as she lived insisted on keeping in touch, and reminding them, whenever she could, of Jonas. "Remember the doctor at

Jonas's funeral?" she had written above the small headline. "Bush Doctor Dead in Air Crash." It was an old picture, surely, blurred in its newspaper reproduction. A rather chunky face, smiling — which she would never have expected him to do for the camera. He hadn't died in his own plane but in the crash of a helicopter on an emergency flight. She showed the clipping to Pierre. She said, "Did you ever figure out why he came to the funeral?"

"They might have been buddies of a sort. All those lost souls up north."

"What did you talk to him about?"

"He told me about one time he took Jonas up to teach him to fly. He said, 'Never again.'"

Then he asked, "Didn't he drive you someplace? Where?"

"To Lynn Valley. To see Aunt Muriel."

"So what did you talk about?"

"I found him hard to talk to."

The fact that he was dead did not seem to have much effect on her daydreams — if that was what you could call them. The ones in which she imagined chance meetings or even desperately arranged reunions, had never had a foothold on reality, in any case, and were not revised because he was dead. They had to wear themselves out in a way she did not control and never understood.

When she was on her way home that night it had started to rain, not very hard. She had stayed out on the deck of the ferry. She got up and walked around and could not sit down again on the lid of the life-jacket bin without getting a big wet spot on her dress. So she stayed looking at the froth stirred up in the wake of the boat, and the thought occurred to her that in a certain kind of story — not the kind that anybody wrote any more — the thing for her to do would be to throw herself into the water. Just as she was, packed full of happiness, rewarded as she would surely never be again, every cell in her body plumped up with a sweet self-esteem. A romantic act that could be seen — from a forbidden angle — as supremely rational.

Was she tempted? She was probably just letting herself imagine being tempted. Probably nowhere near yielding, though yielding had been the order of that day.

It wasn't until after Pierre was dead that she remembered one further detail.

Asher had driven her to Horseshoe Bay, to the ferry. He had got out of the car and come around to her side. She was standing there, waiting to say goodbye to him. She made a move toward him, to kiss him — surely a natural thing to do, after the last few hours — and he had said, "No."

"No," he said. "I never do."

Of course that wasn't true, that he never did. Never kissed out in the open, where anybody could see. He had done it just that afternoon, at Prospect Point.

No.

That was simple. A cautioning. A refusal. Protecting her, you might say, as well as himself. Even if he hadn't bothered about that, earlier in the day.

I never do was something else altogether. Another kind of cautioning. Information that could not make her happy, though it might be intended to keep her from making a serious mistake. To save her from the false hopes and humiliation of a certain kind of mistake.

How did they say goodbye, then? Did they shake hands? She could not remember.

But she heard his voice, the lightness and yet the gravity of his tone, she saw his resolute, merely pleasant face, she felt the slight shift out of her range. She didn't doubt that the recollection was true. She did not see how she could have suppressed it so successfully, for all this time.

She had an idea that if she had not been able to do that, her life might have been different.

How?

She might not have stayed with Pierre. She might not have been able to keep her balance. Trying to match what had been said at the ferry with what had been said and done earlier the same day would have made her more alert and more curious. Pride or contrariness might have played a part — a need to have some man eat those words, a refusal to learn her lesson — but that wouldn't have been all. There was another sort of life she could have had — which was not to say she would have preferred it. It was probably because of her age (something she was always forgetting to take account of) and because of the thin cool air she breathed since Pierre's death, that she could think of that other sort of life simply as a kind of research which had its own pitfalls and achievements.

Maybe you didn't find out so much, anyway. Maybe the same thing over and over — which might be some obvious but unsettling fact about yourself. In her case, the fact that prudence — or at least some economical sort of emotional management — had been her guiding light all along.

The little self-preserving movement he made, the kind and deadly caution, the attitude of inflexibility that had grown a bit stale with him, like an outmoded swagger. She could view him now with an everyday mystification, as if he had been a husband.

She wondered if he'd stay that way, or if she had some new role waiting for him, some use still to put him to in her mind, during the time ahead.

STANDING ON RICHARDS

George Bowering

Richards Street in downtown Vancouver is pretty interesting or pretty boring, depending on your point of view. Of all the people standing on corners along Richards Street, I am probably the only one who knows that it was named after Captain George Harry Richards, the nineteenth-century surveyor who gave False Creek its name.

Try it. Go up to one of the girls on the corner of Richards and, say, Nelson, and ask, "Hey, did you know that this street was named after the nineteenth-century surveyor who gave False Creek its name?"

"Oh, yeah, like I really give a shit about that." That's what she'll say.

Most nights I stand on the corner of Richards and Helmcken. Helmcken, by the way, was a Hudson's Bay Company doctor who made a lot of money on real estate around Victoria in the late nineteenth century. He was cosy with the Americans.

I don't look like anyone else standing on corners along Richards. You go down to Richards and Nelson, and you get your tall young women in high heels. In the summer you can see the cheeks of their asses. In the winter they are nearly freezing because they might have winter coats, but they leave them open so guys in slowly cruising cars can see their long legs. An awful lot of them are blonds of one sort or another, because the Asian businessmen and tourists don't come all the way over here for women with dark hair.

I like Danielle. She has the darkest hair you ever saw, and she doesn't care. She's got eyes that could give a Japanese volleyball coach a heart attack. She's also got a PhD in anthropology. But when it came to selling, she decided to sell her body. I have nothing against her body.

That's a witticism.

I have nothing against her decision. As far as I can see, she's the only girl on Richards who had to make that choice.

A couple blocks in the other direction you'll see the boys and the young men trying to look like boys, around Richards and whatever that street is the other side of Davie. If you want to be one of those boys you have to be skinny. You have to look as if you could get hurt easily, and you have to know what to wear, no T-shirts with designer names on them, no No Fear, no Club Monaco. You don't want to be wearing a baseball cap backward. A nice clean pair of tans and a white shirt with some buttons undone will do the trick. You have to look as if you've done this before, just to be safe, and you have to look as if you haven't been doing this for long. There aren't any real stores or cafés down there past Davie, so you stand out like a sore you know what.

Usually I am the only person standing on the corner of Richards and Helmcken. Hardly anyone pronounces that name right. It is something like "Helmakin." Or it was when it was still attached to Dr. John S. Helmcken, the first doctor to show up in Victoria, in 1850. He married one of Governor Douglas's daughters and started buying up real estate. Doctors have been doing something like that ever since, except maybe the doctors who try to take care of the less lucky people standing on corners along Richards Street.

So I was going to tell you that I look somewhat different from the other people standing on corners along Richards. You won't see my bare legs, that's for certain, and I do not look in any way like a boy. I guess I look like a college professor from about twenty years ago. I'm wearing brown shoes, no sign of recent polishing, laces not as long as they used to be. Gabardine slacks, either dark brown or grey, I'm not sure. A light-blue long-sleeve shirt with an ink stain at the bottom of the pocket, and a tie with stripes on a slant. One of those generic old school ties, somewhat wider than the ties I see salesmen wearing these days. Bifocal glasses that have frames halfway between round and square. And a genuine Harris tweed jacket.

Let me explain why I said "genuine." You see, first of all, a lot of people think that tweeds are called tweeds because they are woven in the Tweed Valley. Well, some of them are woven in the Tweed Valley, but that is not how we got the word "tweed."

Tweeds are made from varieties of the old twill weave, and the old Scottish word for twill is "tweel." In 1826 some clerk in London made an understandable mistake, writing "tweed" instead of "tweel," and it was not long until our jackets were called tweeds, even in Scotland.

So what about Harris? Well, if you go across The Minch from the top of mainland Scotland, you will come to the biggest island in the Outer Hebrides. Stornaway Castle is up there, you may remember. Well, really it is all one island called Lewis Island, but the locals always refer to two islands, Lewis and Harris. No one knows why, but it may be because Lewis is a lot hillier, or mountainous, as they say over there. In any case, if someone had not started the Harris tweed cottage industry, they would have had to get by on fishing, and you know how unlikely that has become over the years.

So that's why I said "genuine." Harris tweeds are the most northerly tweeds, so the sheep they get the wool from have the thickest and toughest texture. That's my theory, anyway. If you are interested in a tweed jacket, have a good look at the label. Look for the word "genuine."

I said that I look like a professor from about twenty years ago. In fact I *was* a professor twenty years ago. I was a professor *five* years ago, professor of English. I was one of those strange ducks who kept reading outside my field of expertise. In fact, most people in my field of expertise, Nineteenth-Century American Literature, knew a lot more about the recent work in the field than I did. I didn't want to stop reading Latin poetry and Japanese novels and provincial history, so I sort of fell behind in the latest theory about criticism of nineteenth century American prose and/or poetry. Every time I started to read some of the latest theory about criticism in my field of expertise, I would run into the word "hegemonic" or the word "template." So I would put the paper aside and pick up Plutarch.

But that is not the real reason I quit being a professor. Not the only one, anyway. I quit because I was finding it difficult to find anyone who wanted to know anything about literature. Once in a while I would have to supervise a graduate student who was interested in hegemonic templates in recent criticism of W. D. Howells, and I would encourage that young person to read *The Atlantic Monthly* from 1871 through 1881. But I was always tabbed to do more than my share of first-year English classes. An Introduction to English Fiction — that sort of thing.

Maybe there's something wrong with me. I still get all excited when I read an author I have never bothered with before, someone like, say, Mrs. Chapone. Or when I find a new book about Fort Simpson and the Christian missionaries along the northern coast.

So you can imagine how I felt when September would slide into October, and it would become apparent that the youngsters in their backward caps and Club Monaco sweatshirts didn't particularly want to learn anything. In fact, more and more of them let it be known that once they had paid their tuition money they thought it was an imposition to make them read anything as well.

So I quit.

I wanted to see whether there was some place where I could sell my mind to someone who wanted to buy it.

I told this story to Danielle. She told me that she understood perfectly. She probably did. She never told me whether she had quit a professor job or whether she had just got a PhD for the fun of it and didn't want to drive cab.

You might say, Who would stop their car and haggle over price with a guy in a tweed jacket who wants to sell his mind on Richards Street? I know I did. But I thought that I would give it a try. If that didn't work, there must be lots of other ways of selling your mind. Well, that's what I had been doing for twenty years at the university on the hill.

In recent years the university had acquired some high-rise space for a campus extension downtown, just off the financial district. Twenty-five tired students and I used to sit in a room with sealed windows every Tuesday night, two hours and a cigarette break and two more hours, not a coffee shop within walking distance because the businessmen were all at home drinking vodka. Then I would walk up Howe Street, turn right on Georgia, turn right into a lane, and get into my professor car. Head home, have a last coffee, and lie in bed, trying to remember what I had to teach in the morning.

When you turned right at Georgia Street in those times, you walked past a number of tall young prostitutes trying to look upscale. One night after four hours of trying to get tired students interested in reading Henry James, I was walking past the genteel windows in front of the Georgia Hotel, when a good-looking young woman with glowing dark-brown skin spoke to me.

"Would you like some company?"

She sounded cheerful.

"No thanks. I'm going to go home and read," I said, still walking.

"I'll read to you," she called out, as I turned in at the lane.

I did not change my pace, but I imagined, not for the last time, bringing that pleasant woman home to read to me. In a negligee, I guess. Say, hanging open in the front. One glowing breast peeking out, let's say.

So one sunny day in June I took along my old flaked briefcase and stood on the corner of Richards and Helmcken. I had books in the briefcase, and the first thing I did was to set the briefcase down and take out Margaret Ormsby's *British Columbia: A History*, and start reading. I would read a paragraph and then scan the windshields of slowly approaching cars for a bit, then bend my whitening head and read another paragraph. Ormsby's book was published in time for the province's centenary in 1858. Well, the province has had a number of centenaries. Some people, unaware of the difference between a noun and an adjective, call them centennials. These are no doubt the same people who thought that the new millennium would start in January 2000. I wonder why they didn't just call it the new millennial?

Anyway, it was not the first time I had read Ormsby's book, but it seemed to me that it would make good reading while I waited for someone to come along and buy an hour of my mind. I had a lot to learn about that. I was already well into chapter 7, "Jewel in Queen Victoria's Diadem," before anyone stopped, and it was already past nine at night.

I had watched what the girls did. When the car came to a stop at the curb in front of me, I went over and bent down, first looking to check for possible violence, then at the open side window, for negotiation. A thirtyish guy with a balding forehead leaned over and asked me what the hell I was doing.

"I been driving by here ten times today, and you're always there," he said.

"Just about," I said, ready to add words about a late lunch and several pees.

"What the hell are you doing?"

"I'm —"

"What's with the book? Always the book."

"I guess two things. How can a person stand around all day without a book to read —"

"Do it all the —"

"And it's kind of what you might call public information. I mean, I wouldn't want people to get the wrong idea," I said.

There was a cop car approaching, slowly. It crossed my mind that this guy I was talking to was also a cop, hoping to entrap me. Thank goodness, I thought, neither of us had mentioned anything about money. The cop on my side of their car looked me up and down. He did not smirk, just kept that blank look the cops favour. The cop car pulled away, changing lanes without signalling.

"What wrong idea?" asked my guy in the car.

"Ah, well, I mean, I wouldn't want anyone to think I was just some low-IQ person blessed with a desirable body."

"Har har," he said. It looked as if he were preparing to drive away.

But he was my first possible sale. I decided to turn on my

special gift for patter, the talent that had kept me in the classroom for two decades without disaster.

"Har har indeed," I said.

"So what would be the right idea?"

"Well," I said, and made the throat sound that is often conveyed with the printed word "harrumph." "The other attractive people you see standing on corners up and down this street are seeking to sell, or rather rent, their bodies. I seek to sell or rent my mind."

"Hardy har har," he said, and drove away.

"Conrad car car," I said into the night, regretting that no one within earshot would recognize the instant and multilevelled word play.

When I was an undergraduate, the English professors let it be known that while they had to teach Hardy and Conrad in the same course, they reserved most of their respect for Conrad. He anticipated the psychological insights that would animate the major novelists and poets and filmmakers in the modern era, while Hardy was a typical Victorian with a ham-handed approach to characterization.

Secretly I had always preferred Hardy. He let you know how sad he was about the world. Conrad was interested in exhibiting moral conflicts, but you never got the sense that he cared all that much when his characters failed the test. Hardy, though blessed with an arch sarcasm, would often turn the screws of fate so hard on his people that you wanted to lament the lack of justice in the mortal world.

I thought about Hardy and Conrad for hours rather than reading in the evening light that made its way through the three layers of cloud over Vancouver. I did not get another prospective client, though several cars slowed as they passed my corner. I tried to look intellectually seductive, which consisted mainly of fiddling with my old brier and looking over the top of my glasses.

When I quit teaching the university gave me the equivalent of two years' salary, which I banked and paid income tax on. I'm still pretty comfortable, though it will be over a decade till my pension kicks in. It was not out of financial desperation that I first stood on my corner. I suppose I might have needed something to fill my days now that I was no longer pretending to write my book on Matthew Arnold. But the main reason for my being there was a kind of curiosity. I wanted to know whether men who drove slowly down certain streets in downtown Vancouver were as lonely for knowledge as they were for physical spasms.

Maybe some of those people driving by in their slow, quiet cars were just too bashful or too little experienced to stop and bargain for knowledge. Maybe they had been enucleated by the popular culture, as people these days were calling it. I am one of the few old codgers who would insist that by "culture" they mean such things as literature, serious music and the Quatroccento.

Danielle stopped to say hello on her way back from her coffee break at a shop next to the library. She was gorgeous in patent leather boots that zipped up to her thighs. She had a form-fitting jacket that seemed to be made principally of red egret feathers.

"Aubrey, how long are you going to carry out this feckless experiment?" she asked. "Why don't you go home, have a nice chocolate Ovaltine, and snuggle up with *The Decline and Fall of the Roman Empire*?"

"I've read it four times. I know it off by heart."

"Aubrey, you're going to give Richards Street a bad name," she said.

"Did you ever consider that I am hanging out here so that I can gaze at you just a block away?"

"I charge two hundred dollars an hour for gazing, chum."

She gave me her nicest smile, professional as it was, and patted my tweed shoulder with her long fingers, then headed toward her corner with a stride that would make a prelate pee his trousers.

The next night I was standing there with a cardboard coffee warming one hand, and a leather-bound copy of *Maud* in the other, when the same fellow stopped his car in front of me. The passenger-side window lowered without a sound, and he leaned over as best he could with his seat belt on.

"How much?" he asked.

Of course I had thought about this, and had even come to a decision, but at that moment I could not remember what decision I had come to.

"Negotiable," I said.

"So, negotiate," he said.

"Hundred dollars."

"Fifty."

"Okay." I had been standing on that corner for two weeks without a sale.

"Get in."

I was as awkward as always, what with my briefcase, and

Maud and coffee. Over the past two weeks, and during my research the week before that, I had seen tall young women on high spiky shoes slip into the passenger seats of sedans and Jeeps and convertibles with a flourish of long naked legs and rippling hair. I banged my knee, dropped my coffee to the curb, and took three tries at closing the door. I didn't even try to do the seat belt.

"Are we going to your place or a dark parking lot?" the guy asked.

"What? I mean what?" Things were still falling off my lap, et cetera.

"Usually we go to their place or a dark parking lot," he said. "Some of them don't want anyone going to their place. I never go to my place."

"Oh, I never go to my place on a first date," I said.

Which didn't make a lot of sense, because if I was going to sell my mind for fifty dollars the least I could do was let my reference books do half the work.

He pulled the car, and now I saw that it was a sports utility vehicle, into a lot down by the north side of False Creek.

"What sports do you find your vehicle useful for?"

"I don't know what you're talking about," he said, and he turned off the key. The lights went out and a glimmer was noticeable on the water. On the south side of False Creek young marrieds put their white plastic bags of fresh farm vegetables on the floor and began to consume three-dollar cups of coffee.

"I don't do any sports," said the guy. He was ducking his head under his retracting seat belt.

"Well, you have a sports utility vehicle," I said.

"I don't know what you're talking about," he said. "This don't seem much like fifty dollars' worth of mind to me."

I seized the opportunity to appear on top of the moment.

"The transaction starts when you hand me fifty dollars," I said.

He was a little overweight, and probably short, and shifted and heaved in the bucket seat as he reached into a side pants pocket for his thick wallet. He gave me two twenties, a five, three loonies and some silver.

"That's what I've got," he said.

"I'll go fifty-five minutes," I said. I was wondering every second, what happens next, what do I do? I remembered certain experiences in the classroom.

"Okay, start," he said, and he might as well have looked at his wristwatch.

"You interested in the Austro-French Piedmontese war?" I asked, and a voice inside me asked why the hell I would come up with that.

He eyeballed me, then looked ahead at the shimmer in the black water. He shuffled his body behind the driver's wheel, and put the palm of his right hand on his right thigh. Was he getting ready to put it on my left thigh? What the hell is the protocol, I asked myself.

I shuffled my body in the passenger seat.

"Well, it seems that an Italian patriot named Felice Orsini tried to assassinate the Habsburg emperor Franz-Josef. People were always trying to assassinate the Habsburg emperor. But when Napoléon III of France found out about it, he remembered that in his youth he too had fought for Italian independence.

The Napoléons were always crying for liberty and such, while pulling off coups d'état, and here was a chance for Louis-Napoléon to get in good with the senators he had recently dumped. So in a secret meeting at Plombières, in July of 1858, he pledged support for the Italian forces in the effort to free Lombardy and Venetia from the Austrian yoke. There are two villages called Plombières, in fact. There is Plombières-les-Bains, a dicky little place somewhat south of Nancy, and Plombières-les-Dijon, just west of Dijon. Anyway, the Italians also had England on their side, and could probably count on the Russians, who were pissed off with the Austrians for not being grateful enough for their help in an earlier scrap. Well, the Austrians blew this one. They should have just let well enough alone, but the emperor sent tough messages to Sardinia and Piedmont and ordered the Italians to forget it. This gave Napoléon III and Cavour all the excuse they needed to start the Austro-Piedmontese war. Well, both sides fought with stupidity and gallantry, and thousands of nicely dressed soldiers were killed, but eventually Napoléon beat Franz-Josef, and a little more of the Italian peninsula was removed from Austrian ownership. Then, of course the Austrians had to worry about war with Prussia concerning territory in Denmark."

"Fascinating but confusing," said my client, still looking at the shimmer. The fingers of his right hand were tapping on his right knee.

"Interested in how the rumours of liberty in the north of Italy seemed to threaten the hegemony of the Pope?"

"I would find it fascinating."

"The Pope's people in Paris were concerned that —"

"I would find it fascinating, but I have to bring up a question that is bothering me," said my client, with forty-some-odd minutes still on the clock.

The thought went through my mind that if I had had students more like him I might have still been in the classroom. Imagine: a student that brings up a question. Of course I smiled now, and shuffled in my seat so that I was nearly facing him.

"Bring up your question, Mr. —"

"We don't do names in this kind of situation," he said.

"Of course not," I said. "What is your question?"

Unconsciously, probably, he now had his hands on the steering wheel. He did not, at first, look like the kind of man who spends a lot of time in reflective thought, but perhaps the species accommodates to the individual — a look of systematic consideration fitted itself to his very high forehead, and he spoke, still looking straight ahead through the windshield into patterns of exterior artificial light.

"You claim to be selling your mind," he said.

"Correct."

"You're a mind whore."

"If you have to put it in those terms."

He took a quick look at me and then looked back at his shimmer. Then back at me, briefly.

"It seems to me," he said, "that with this Napoléon war in Italy, you are reciting a chain of events, a chain of events with a kind of cause and effect process, implied cause and effect, wouldn't you say?"

"Well, teaching is more than —"

"Teaching?"

"I mean."

"Here's what I'm thinking," he said. "All that stuff about alliances and battles and emperors, you could store it in your brain. Store it in your brain, and then bring some out whenever you need it."

"Ah, but it entails more than that. There's analytical thought and —"

"Bring it out whenever you want," he said.

"Sometimes it's easier than other times," I said.

His fingers were tapping fast on his thigh, both hands, both thighs. I was beginning to remember the stories I had heard from Danielle about bad tricks. No, that was an exaggeration, I decided. My client was still looking straight ahead, out the windshield, at the gleam. That did not make me comfortable, though.

"So what I'm saying is: that's brain, that's not mind."

"Tell us what you mean by the distinction," I suggested.

"Us? Us? This isn't a classroom, professor, this is a date," said my client. I was really wishing that I knew his name, so that I could say his name at the beginning of each sentence from now on.

"Me," I said.

His fingers calmed down. Now he was running the palms of his hands up and down the dark cloth on his thighs. I reached inside my sweater and retrieved a roll of coughdrops from my shirt pocket. I extended it toward him and he looked and shook his head. So I popped two into my mouth.

I looked surreptitiously at my watch. Half an hour.

"The distinction," he said at last. "The distinction is this. Your brain is a network of gooey meat inside your head, very physical. But you do a million calculations, memory storing, arithmetic, sexual fantasies, and so on, with your brain. And it's your brain. It's a personal thing, an individual thing, private. You follow me?"

I nodded, sort of forcing him to look over at me for a second.

"I got a brain. You got a brain. All God's children got brains. One each. Some better than others. When you die, that's it. That brain is toast."

"So to speak," I offered.

"Whereas the mind — that is a: not personal, and b: not physical."

He sounded a little smug. Maybe a little apprehensive regarding how well he was doing, but also a little smug. Professors are used to getting that combination from people who want to argue with them.

"Proceed," I said. I had heard about johns who pay prostitutes a lot of money just so they can have someone to talk to. But this was a little complicated, this date. I mean it was I who was supposed to be talking for money.

He proceeded.

"Well, the way I look at it, the mind is something that just — exists — out there, and we tap into it. With our brains, I guess."

"I think I see where you're going," I said.

"Each of us can tap into various minds."

"Uh-huh?"

"You've heard about them. The seventeenth-century mind. The female mind. The Northern European mind. Et cetera et cetera."

"The Habsburg mind and the Piedmontese mind," I suggested.

"Ha ha. So what does it mean when you 'change your mind'? I guess it's like changing your address or changing your pants. You move out of one and into another. That's mind. So that's why you can't really say that you're selling your mind on the street, eh?"

"Well," I said in my defence, "I can't very well say I've got brain for sale, can I?"

"Climb the stairs, try my wares."

"What?" I didn't know what he was saying.

Now his fingers were tapping like crazy.

"I figure you ought to give me back half my money," he said.

"Why?"

"Well, I figure brain is worth a lot less than mind, it being just — a: physical, and b: personal."

"Ah," I countered, making the "ah" last as long as possible while I thought about my next move. "Ah, but mind, well, you can just tap into mind, like the Internet. But brain is individual. If you get someone to deliver brain, that's a service. The provider has to make a living, eh?"

He was looking at me now, instead of his old shimmer.

"Okay, I guess you're right," he said.

I smiled.

"How about a kiss?" he said.

What the hell. I gave him a kiss.

THE JADE PEONY

Wayson Choy

Excerpt from the novel *The Jade Peony*

The old man first visited our house when I was five, in 1933. At that time, I had only two brothers to worry about. Kiam and Jung were then ten and seven years old. Sekky was not yet born, though he was on his way. Grandmother, or Poh-Poh, was going regularly to our family Tong Association Temple on Pender Street to pray for a boy.

Decades later, our neighbour Mrs. Lim said that I kept insisting on another girl to balance things, but Stepmother told me that these things were in the hands of the gods.

Stepmother was a young woman when she came to Canada, barely twenty and a dozen years younger than Father. She came with no education, with a village dialect as poor as she was. Girls were often left to fend for themselves in the streets, so she was lucky to have any family interested in her fate. Though my face was round like Father's, I had her eyes and delicate mouth, her high forehead but not her high cheekbones.

This slim woman, with her fine features and genteel posture, was a seven-year-old girl in war-torn China when bandits killed most of her family. Found hiding between two trunks of clothes, she was taken to a Mission House, then taken away again, reclaimed by the village clan, and eventually sold into Father's Canton merchant family. For years they fed her, taught her house duties, and finally put her on a steamship to Canada. She was brought over to help take care of Poh-Poh and to keep Father appropriate wifely company; but soon the young woman became more a wife than a concubine to Father, more a stepdaughter than a house servant to Grandmother. And a few years later, I, Jook-Liang, was born to them. Now, in our rented house, she was big with another child.

Poh-Poh, being one of the few elder women left in Vancouver, took pleasure in her status and became the arbitrator of the old ways. Poh-Poh insisted we simplify our kinship terms in Canada, so my mother became "Stepmother." That is what the two boys always called her, for Kiam was the First Son of Father's First Wife who had died mysteriously in China; and Jung, the Second Son, had been adopted into our family. What the sons called my mother, my mother became. The name "Stepmother" kept things simple, orderly, as Poh-Poh had determined. Father did not protest. Nor did the slim, pretty woman that was my mother seem to protest, though she must have cast a glance at the Old One and decided to bide her time. That was the order of things in China.

"What will be, will be," all the *lao wah-kiu*, the Chinatown old-timers, used to say to each other. "In Gold Mountain, simple is best."

There were, besides, false immigration stories to hide, secrets to be kept.

Stepmother was sitting on a kitchen chair and helping me to dress my Raggedy Ann; I touched her protruding tummy, I wanted the new baby all to myself. The two boys were waving toy swords around, swinging them in turn at three cutout hardboard nodding heads set up on the kitchen table. *Whack!* The game was to send the flat heads flying into the air to fall on a roll-out floor map of China. Whack! The game was Hong Kong-made and called Enemies of Free China.

One enemy head swooped up and clacked onto the linoleum floor, missing its target by three feet. Jung started to swear when Father looked up from his brush-writing in the other room. He could see everything we were doing in the kitchen. Poh-Poh sat on the other side of the table, enjoying Kiam and Jung's new game. Bags of groceries sat on the kitchen counter ready for supper preparations.

"I need a girl-baby to be my slave," I insisted, remembering Poh-Poh's stories of the time she herself once had a girl-helper in the dank, steamy kitchen of the cruel, rich Chin family in Old China. The Chins were refugees from Manchuria after the Japanese seized the territory. Not knowing any better, Poh-Poh treated the younger girl, her kitchen assistant, as unkindly as she herself had been treated; the women of the rich Chin family who "owned" Poh-Poh were used to wielding the whip and bamboo rods as freely on their fourteen servants as on the oxen and pigs.

"Too much bad memory," Poh-Poh said, and then, midway in its telling, would suddenly end a story of those old days. She would make a self-pitying face and complain how her arteries felt cramped with pain, how everything frustrated her, "*Ahyaii, ho git-sum!* How heart-cramp!" Though she was years younger than Poh-Poh, Mrs. Lim would shake her head in agreement, both of them clutching their left sides in common sympathy. It was a gesture I'd noticed in the Chinese Operas that Poh-Poh took me and my brothers to see in Canton Alley.

Whack! Another head rolled onto the floor. Kiam swung his toy sword like an ancient warrior-king from the Chinese Opera. Jung preferred to use his sword like a bayonet first, and then, *Whack!*

"Maybe Wong Bak — Old Wong — keep you company later, Liang-Liang," Poh-Poh said, happily stepping over one of the enemies of Free China to get some chopsticks from the table drawer. She was proud of her warrior grandsons. "Kill more," she commanded.

Poh-Poh spoke her *Sze-yup*, Four County village dialect, to me and Jung, but not always to Kiam, the First Son. With him, she spoke Cantonese and a little Mandarin, which he was studying in the Mission Church basement. Whenever Stepmother was around, Poh-Poh used another but similar village dialect, in a more clipped fashion, as many adults do when they think you might be the village fool, too worthless or too young, or not from their district. The Old One had a wealth of dialects which thirty-five years of survival in China had taught her, and each dialect hinted at mixed shades of status and power, or the lack of both. Like many Chinatown old-timers, the *lao wah-kiu,* Poh-Poh could eloquently praise someone in one dialect and ruthlessly insult them in another.

"An old mouth can drop honey or drop shit," Mrs. Lim once commented, defeated by the acrobatics of Grandmother's twist-punning tongue. The Old One roared with laughter and spat into the kitchen sink.

Whack!

Another head fell.

Stepmother rubbed her forehead, as if it were driving her mad. "Wong Bak come for supper tonight," Poh-Poh said, signalling Stepmother to start preparing the supper. The kitchen light caught something gleaming on the back of her old head; Poh-Poh had put on her jade hair ornament for Wong Bak's visit tonight. He was an Old China friend of Grandmother's; they were both now in their seventies.

Wong Bak had been sent from the British Columbia Interior by a group of small-town Chinese in a place called Yale. He was too old to live a solitary existence any longer. Someone in our Tong Association gave Father's name as a possible Vancouver contact, because Old Wong might know Poh-Poh, who had once lived in the same ancestral district village.

Most Chinatown people were from the dense villages of southern Kwangtung province, a territory racked by cycles of famine and drought. When the call for railroad workers came from labour contract brokers in Canada in the 1880s, every man who was able and capable left his farm and village to be indentured for dangerous work in the mountain ranges of the Rockies. There had also been rumours of gold in the rivers that poured down those mountain cliffs, gold that could make a man and his family wealthy overnight.

"Go to Gold Mountain," they told one another, promising to send wages home, to return rich or die. Thousands came in the decades before 1923, when on July 1st the Dominion of Canada passed the Chinese Exclusion Act and shut down all ordinary bachelor-man traffic between Canada and China, shut off any women from arriving, and divided families. Poverty-stricken bachelor-men were left alone in Gold Mountain, with only a few dollars left to send back to China every month, and never enough dollars to buy passage home. Dozens went mad; many killed themselves. The Chinatown Chinese call July 1st, the day celebrating the birth of Canada, the Day of Shame.

Some, like Old Wong, during all their hard time in British Columbia, still hoped to return to China if they could somehow win the numbers lottery or raise enough money from gambling. But now there was the growing war with the Japanese, more civil strife between the Communists and the Nationalists, and even more bitter starvation. Hearing all this, Poh-Poh gripped her left side, just below her heart, and said she only wanted her bones shipped back.

Father always editorialized in one of the news sheets of those Depression years how much the Chinese in Vancouver must help the Chinese. Because, he wrote, "No one else will."

In the city dump on False Creek Flats, living in makeshift huts, thirty-two Old China bachelor-men tried to shelter themselves;

dozens more were dying of neglect in the overcrowded rooms of Pender Street. There were no Depression jobs for such men. They had been deserted by the railroad companies and betrayed by the many labour contractors who had gone back to China, wealthy and forgetful. There was a local Vancouver bylaw against begging for food, a federal law against stealing food, but no law in any court against starving to death for lack of food. The few churches that served the Chinatown area were running out of funds. Soup kitchens could no longer safely manage the numbers lining up for nourishment, fighting each other. China men were shoved aside, threatened, forgotten.

During the early mornings, in the 1920s and '30s, nuns came out regularly from St. Paul's Mission to help clean and take the bodies away. In the crowded rooming houses of Chinatown, until morning came, living men slept in cots and on floors beside dead men.

Could we help out with Wong Bak? Perhaps a meal now and then, a few visits with the family ...? asked the officer from the Tong Association. It turned out that Poh-Poh indeed knew Wong Bak when they were in China, more than thirty years ago.

"Old-timers know all the old-timers," Third Uncle Lew said, taking inventory on his warehouse stock with an abacus. "Why not? The same bunch came over from the same damn districts," he laughed. "We all pea-pod China men!"

And now, tonight, Wong Bak was coming for dinner.

I looked up past Stepmother's swelling stomach, at the kitchen counter beside the sink with the pots and pans. Father had splurged on groceries: a bare long-necked chicken's head, freshly killed, hung out of the bag he had carried home. Poh-Poh also unwrapped a fresh fish, its eyes still shiny. Once it was cooked, Kiam and Jung would fight over who would get to suck on the hard-as-marble calcified fish eyes. I wanted the chicken feet. I wondered which part Wong Bak would want.

Father was worried about our meeting him for the first time. Wong Bak, I sensed from Father's overpreparation and nervousness, was indeed not an ordinary human being. He was an elder, so every respect must be paid to him, and *especially* as he knew the Old One herself. Grandmother must not lose face; we must not fail in our hospitality. Excellent behaviour on the part of my two brothers and me would signal our family respect and honour for the old ways.

Father looked at his watch and put down his writing brush.

"Let us talk a moment," he said to my brothers, and they left their game and stood before him. He told Kiam and Jung that Wong Bak might appear "very strange," especially to me, as I was so young, and a girl, and therefore might be more easily frightened.

"Frightened?" Stepmother said.

My ears perked up.

Father answered that the boys, being boys, would not be as easily scared about you-know-what. He spoke in code to Stepmother but whispered details to Kiam first, then Jung, whose eyes widened. After the whispering, Father delivered to the three of us a stern lecture about respect and we must use the formal term *Sin-saang*, Venerable Sir, as if Wong Bak were a "teacher" to be highly respected, as much as the Old Buddha or the Empress of China.

Respect meant you dared not laugh at someone because they were "different"; you did not ask stupid questions or stare rudely. You pretended everything was normal. That was respect. Father tried to simplify things for my five-year-old brain. Respect was what I gave my Raggedy Ann doll. I knew respect.

"I don't want you boys to stare at Wong Sin-saang's face," Father warned, which I thought was odd. Old people's faces were all the same to me, wrinkled and craggy. "Wong Sin-saang's had a very tough life."

"We know how to behave," First Brother Kiam insisted, waving the toy sword over the buck-toothed "Warlord" nodding on the edge of the kitchen table. Jung poked his sword, bayonet-fashion, and two other heads nodded away, waiting for decapitation.

Third Uncle Lew had given Kiam the Enemies of Free China game for his tenth birthday. Third Uncle had imported some samples from Hong Kong with the idea of selling them in Chinatown. Kiam read the game instructions written in English: USE SWORD TO SMACK HEAD. COUNT POINTS. MOVE VICTORIOUS CHINESE AHEAD SAME NUMBER.

The Warlord was one of three enemy-of-China "heads." The other two were a Communist and a Japanese soldier named Tojo. All three had ugly yellow faces, squashed noses and impossible buck teeth. It was a propaganda toy to encourage overseas Chinese fund-raising for Free China.

Watching Kiam and Jung jump up and down was far better than having them force me to play dumb games like Tarzan and Jane and Cheetah. Kiam had seen the picture *Tarzan* three times. Kiam got to be Tarzan; Jung, Cheetah; and I got to be Jane doing nothing. I embraced my Raggedy Ann and watched another swing of Jung's sword — *Whack!* — take off Tojo's head. Father said that Tojo, a Japanese, was in command of the plot to enslave China for the Japanese.

Whack!

The third head went flying.

"Don't forget," Father repeated, thinking of the worst, "no staring at Wong Sin-saang's face. No laughing."

"Tell Liang-Liang," said Jung, waving the wooden sword at me. "She'll stare at Wong Sin-saang's face and behave like a brat."

"Jook-Liang will be too shy," Stepmother said. "I promise she'll do nothing but run away. At five, I would."

"Jook-Liang almost six," Grandmother interjected. "She look. I look."

Stepmother turned away. Jung swung. *Whack!*

"Liang-Liang'll say something to Wong Sin-saang," Kiam said. "She'll say something about Wong Sin-saang's face."

"You will, won't you, Liang-Liang?" Jung said, following First Brother's cue to be superior at my expense.

I looked up at them through the flowered wall and tiny windows of my Eaton's Toyland doll house. I put Tarzan's Jane, whose doll legs would not bend, in the front room. At Sunday School, I had learned how all visitors, like the Lord Jesus, for example, and even Tarzan and his pet chimpanzee, Cheetah, should always politely knock first, before you invited them into the front room of your house. At Kingdom Church Kindergarten, I also learned to say the words "fart face," and that upset Miss Bigley.

"Fart face," I said.

Jung opened his mouth to reply. Kiam looked darkly at me.

"If you have eyes, stare," Poh-Poh said to me. "Eyes for looking."

Just as Jung was putting away the game box and taking my Raggedy Ann from me, and Stepmother and Kiam were setting the oak table, someone banged on our front door. A rumbling *Boom ... Boom ...* tumbled all the way from dark hallway to kitchen. Grandmother and I were waiting for the rice pot to finish cooking.

"Thunder," Poh-Poh commented, sniffing the air. The autumn damp would tighten her joints. She was midway through telling me a story about the Monkey King, who was being sent on another adventure by the Buddha. This time, the Monkey King took on the disguise of a lost boatman, and with his companion, Pig, they rode the back of a giant sea turtle to escape the fire-spouting River Dragon. "No one crosses my border," Poh-Poh said, in the deep voice of the River Dragon.

Boom ... Boom ...

"It's the front door," I said, comfortable against Poh-Poh's quilted jacket, listening.

"Thunder," Poh-Poh insisted, "ghost thunder."

There were in Grandmother's stories, always, wild storms and parting clouds, thunder, and after much labour, mountains that split apart, giving birth to demons who were out to kill you or to spirits who ached to test your courage. Until the last moment, you could never know for sure whether you were dealing with a demon or a spirit.

"Liang, stay in the kitchen," Stepmother said, wiping her hands on her apron. I heard Father struggling with the swollen front door, pulling, until the door surrendered and slammed open. "Step in, step in ..."

I jumped off Poh-Poh's knee. Everything in our musky hallway was suddenly lit by the outside street lamp. I could make out a hunched-up shadow standing on the porch, much shorter than Father. I thought of the burnished light that lingers after thunder; a mountain, after much labour, yawning wide.

"It's Wong Sin-saang," Father nervously called back to us, as if the shifting darkness might otherwise have no name.

Is it a demon or spirit? I thought, and nervously darted back to join Stepmother standing quietly at the end of the parlour. Jung and Kiam raced to crowd around Father; he waved them away. I grabbed Stepmother's apron.

In the bluish light cast by the street lamp, a dark figure with an enormous hump shook off its cloak. My eyes opened wide. The large hump continued shaking, struggling, quaking. Something dark lifted into the air. The mysterious mass turned into a sagging knapsack with tangled straps. Father hoisted the knapsack above the visitor's head and took away a black cloak.

The obscure figure gave one more shudder, as if to resettle its bones; now I could see, against the pale light, someone old and angular, someone bent over, his haggard weight bearing down on two sticks.

"This way to the parlour," Father said, turning to put the cloak and knapsack away in the hall closet.

The stooped stranger, leaning on his walking sticks, confidently push-pulled, push-pulled himself into our parlour. My eyes widened. Everyone was anxious to see his face, but so sloped was the visitor, yanking his walking sticks about, that at first only the top of a balding grey crown greeted us. Finally, he stopped, half-standing in the parlour, a runty frame rising just under First Brother Kiam's chin; the narrow torso, fitted with a grown man's broad shoulders, thrust against an oversized patched shirt. Powerful legs angled out from his suspendered work pants. He looked like a half-flopped puppet with its head way down, but there were no strings moving him about. Suddenly, the old man snorted, cleared his throat, but did not spit. The force of his breathing told you he was ready for anything to happen next. Now it was your turn to breathe or to speak. Or to clear your throat. Your turn.

No one moved except Jung. He tried secretly bending his knees to peek at the very face we had been warned not to stare at; Kiam quickly elbowed Jung up again. Did the old man notice? No one said a word. The old man began to breathe more heavily, sawing, as if to inhale strength back into his lungs. Still no one could see the face. We examined the rest of him. Sleeves were rolled up over frayed longjohn cuffs; dark pants, freshly pressed. Gnarled thick fingers curled tightly onto bamboo canes. Scuffed boots pointed in skewed directions. Except for a cane on each side of him, his crooked legs looked no worse than some of the one-cane bachelor-men I'd seen sitting on the steps of Chinatown, hacking, always hacking, with grey-goateed heads bowed to their knees.

"*Sihk faahn mai-ahh?* Have you had your rice yet?" Father asked, using a more formal phrase than Stepmother's village *Haeck chan mai-ah!* greeting — Eat dinner, yet!

To answer, the visitor straightened himself as far as he could, which was not far, and shook his head sideways: the overhead light bluntly hit Wong Sin-saang's face. A broad furrowed brow came into view. Wrinkles deepened. Jung gasped; the back of Kiam's neck stiffened. Father's warnings echoed in our minds: *Remember not to stare.* How could we help it? We all stared. Even Stepmother stared. I stared until I felt my eyes bulge out. The old man's face was like no other human one we had seen before: a wide-eyed, wet-nosed creature stared back at us.

A thrill went through me: this face, narrow at the top and wide at the bottom; this face, like those carved wooden masks sold during the Year of the Monkey; this wizened face looked directly back at me, perhaps like Cheetah, but more royal. I heard ghost thunder. A mountain opened, and here, right in our parlour, staring back at me, stood *Monkey,* the Monkey King of Poh-Poh's stories, disguised as an old man bent over two canes. But I, Jook-Liang, was not fooled. It could not be anyone but mischievous *him.* The air intensified; the world seemed more real than it had ever been for me. Poh-Poh was right: she heard ghost thunder when I heard only the door. A spell was cast in our parlour. Kiam pushed against it, trying to be sensible; First Brother asked the Monkey King, "Have you eaten, venerable sir?" Kiam used the formal dialect, just as Father had instructed him.

Monkey grimaced, showing large tobacco-stained teeth.

"No, not yet, thank you, so good of you to ask," he said, with Monkey smoothness, in a Toisan dialect, meaning that we, the family, needn't be so formal. Kiam tried discreetly to clear his throat, gulped, and stepped back, leaving Jung to stand alone. Now Monkey King, exactly as if he were holding court, looked steadily at Jung.

Jung said nothing. There was a long silence; it was Jung's turn as the Second Son to give his own greeting. Jung kept staring, open-mouthed. I thought of a sword flying through the air — *Whack!* — Jung's head, tumbling. I laughed, a short unstoppable titter. Stepmother's hand quickly covered my mouth.

"Wong Sin-saang," I heard Stepmother say, "you must be hungry."

Pulling a red handkerchief from his shirt pocket, Wong Sin-saang blew his nose noisily. Perhaps to signal his companion, Pig, waiting outside for instructions. I looked past the lace curtains, saw only the one-eyed street lamp.

"Who's there?" Poh-Poh shouted from the kitchen, all this time waiting for one of us to call her politely to come and meet the visitor, so she wouldn't seem too rude or too anxious. We'd forgotten. She banged on a bowl and banged on a plate and stayed in the kitchen, waiting.

The Monkey King seemed to hear nothing; he had turned his sable eyes on me. I let go of Stepmother's apron and slowly walked toward him. Stepmother reached out to grab me; I slipped past her. I pushed Jung and Kiam aside. Father began to fidget in the hall.

Across the room, Wong Sin-saang seemed not much bigger than me. His grey head drooped, as if it needed to bend lower. I stepped toward him. Stopped.

"This must be Jook-Liang," Monkey finally said, and his voice trembled, "the pr-pretty one."

I ran the last few steps and reached out to him, at once burying my head against his bone-thin body: *Here was the Monkey King!* After all, I heard his voice tremble — *the pr-pretty one* — a signal to any child not to be afraid of him. Not to doubt him. His disguise as an old man and his two canes were not meant to fool me, especially the canes. I knew what these really were: the two walking sticks, which he could instantly rejoin to become the powerful bamboo pole Monkey used to propel himself across canyons and streams; the same pole he employed to battle monsters, mock demons, shake at courage-testing spirits. I laughed and felt Monkey awkwardly embrace me; very awkwardly of course, so as not to betray his disguise as an Old One with two canes.

His gesture broke the ice; everything was familiar again.

I heard Stepmother and Father welcoming Wong Sin-saang in a jumble of ritual phrases: "Stay, stay for dinner!" "No, please don't stand on ceremony." "How good of you to visit." Even Jung finally spoke, though he did not remember every word.

"Have you your rice?" No one felt it necessary to notice how Monkey blew his nose again — and again — or how quickly he wiped his eyes. A signal to Pig, hiding under our porch.

The aroma of twice-cooked chicken filled the air; we could hear Grandmother preparing the food for the table; she stepped into the parlour and boldly stared at Monkey. *Eyes for looking.*

"*Aiiiyah!* Wong Kimlein!" Poh-Poh exclaimed, calling him by his birth-name in a voice loud enough to break up the hubbub. "It's truly you! They say you come back from Yale. Not die there. Die here, in Salt Water City, in Vancouver."

"Die here, maybe," Monkey said, looking up. "How goes your old years? Are you well?"

"Die soon," Poh-Poh said. "You and me too old for these days."

Stepmother took my hand and led the way to the dining room.

"You hear from Old China?" Poh-Poh took Monkey's arm, as if she would lean on his walking stick, too.

"We must talk, Wong Kimlein, just you and me," Poh-Poh commanded. "Come, come, sit for dinner."

I rushed to take the seat beside Monkey, and Poh-Poh pulled back a chair for him and sat down to be on his other side. She suddenly spoke to him in a different dialect, more pitched and strange than I had ever heard. *Monkey talk.* Poh-Poh waved Father into the kitchen to bring the food. Monkey chattered back to Grandmother, matching her odd, lurching vowels. Stepmother and Kiam and Jung brought in bowls of rice and steaming dishes of pork and vegetables and fish and bitter melon soup.

"Let's all sit and eat," Father said, bringing in the twice-cooked chicken.

All through dinner, I sat next to Wong Sin-saang, looking up at Monkey devouring his rice. He was careful not to miss a single grain so he would not have a pock-marked bride, and kept monkey-talking in that strange way with Poh-Poh. Jung could see what I was thinking. Being seven, he could still think like a kid, but not completely. When Jung brought over my own bowl of bitter melon soup, he whispered to me, "He's just a man, stupid."

I admit I was still not entirely sure and I kept arguing with myself: if Wong Sin-saang knew Poh-Poh — who said *she* felt older than even Miss Bigley's Bible friends, like Moses — how could Monkey be just a man? An ordinary man?

I drank all my soup, but hardly ate any rice. I was too excited, though Poh-Poh was drawing away most of the Monkey King's attention. She grew more animated, grew flushed with excitement to hear a voice matching the servant dialects of Old China. She listened with glee to the resonant *slurrph* the old man sounded at the edge of his soup spoon, a sound not encouraged at our table. (Father had taught us to sip our soup slowly, noiselessly, in the Western way.) Poh-Poh hardly ate anything, barely touched the green vegetables Father dropped into her bowl. She had turned her attention completely to the old man, speaking Old China secrets. Poh-Poh nodded, sometimes laughed, but both of them — more often than not — sighed with longtime sadness. Grandmother's eyes grew wide with remembering; the more she talked, the more she had to say.

Monkey kept eating, nodding; between bites, he spoke a moment or two, then let Poh-Poh chatter on. He was hungry.

I thought of all the stories Poh-Poh had told me since I was two: Monkey King, in all kinds of disguises, adventuring through the world of ordinary people: "He could look like an old woman with a hooked nose and crooked fingers, or turn as lovely as Kwan Yin standing in a white silk gown; sometimes it suited him to be a country farmer with dirt on his brows ... but all the time he was as hungry as a bear from his travels. You could trick the Monkey King with food, especially if you offered him ripe peaches." Poh-Poh smacked her lips. "Lunch and dinner were perilous times for Monkey."

My eyes were in pain from so much staring. I could not help myself: *here* beside me, the Monkey King sat, playing at being an old man as ancient as Poh-Poh, yet wielding chopsticks with youthful ease. I imagined juicy peach slices, delicately held by those same chopsticks, skinned slice after skinned slice, smoothly disappearing into his mouth. Wong Sin-saang ate every piece of stir-fried celery, bean cake, carrot, bok choi, eggplant, pork, fish and twice-cooked chicken offered to him, and ate, and ate, into his third brimming bowl of rice. *Hungry as a bear.* When the Monkey King ate, not a drop of sauce fell, not one grain of rice was lost. Father nudged Jung to stop staring at the old man.

I fidgeted with joy. Looking up at Wong Sin-saang, watching him carry his third bowl of rice to his mouth with such a sigh of pleasure, I sensed no one knew what else I knew: here, too, right beside me in his patched-up shirt, with his soft eyes, like liquid — sat the marvellous Cheetah of the matinee movies; Cheetah,

Tarzan's friend. Poh-Poh had educated me about this. After Jung took Grandmother and me to the Lux to see my first Tarzan movie, Poh-Poh announced that Cheetah was another one of the Monkey King's disguises. It was a way for the Monkey King to be with his monkey tribe and still keep in touch with Buddha's commands, for Monkey could not do without human company, black or white or yellow. After all, people were closest to Buddha, Poh-Poh told me.

First Brother Kiam always argued that Poh-Poh's stories were just *stories*, nothing more, like the stories about the blond Jesus Miss Bigley told us. At home, after Sunday School, Kiam always demanded to know: "How can anyone walk on water? How can so few baskets of bread and fish feed hundreds?" And Santa Claus never once visited our house. Doubt grew in me. Jung's insidious whisper was doing its job: *He's just a man, stupid.* The more I looked at Wong Sin-saang's animated face, his cheeks flushed with food, the more I felt I needed to know for sure. Slowly, a single question began to disturb my child's mind: *He's wearing a mask ...* I thought ... *like one of those Halloween demons* ... I wanted all at once to make sure he was not tricking me, not wearing a monkey mask, like those demons who came banging on our door and sent me crying with fright back into the kitchen. At once, I stood up on my chair. I dropped my chopsticks, turned, and grabbed Wong Sin-saang's large ear, tugging his Cheetah face toward me. Father banged his hand on the table.

"You Tarzan monkey," I said to Wong Sin-saang. "You Cheetah ..."

Stepmother gasped.

Poh-Poh reached across to stop me. "Let go!"

Wong Sin-saang started laughing.

"Let her pull, Old One," Monkey said, "let her pull away. Jook-Liang has your *lao foo* spirit." He looked into my eyes and announced, "Liang is tiger-willed."

I looked into his eyes. His dark eyes focussed and refocussed. They were real, reflecting life. I touched his deeply wrinkled forehead, studied both sides of his head to look for a telltale string. Nothing but straggly hair. Even the pen-brush tufts that stuck out from his ears were honest. I felt proud of myself, unable to hold back the news: *"Gene-goh Mau-lauh Bak!"* I said to the soft eyes. "A *for-real* Monkey Man!"

Stepmother swallowed deeply. Jung giggled. Wong Sin-saang pushed himself a foot away from my chair. Father tried to say something, but Monkey shook his head. Everyone sat with chopsticks poised. Silent.

The old man bent his head lower. We were eye to eye. He knew I knew his real name. My lips soundlessly mouthed the words: *Monkey Man. Mau-lauh Bak. Monkey Man.* He denied nothing. But he said, "Will you call me Wong *Suk?*"

I tried out the name: "Wong *Suk.*"

Suk meant someone about Father's age, or much younger. *Suk* was more informal than *Sin-saang. Suk,* I thought, and knew he was younger than Father even if he was very old on the outside.

"I like *Suk* very, very much," he said. "Oh, much better than Wong *Bak* — *Old* Wong. Make me feel younger. Call me Wong

Suk. Okay? Maybe everyone call me that. Okay?"

I nodded. He was giving us his secret magic name as a blessing.

Then I said the next thing Father insisted no one was supposed to say out loud.

"Wong Suk," I said, loudly, in Chinese, "you all twisted up, *crooked.*"

Wong Suk swallowed; he reached out and held me gently at arms' length, though it seemed to me his long fingers, his wide palms, were too awkward to hold an almost-six-year-old with such unearthly gentleness. Wong Suk's eyes grew strange. He spoke to me in the family dialect:

"M-pai Mau-lauh Bak?" Wong Suk's voice was a half-whisper. "You not *scared* of Monkey Man?" I shook my head, took a closer look at Wong Suk, touched his for-real wide nose, delicately tugged at the curving tufts of salt-and-pepper hair that formed his bushy eyebrows. I recognized his hair tonic; it smelled of the stuff Father always used. I leaned closer. Crooked arms enfolded me. *M-pai ... m-pai ...?* I heard Wong Suk chant. *Not afraid ... you not afraid ... m-pai ...?*

It seemed he could not stop his chanting nor his heart's rapid beat, nor could he let go his hold on me. I only knew to hold him tighter, lean into him like a cat, a tiger, catching the herbal scent of his body. The air felt hot.

"This child not afraid of me," I heard him say to everyone. "She not afraid."

"Don't be foolish," I heard Poh-Poh saying, in the dialect I understood, and I could feel her tugging away at my arm. "Don't be foolish."

He's mine, I wanted to shout. *He's mine!* Something old sprang from me, something struggled to defy even Poh-Poh. I pulled my head away from Wong Suk and looked back at her. Something like an ancient sword swooped — *Whack!* — striking her against the wall, though outwardly nothing happened to Grandmother, or to Wong Suk, or to me.

Wong Suk let me go. I slumped back into my chair and picked up my chopsticks. Poh-Poh turned back to the table. Everyone went back to steadily eating supper, went on breathing the heated air. After Wong Suk settled back and slurped his soup, loudly, he and Poh-Poh spoke no more in their secret language to one another, though their lips smiled and moved with the memory of something deep and savoury.

TIME ZONE

Stephen Osborne

Excerpt from the novel *For You Who
Grow Pale at the Mention of Vancouver*

A taxi carried me north into the city over a bridge named for an unremembered government functionary, no doubt a man with a family and a history of his own; I cracked open the window and the tang of cedar and fish tugged at my nostrils. We swept down Cambie Street at great speed and I gazed onto wet pavement and gleaming boulevards into a world of muted greens and greys, and then the cloud broke apart overhead and sunlight burst into the street. Glistening shrubs that I had never learned the names of sprang into view in the sudden radiance, in shades of emerald and jade, and tiny purple flowers popped into the foreground; in an instant things had become overspoken: the grass was too green, the pavement unacceptably lustrous; all was saturated in colour and light. I looked again and saw daffodils fluorescent and tumescent and then things became in a moment, as they so frequently do, merely familiar. Daffodils are a member of the narcissus family, a little known fact of interest that enters the mind and is as suddenly gone again. We stopped for a red light at City Hall, whose looming towers resembled the *Daily Planet* building in Superman comics, with its pontifical air of all-knowing and even all-seeing, lacking only talk bubbles emerging from a window near the top in a long shot, and on past an enormous stadium with an inflated roof that made it look like an elephantine marshmallow. The driver, who wore a turban, swept out a hand as if to say behold or hark or perhaps to ease a cramp in the back of his neck, and swung over onto Pacific Boulevard and around to the West End through antiseptic corridors of glass and steel apartment buildings, to the lawns and the beaches of English Bay and the Sylvia Hotel, where I had booked a room on the fifth floor facing the sea. Years ago I had envied friends from out of town who stayed at the Sylvia, an anachronistic stone structure of eight storeys covered in an immense growth of gnarled ivy that gave it the air of a literary personage wearing tweeds and leather patches on the elbows, and now on my return I would stay there myself, a visitor and an outsider in my adopted city. The tiny lobby of the Sylvia was crowded with enormous piles of luggage, groups of elderly travellers costumed in creamy safari outfits with big pockets and pocket flaps. An elevator door opened and a middle-aged man wearing a fedora and a leather windbreaker stepped out and took hold of the only luggage rack in evidence. I need this right away, he said in an Australian or perhaps a New Zealand accent, and then he disappeared into the elevator. A tiny white-haired woman cried out rather sweetly or painfully, what shall we do now? and another woman called back: you'll have to manage without, dear. My room contained a flowered sofa and a kitchen table with chrome legs; the walls had been painted the colour of the filling in a pumpkin pie and hung upon them were pictures of shy maidens languishing in pastoral settings. I went over and looked out the window at the sunlight pouring into the bay through a distant patch of sky torn from the clouds, and at the freighters floating in the distance. Beyond that nothing could be seen in the west, where the clouds ended and the sea began. I went out to the beach and walked in wet grass over to the bathhouse and peered into the gloom within. I might have been looking into a bunker on the beaches of Dunkirk. Then for the first time I tasted the long damp molecules of that particular air of the west coast. A permanent signpost had been sunk into the ground next to a Mr. Tube Steak at one end of the bathhouse: WARNING, COYOTES IN THE AREA, it said, and below that, in rather fierce lettering: KEEP THEM AT A DISTANCE, punctuated with an exclamation mark. Had we ever known coyotes in the city before? And how does one keep them at a distance, as Confucius in his analects, if I am not mistaken, advises us in the same terms to do upon encountering supernatural beings? Overlooking the beach stood a sundial mounted on a granite plinth; as the clouds broke up over the bay, the shade retreated and in a moment I was able to reset my watch in a pool of sunshine by reading off the position of the shadow cast by the narrow blade of the sundial designed for that purpose and given an exotic name which I could not recall, onto a curved armature marked out in quarter hours, and in that moment I recovered four and a half hours of my day across the time zones, an illusion perhaps but nevertheless a sensation that I was collecting something due to me, for want of a better metaphor, and the metaphors of business so rarely do the job. The sundial was a memorial, according to the plaque set into its base, to a drugstore that had long ago disappeared from the neighbourhood. What species of civic memory was this? I wanted to ask but there was no one to answer. Later I remembered the name of the blade on the sundial and when I pronounced it aloud, *gnomon*, I was overtaken by an inordinate sense of satisfaction, perhaps an effect of the elongation of a day that had stretched across a continent: I reminded myself that I was alone by choice. I went into a taverna and ate a Greek salad and drank a glass of retsina and a thimbleful of ouzo. Later a trolley slipped from its wire as a bus turned from Davie onto Denman Street and I saw bus lightning for the first time in years, and the tiny shower of blue sparks overhead confirmed that I had come home again for the first time. Who could know this place as superficially as I? In the liquor store on Davie Street I purchased a bottle of Chardonnay, and took it back to my room and when I couldn't find a corkscrew called down to the desk, and a woman with a magnificent gravelly voice told me I might find a corkscrew in the bar so I went down to the bar, which at first glance appeared to be deserted save for a well-dressed woman of advanced years sitting at a table by the door with a carafe of white wine in front of her. She seemed to be thinking fiercely, I was tempted to say thinking to herself, but can we presume to know such things about other people without asking them, without getting to know them at least, perhaps by observation, although a simple interview would certainly suffice. Sonorous funereal music filled the room; had I been with a companion I would have uttered the word *lugubrious* aloud. In a far corner a younger woman with a swath of bright pink running through her black hair peered into a notebook; she held a pen in her hand. Later I must have glimpsed her nose, which was slightly misshapen, like a boxer's nose, rather lovely and strange. I advanced toward the street door where a notice on the wall said simply, NO POPCORN: a warning, perhaps, or could it be a statement of fact? It was impossible for the bartender, a smiling dignified man with an accent, to part with his corkscrew under any circumstances, as he said with no loss of dignity, if only as a point of professional pride, so I went back up to my room to get the bottle and realized that there was no fridge in the room and therefore no ice, so when I got back to the bar I asked the bartender for ice and he congratulated me on my good taste in the Chardonnay, I have forgotten what the label was, and advised me to chill it before drinking. I reminded him that that was why I wanted the ice and he lowered his voice to a near whisper to say that I would be well advised to invest in a proper, that is to say, and he repeated himself for emphasis, proper corkscrew like the one with which he was extracting the cork from my bottle of Chardonnay, with an effortless twist of the wrist that produced, as he expressed it, and it may have been at that moment that I glimpsed the slight indentation and then the subtle and perhaps tender widening in the form of the nose belonging to the woman with the pink streak in her thick black hair as she continued to write in her notebook at the table against the far wall, no embarrassing cork crumbs to be scooped up with the tip of the finger when you pour out the first glass. I went back to my room and put the wine into the ice in the bucket that the bartender had given me and turned on the radio and gave the wine time to cool as I looked out over the darkened prospect of English Bay, the waters of which were now sparkling in appropriately silvery light, and when the moon drifted into view in the southwest and I could see, in the words of the poet, that everything near had become far, I began waiting for Thursday to end. Sometime after midnight I switched off the light.

THE WINTER MARKET

William Gibson

It rains a lot, up here; there are winter days when it doesn't really get light at all, only a bright, indeterminate grey. But then there are days when it's like they whip aside a curtain to flash you three minutes of sunlit, suspended mountain, the trademark at the start of God's own movie. It was like that the day her agents phoned, from deep in the heart of their mirrored pyramid on Beverly Boulevard, to tell me she'd merged with the net, crossed over for good, that *Kings of Sleep* was going triple-platinum. I'd edited most of *Kings*, done the brain-map work and gone over it all with the fast-wipe module, so I was in line for a share of royalties.

No, I said, no. Then yes, yes, and hung up on them. Got my jacket and took the stairs three at a time, straight out to the nearest bar and an eight-hour blackout that ended on a concrete ledge two metres above midnight. False Creek water. City lights, that same grey bowl of sky smaller now, illuminated by neon and mercury-vapour arcs. And it was snowing, big flakes but not many, and when they touched black water, they were gone, no trace at all. I looked down at my feet and saw my toes clear of the edge of concrete, the water between them. I was wearing Japanese shoes, new and expensive, glove-leather Ginza monkey boots with rubber-capped toes. I stood there for a long time before I took that first step back.

Because she was dead, and I'd let her go. Because, now, she was immortal, and I'd helped her get that way. And because I knew she'd phone me, in the morning.

My father was an audio engineer, a mastering engineer. He went way back, in the business, even before digital. The processes he was concerned with were partly mechanical, with that clunky quasi-Victorian quality you see in twentieth-century technology. He was a lathe operator, basically. People brought him audio recordings and he burned their sounds into grooves on a disk of lacquer. Then the disk was electroplated and used in the construction of a press that would stamp out records, the black things you see in antique stores. And I remember him telling me, once, a few months before he died, that certain frequencies — transients, I think he called them — could easily burn out the head, the cutting head, on a master lathe. These heads were incredibly expensive, so you prevented burnouts with something called an accelerometer. And that was what I was thinking of, as I stood there, my toes out over the water: that head, burning out.

Because that was what they did to her.

And that was what she wanted.

No accelerometer for Lise.

I disconnected my phone on my way to bed. I did it with the business end of a West German studio tripod that was going to cost a week's wages to repair.

Woke some strange time later and took a cab back to Granville Island and Rubin's place.

Rubin, in some way that no one quite understands, is a master, a teacher, what the Japanese call a sensei. What he's the master of, really, is garbage, kipple, refuse, the sea of cast-off goods our century floats on. *Gomi no sensei.* Master of junk.

I found him, this time, squatting between two vicious-looking drum machines I hadn't seen before, rusty spider arms folded at the hearts of dented constellations of steel cans fished out of Richmond dumpsters. He never calls the place a studio, never refers to himself as an artist. "Messing around," he calls what he does there, and seems to view it as some extension of boyhood's perfectly bored backyard afternoons. He wanders through his jammed, littered space, a kind of minihangar cobbled to the water side of the Market, followed by the smarter and more agile of his creations, like some vaguely benign Satan bent on the elaboration of still stranger processes in his ongoing Inferno of *gomi.* I've seen Rubin program his constructions to identify and verbally abuse pedestrians wearing garments by a given season's hot designer; others attend to more obscure missions, and a few seem constructed solely to deconstruct themselves with as much attendant noise as possible. He's like a child, Rubin; he's also worth a lot of money in galleries in Tokyo and Paris.

So I told him about Lise. He let me do it, get it out, then nodded. "I know," he said. "Some CBC creep phoned eight times." He sipped something out of a dented cup. "You wanna Wild Turkey sour?"

"Why'd they call you?"

"'Cause my name's on the back of *Kings of Sleep*. Dedication."

"I didn't see it yet."

"She try to call you yet?"

"She will."

"Rubin, she's dead. They cremated her already."

"I know," he said. "And she's going to call you."

Gomi.

Where does the *gomi* stop and the world begin? The Japanese, a century ago, had already run out of *gomi* space around Tokyo, so they came up with a plan for creating space out of *gomi*. By the year 1969 they had built themselves a little island in Tokyo Bay, out of *gomi*, and christened it Dream Island. But the city was still pouring out its nine thousand tons per day, so they went on to build New Dream Island, and today they coordinate the whole process, and new Nippons rise out of the Pacific. Rubin watches this on the news and says nothing at all.

He has nothing to say about *gomi*. It's his medium, the air he breathes, something he's swum in all his life. He cruises Greater Van in a spavined truck-thing chopped down from an ancient Mercedes airporter, its roof lost under a wallowing rubber bag half-filled with natural gas. He looks for things that fit some strange design scrawled on the inside of his forehead by whatever serves him as Muse. He brings home more *gomi*. Some of it still operative. Some of it, like Lise, human.

I met Lise at one of Rubin's parties. Rubin had a lot of parties. He never seemed particularly to enjoy them, himself, but they were excellent parties. I lost track, that fall, of the number of times I woke on a slab of foam to the roar of Rubin's antique espresso machine, a tarnished behemoth topped with a big chrome eagle, the sound outrageous off the corrugated steel walls of the place, but massively comforting, too: There was coffee. Life would go on.

First time I saw her: in the Kitchen Zone. You wouldn't call it a kitchen, exactly, just three fridges and a hot plate and a broken convection oven that had come in with the *gomi*. First time I saw her: She had the all-beer fridge open, light spilling out, and I caught the cheekbones and the determined set of that mouth, but I also caught the black glint of polycarbon at her wrist, and the bright slick sore the exoskeleton had rubbed there. Too drunk to process, to know what it was, but I did know it wasn't partytime. So I did what people usually did, to Lise, and clicked myself into a different movie. Went for the wine instead, on the counter beside the convection oven. Never looked back.

But she found me again. Came after me two hours later, weaving through the bodies and junk with that terrible grace programmed into the exoskeleton. I knew what it was, then, as I watched her homing in, too embarrassed now to duck it, to run, to mumble some excuse and get out. Pinned there, my arm

around the waist of a girl I didn't know, while Lise advanced —
was advanced, with that mocking grace — straight at me now,
her eyes burning with wizz, and the girl had wriggled out and
away in a quiet social panic, was gone, and Lise stood there in
front of me, propped up in her pencil-thin polycarbon prosthetic.
Looked into those eyes and it was like you could hear her
synapses whining, some impossibly high-pitched scream as the
wizz opened every circuit in her brain.

"Take me home," she said, and the words hit me like a whip.
I think I shook my head. "Take me home." There were levels of
pain there, and subtlety, and an amazing cruelty. And I knew
then that I'd never been hated, ever, as deeply or thoroughly as
this wasted little girl hated me now, hated me for the way I'd
looked, then looked away, beside Rubin's all-beer refrigerator.

So if that's the word I did one of those things you do and
never find out why, even though something in you knows you
could never have done anything else.

I took her home.

I have two rooms in an old condo rack at the corner of Fourth
and MacDonald, tenth floor. The elevators usually work, and if
you sit on the balcony railing and lean out backward, holding
on to the corner of the building next door, you can see a little
upright slit of sea and mountain.

She hadn't said a word, all the way back from Rubin's, and I
was getting sober enough to feel very uneasy as I unlocked the
door and let her in.

The first thing she saw was the portable fast-wipe I'd brought home from the Pilot the night before. The exoskeleton carried her across the dusty broadloom with that same walk, like a model down a runway. Away from the crash of the party, I could hear it click softly as it moved her. She stood there, looking down at the fast-wipe. I could see the thing's ribs when she stood like that, make them out across her back through the scuffed black leather of her jacket. One of those diseases. Either one of the old ones they've never quite figured out or one of the new ones the all too obviously environmental kind that they've barely even named yet. She couldn't move, not without that extra skeleton, and it was jacked straight into her brain, myoclectric interface. The fragile-looking polycarbon braces moved her arms and legs, but a more subtle system handled her thin hands, galvanic inlays. I thought of frog legs twitching in a high-school lab tape, then hated myself for it.

"This is a fast-wipe module," she said, in a voice I hadn't heard before, distant, and I thought then that the wizz might be wearing off. "What's it doing here?"

"I edit," I said, closing the door behind me.

"Well, now," and she laughed. "You do. Where?"

"On the Island. Place called the Autonomic Pilot."

She turned; then, hand on thrust hip, she swung — it swung her — and the wizz and the hate and some terrible parody of lust stabbed out at me from those washed-out grey eyes.

"You wanna make it, editor?"

And I felt the whip come down again, but I wasn't going to

take it, not again. So I cold-eyed her from somewhere down in the beer-numb core of my walking, talking, live-limbed, and entirely ordinary body and the words came out of me like spit: "Could you feel it, if I did?"

Beat. Maybe she blinked, but her face never registered. "No," she said, "but sometimes I like to watch."

Rubin stands at the window, two days after her death in Los Angeles, watching snow fall into False Creek. "So you never went to bed with her?"

One of his push-me-pull-you's, little roller-bearing Escher lizards, scoots across the table in front of me, in curl-up mode.

"No." I say, and it's true. Then I laugh. "But we jacked straight across. That first night."

"You were crazy," he said, a certain approval in his voice. "It might have killed you. Your heart might have stopped, you might have stopped breathing ..." He turns back to the window. "Has she called you yet?"

We jacked, straight across.

I'd never done it before. If you'd asked me why, I would have told you that I was an editor and that it wasn't professional.

The truth would be something more like this.

In the trade, the legitimate trade — I've never done porno — we call the raw product dry dreams. Dry dreams are neural output from levels of consciousness that most people can only access in sleep. But artists, the kind I work with at the Autonomic Pilot, are able to break the surface tension, dive down deep, down and out, out into Jung's sea, and bring back — well, dreams. Keep it simple. I guess some artists have always done that, in whatever medium, but neuroelectronics lets us access the experience, and the net gets it all out on the wire, so we can package it, sell it, watch how it moves in the market. Well, the more things change ... That's something my father liked to say.

Ordinarily I get the raw material in a studio situation, filtered through several million dollars' worth of baffles, and I don't even have to see the artist. The stuff we get out to the consumer, you see, has been structured, balanced, turned into art. There are still people naive enough to assume that they'll actually enjoy jacking straight across with someone they love. I think most teenagers try it, once. Certainly it's easy enough to do; Radio Shack will sell you the box and the trodes and the cables. But me, I'd never done it. And now that I think about it, I'm not so sure I can explain why. Or that I even want to try.

I do know why I did it with Lise, sat down beside her on my Mexican futon and snapped the optic lead into the socket on the spine, the smooth dorsal ridge, of the exoskeleton. It was high up, at the base of her neck, hidden by her dark hair.

Because she claimed she was an artist, and because I knew that we were engaged, somehow, in total combat, and I was not going to lose. That may not make sense to you, but then you never knew her, or know her through *Kings of Sleep*, which isn't the same at all. You never felt that hunger she had, which was pared down to a dry need, hideous in its singleness of purpose. People who know *exactly* what they want have always frightened me, and Lise had known what she wanted for a long time, and wanted nothing else at all. And I was scared, then, of admitting to myself that I was scared, and I'd seen enough strangers' dreams, in the mixing room at the Autonomic Pilot, to know that most people's inner monsters are foolish things, ludicrous in the calm light of one's own consciousness. And I was still drunk.

I put the trodes on and reached for the stud on the fast-wipe. I'd shut down its studio functions, temporarily converting eighty thousand dollars' worth of Japanese electronics to the equivalent of one of those little Radio Shack boxes. "Hit it," I said, and touched the switch.

Words. Words cannot. Or, maybe, just barely, if I even knew how to begin to describe it, what came up out of her, what she did ...

There's a segment on *Kings of Sleep*; it's like you're on a motorcycle at midnight, no lights but somehow you don't need them, blasting out along a cliff-high stretch of coast highway, so fast that you hang there in a cone of silence, the bike's thunder lost behind you.

Everything, lost behind you ... It's just a blink, on *Kings*, but it's one of the thousand things you remember, go back to, incorporate into your own vocabulary of feelings. Amazing. Freedom and death, right there, right there, razor's edge, forever.

What I got was the big-daddy version of that, raw rush, the king hell killer uncut real thing, exploding eight ways from Sunday into a void that stank of poverty and lovelessness and obscurity.

And that was Lise's ambition, that rush, *seen from the inside.*

It probably took all of four seconds.

And, course, she'd won.

I took the trodes off and stared at the wall, eyes wet, the framed posters swimming.

I couldn't look at her. I heard her disconnect the optic lead. I heard the exoskeleton creak as it hoisted her up from the futon. Heard it tick demurely as it hauled her into the kitchen for a glass of water.

Then I started to cry.

Rubin inserts a skinny probe in the roller-bearing belly of a sluggish push-me-pull-you and peers at the circuitry through magnifying glasses with miniature headlights mounted at the temples.

"So? You got hooked." He shrugs, looks up. It's dark now and the twin tensor beams stab at my face, chill damp in his steel barn and the lonesome hoot of a foghorn from somewhere across the water. "So?"

My turn to shrug. "I just did ... There didn't seem to be anything else to do."

The beams duck back to the silicon heart of his defective toy. "Then you're okay. It was a true choice. What I mean is, she was set to be what she is. You had about as much to do with where she's at today as that fast-wipe module did. She'd have found somebody else if she hadn't found you ..."

I made a deal with Barry, the senior editor, got twenty minutes at five on a cold September morning. Lise came in and hit me with that same shot, but this time I was ready, with my baffles and brain maps, and I didn't have to feel it. It took me two weeks, piecing out the minutes in the editing room, to cut what she'd done down into something I could play for Max Bell, who owns the Pilot.

Bell hadn't been happy, not happy at all, as I explained what I'd done. Maverick editors can be a problem, and eventually most editors decide that they've found someone who'll be it, the next monster, and then they start wasting time and money. He'd nodded when I'd finished my pitch, then scratched his nose with the cap of his red feltpen. "Uh-huh. Got it. Hottest thing since fish grew legs, right?"

But he'd jacked it, the demo soft I'd put together, and when it clicked out of its slot in his Braun desk unit, he was staring at the wall, his face blank.

"Max?"

"Huh?"

"What do you think?"

"Think? I ... What did you say her name was?" He blinked. "Lisa? Who you say she's signed with?"

"Lise. Nobody, Max. She hasn't signed with anybody yet."

"Jesus Christ." He still looked blank.

"You know how I found her?" Rubin asks, wading through ragged cardboard boxes to find the light switch. The boxes are filled with carefully sorted *gomi*: lithium batteries, tantalum capacitors, RF connectors, breadboards, barrier strips, ferro-resonant transformers, spools of bus bar wire ... One box is filled with the severed heads of hundreds of Barbie dolls, another with armoured industrial safety gauntlets that look like spacesuit gloves. Light floods the room and a sort of Kandinski mantis in snipped and painted tin swings its golfball-size head toward the bright bulb. "I was down Granville on a *gomi* run, back in an alley, and I found her just sitting there. Caught the skeleton and she didn't look so good, so I asked her if she was okay. Nothin'. Just closed her eyes. Not my lookout, I think. But I happen back by there about four hours later and she hasn't moved. 'Look, honey,' I tell her, 'maybe your hardware's buggered up. I can help you, okay?' Nothin'. 'How long you been back here?' Nothin'. So I take off." He crosses to his workbench and strokes the thin metal limbs of the mantis thing with a pale forefinger. Behind the bench, hung on damp-swollen sheets of ancient pegboard, are pliers, screwdrivers, tie-wrap guns, a rusted Daisy BB rifle, coax strippers, crimpers, logic probes, heat guns, a pocket oscilloscope, seemingly every tool in human history, with no attempt ever made to order them at all, though I've yet to see Rubin's hand hesitate.

"So I went back," he says. "Gave it an hour. She was out by then, unconscious, so I brought her back here and ran a check on the exoskeleton. Batteries were dead. She'd crawled back there when the juice ran out and settled down to starve to death, I guess."

"When was that?"

"About a week before you took her home."

"But what if she'd died? If you hadn't found her?"

"Somebody was going to find her. She couldn't ask for anything, you know? Just *take*. Couldn't stand a favour."

Max found the agents for her, and a trio of awesomely slick junior partners Leared into YVR a day later. Lise wouldn't come down to the Pilot to meet them, insisted we bring them up to Rubin's, where she still slept.

"Welcome to Couverville," Rubin said as they edged in the door. His long face was smeared with grease, the fly of his ragged fatigue pants held more or less shut with a twisted paper clip. The boys grinned automatically, but there was something marginally more authentic about the girl's smile. "Mr. Stark," she said, "I was in London last week. I saw your installation at the Tate."

"*Marcello's Battery Factory*," Rubin said. "They say it's scatological, the Brits ..." He shrugged. "Brits. I mean, who knows?"

"They're right. It's also very funny."

The boys were beaming like tabled-tanned lighthouses, standing there in their suits. The demo had reached Los Angeles. They knew.

"And you're Lise," she said, negotiating the path between Rubin's heaped *gomi*. "You're going to be a very famous person soon, Lise. We have a lot to discuss ..."

And Lise just stood there, propped in polycarbon, and the look on her face was the one I'd seen that first night, in my condo, when she'd asked me if I wanted to go to bed. But if the junior agent lady saw it, she didn't show it. She was a pro.

I told myself that I was a pro, too.

I told myself to relax.

Trash fires gutter in steel canisters around the Market. The snow still falls and kids huddle over the flames like arthritic crows, hopping from foot to foot, wind whipping their dark coats. Up in Fairview's arty slum-tumble, someone's laundry has frozen solid on the line, pink squares of bedsheet standing out against the background dinge and the confusion of satellite dishes and solar panels. Some ecologist's eggbeater windmill goes round and round, round and round, giving a whirling finger to the Hydro rates.

Rubin clumps along in paint-spattered L. L. Bean gumshoes, his big head pulled down into an oversize fatigue jacket. Sometimes one of the hunched teens will point him out as we pass, the guy who builds all the crazy stuff, the robots and shit.

"You know what your trouble is?" he says when we're under the bridge, headed up to Fourth. "You're the kind who *always reads the handbook*. Anything people build, any kind of technology, it's going to have some specific purpose. It's for doing something that somebody already understands. But if it's new technology, it'll open areas nobody's ever thought of before. You read the manual, man, and you won't play around with it, not the same way. And you get all funny when somebody else uses it to do something you never thought of. Like Lise."

"She wasn't the first." Traffic drums past overhead.

"No, but she's sure as hell the first person you ever met who went and translated themselves into a hardwired program. You lose any sleep when whatsisname did it, three-four years ago, the French kid, the writer?"

"I didn't really think about it, much. A gimmick. PR ..."

"He's still writing. The weird thing is, he's going to be writing, unless somebody blows up his mainframe ..."

I wince, shake my head. "But it's not him, is it? It's just a program."

"Interesting point. Hard to say. With Lise, though, we find out. She's not a writer."

She had it all in there, *Kings*, locked up in her head the way her body was locked in that exoskeleton.

The agents signed her with a label and brought in a production team from Tokyo. She told them she wanted me to edit. I said no; Max dragged me into his office and threatened to fire me on the spot. If I wasn't involved, there was no reason to do the studio work at the Pilot. Vancouver was hardly the centre of the world, and the agents wanted her in Los Angeles. It meant a lot of money to him, and it might put the Autonomic Pilot on the map. I couldn't explain to him why I'd refused. It was too crazy, too personal; she was getting a final dig in. Or that's what I thought then. But Max was serious. He really didn't give me any choice. We both knew another job wasn't going to crawl into my hand. I went back out with him and we told the agents that we'd worked it out: I was on.

The agents showed us lots of teeth.

Lise pulled out an inhaler full of wizz and took a huge hit. I thought I saw the agent lady raise one perfect eyebrow, but that was the extent of censure. After the papers were signed, Lise more or less did what she wanted.

And Lise always knew what she wanted.

We did *Kings* in three weeks, the basic recording. I found any number of reasons to avoid Rubin's place, even believed some of them myself. She was still staying there, although the agents weren't too happy with what they saw as a total lack of security. Rubin told me later that he'd had to have his agent call them up and raise hell, but after that they seemed to quit worrying. I hadn't known that Rubin had an agent. It was always easy to forget that Rubin Stark was more famous, then, than anyone else I knew, certainly more famous than I thought Lise was ever likely to become. I knew we were working on something strong, but you never know how big anything's liable to be.

But the time I spent in the Pilot, I was *on*. Lise was amazing.

It was like she was born to the form, even though the technology that made that form possible hadn't even existed when she was born. You see something like that and you wonder how many thousands, maybe millions, of phenomenal artists have died mute, down the centuries, people who could never have been poets or painters or saxophone players, but who had this stuff inside, these psychic waveforms waiting for the circuitry required to tap in ...

I learned a few things about her, incidentals, from our time in the studio. That she was born in Windsor. That her father was American and served in Peru and came home crazy and half-blind. That whatever was wrong with her body was congenital. That she had those sores because she refused to remove the exoskeleton, ever, because she'd start to choke and die at the thought of that utter helplessness. That she was addicted to wizz and doing enough of it daily to wire a football team.

Her agents brought in medics, who padded the polycarbon with foam and sealed the sores over with micropore dressings. They pumped her up with vitamins and tried to work on her diet, but nobody ever tried to take that inhaler away.

They brought in hairdressers and makeup artists, too, and wardrobe people and image builders and articulate little PR hamsters, and she endured it with something that might almost have been a smile.

And, right through those three weeks, we didn't talk. Just studio talk, artist-editor stuff, very much a restricted code. Her imagery was so strong, so extreme, that she never really needed to explain a given effect to me. I took what she put out and worked with it, and jacked it back to her. She'd either say yes or no, and usually it was yes. The agents noted this and approved, and clapped Max Bell on the back and took him out to dinner, and my salary went up.

And I was pro, all the way. Helpful and thorough and polite. I was determined not to crack again, and never thought about the night I cried, and I was also doing the best work I'd ever done, and knew it, and that's a high in itself.

And then, one morning, about six, after a long, long session — when she'd first gotten that eerie cotillion sequence out, the one the kids call the Ghost Dance — she spoke to me. One of the two agent boys had been there, showing teeth, but he was gone now and the Pilot was dead quiet, just the hum of a blower somewhere down by Max's office.

"Casey," she said, her voice hoarse with the wizz, "sorry I hit on you so hard."

I thought for a minute she was telling me something about the recording we'd just made. I looked up and saw her there, and it struck me that we were alone, and hadn't been alone since we'd made the demo.

I had no idea at all what to say. Didn't even know what I felt.

Propped up in the exoskeleton, she was looking worse than she had that first night, at Rubin's. The wizz was eating her, under the stuff the makeup team kept smoothing on, and sometimes it was like seeing a death's-head surface beneath the face of a not very handsome teenager. I had no idea of her real age. Not old, not young.

"The ramp effect," I said, coiling a length of cable.

"What's that?"

"Nature's way of telling you to clean up your act. Sort of mathematical law, says you can only get off real good on a stimulant x number of times, even if you increase the doses. But you can't *ever* get off as nice as you did the first few times. Or you shouldn't be able to, anyway. That's the trouble with designer drugs; they're too clever. That stuff you're doing has some tricky tail on one of its molecules, keeps you from turning the decomposed adrenaline into adrenochrome. If it didn't, you'd be schizophrenic by now. You got any little problems, Lise? Like apnea? Sometimes maybe you stop breathing if you go to sleep?"

But I wasn't even sure I felt the anger that I heard in my own voice.

She stared at me with those pale grey eyes. The wardrobe people had replaced her thrift-shop jacket with a butter-tanned matte black blouson that did a better job of hiding the poly-carbon ribs. She kept it zipped to the neck, always, even though it was too warm in the studio. The hairdressers had tried something new the day before, and it hadn't worked out, her rough dark hair a lopsided explosion above that drawn, triangular face. She stared at me and I felt it again, her singleness of purpose.

"I don't sleep, Casey."

It wasn't until later, much later, that I remembered she'd told me she was sorry. She never did again, and it was the only time I ever heard her say anything that seemed to be out of character.

Rubin's diet consists of vending-machine sandwiches, Pakistani takeout food, and espresso. I've never seen him eat anything else. We eat samosas in a narrow shop on Fourth that has a single plastic table wedged between the counter and the door to the can. Rubin eats his dozen samosas, six meat and six veggie, with total concentration, one after another, and doesn't bother to wipe his chin. He's devoted to the place. He loathes the Greek counterman; it's mutual, a real relationship. If the counterman left, Rubin might not come back. The Greek glares at the crumbs on Rubin's chin and jacket. Between samosas, he shoots daggers right back, his eyes narrowed behind the smudged lenses of his steel-rimmed glasses.

The samosas are dinner. Breakfast will be egg salad on dead white bread, packed in one of those triangles of milky plastic, on top of six little cups of poisonously strong espresso.

"You didn't see it coming, Casey." He peers at me out of the thumbprinted depths of his glasses. "'Cause you're no good at lateral thinking. You read the handbook. What else did you think she was after? Sex? More wizz? A world tour? She was past all that. That's what made her so strong. She was past it. That's why *Kings of Sleep*'s as big as it is, and why the kids buy it, why they believe it. They know. Those kids back down the Market, warming their butts around the fires and wondering if they'll find someplace to sleep tonight, they believe it. It's the hottest soft in eight years. Guy at a shop on Granville told me he gets more of the damned things lifted than he sells of anything else. Says it's a hassle to even stock it ... She's big because she was what they are, only more so. She knew, man. No dreams, no hope. You can't see the cages on those kids, Casey, but more and more they're twigging to it, that they aren't going *anywhere*." He brushes a greasy crumb of meat from his chin, missing three more. "So she sang it for them, said it that way they can't, painted them a picture. And she used the money to buy herself a way out, that's all."

I watch the steam bead roll down the window in big drops, streaks in the condensation. Beyond the window I can make out a partially stripped Lada, wheels scavenged, axles down on the pavement.

"How many people have done it, Rubin? Have any idea?"

"Not too many. Hard to say, anyway, because a lot of them are probably politicians we think of as being comfortably and reliably dead." He gives me a funny look. "Not a nice thought. Anyway, they had first shot at the technology. It still costs too much for any ordinary dozen millionaires, but I've heard of at least seven. They say Mitsubishi did it to Weinberg before his immune system finally went tits up. He was head of their hybridoma lab in Okayama. Well, their stock's still pretty high, in monoclonals, so maybe it's true. And Langlais, the French kid, the novelist ..." He shrugs. "Lise didn't have the money for it. Wouldn't now, even. But she put herself in the right place at the right time. She was about to croak, she was in Hollywood, and they could already see what *Kings* was going to do."

The day we finished up, the band stepped off a JAL shuttle out of London, four skinny kids who operated like a well-oiled machine and displayed a hypertrophied fashion sense and a total lack of affect. I set them up in a row at the Pilot, in identical white IKEA office chairs, smeared saline paste on their temples, taped the trodes on, and ran the rough version of what was going to become *Kings of Sleep*. When they came out of it, they all started talking at once, ignoring me totally, in the British version of that secret language all studio musicians speak, four sets of pale hands zooming and chopping the air.

I could catch enough of it to decide that they were excited. That they thought it was good. So I got my jacket and left. They could wipe their own saline paste off, thanks.

And that night I saw Lise for the last time, though I didn't plan to.

Walking back down to the Market, Rubin noisily digesting his meal, red taillights reflected on wet cobbles, the city beyond the

Market a clean sculpture of light, a lie, where the broken and the lost burrow into the *gomi* that grows like humus at the bases of the towers of glass ...

"I gotta go to Frankfurt tomorrow, do an installation. You wanna come? I could write you off as a technician." He shrugs his way deeper into the fatigue jacket. "Can't pay you, but you can have airfare, you want ..."

Funny offer, from Rubin, and I know it's because he's worried about me, thinks I'm too strange about Lise, and it's the only thing he can think of, getting me out of town.

"It's colder in Frankfurt now than it is here."

"You maybe need a change, Casey. I dunno ..."

"Thanks, but Max has a lot of work lined up. Pilot's a big deal now, people flying in from all over ..."

"Sure."

When I left the band at the Pilot, I went home. Walked up to Fourth and took the trolley home, past the windows of the shops I see every day, each one lit up jazzy and slick, clothes and shoes and software, Japanese motorcycles crouched like clean enamel scorpions, Italian furniture. The windows change with the seasons, the shops come and go. We were into the preholiday mode now, and there were more people on the street, a lot of couples, walking quickly and purposefully past the bright windows, on their way to score that perfect little whatever for whomever, half the girls in those padded thigh-high nylon boot things that came out of New York the winter before, the ones that Rubin said made them look like they had elephantiasis.

I grinned, thinking about that, and suddenly it hit me that it really was over, that I was done with Lise, and that now she'd be sucked off to Hollywood as inexorably as if she'd poked her toe into a black hole, drawn by the unthinkable gravitic tug of Big Money. Believing that, that she was gone — probably was gone, by then — I let down some kind of guard in myself and felt the edges of my pity. But just the edges, because I didn't want my evening screwed up by anything. I wanted partytime. It had been a while.

Got off at my corner and the elevator worked on the first try. Good sign, I told myself. Upstairs, I undressed and showered, found a clean shirt, microwaved burritos. Feel normal, I advised my reflection while I shaved. You have been working too hard. Your credit cards have gotten fat. Time to remedy that.

The burritos tasted like cardboard, but I decided I liked them because they were so aggressively normal. My car was in Burnaby, having its leaky hydrogen cell repacked, so I wasn't going to have to worry about driving. I could go out, find partytime, and phone in sick in the morning. Max wasn't going to kick; I was his starboy. He owed me.

You owe me, Max, I said to the subzero bottle of Moskovskaya I fished out of the freezer. Do you ever owe me. I have just spent three weeks editing the dreams and nightmares of one very screwed-up person, Max. On your behalf. So that you can grow and prosper, Max. I poured three fingers of vodka into a plastic glass left over from a party I'd thrown the year before and went back into the living room.

Sometimes it looks to me like nobody in particular lives there. Not that it's that messy; I'm a good if somewhat robotic housekeeper, and even remember to dust the tops of framed posters and things, but I have these times when the place abruptly gives me a kind of low-grade chill, with its basic accumulation of basic consumer goods. I mean, it's not like I want to fill it up with cats or houseplants or anything, but there are moments when I see that anyone could be living there, could own those things, and it all seems sort of interchangeable, my life and yours, my life and anybody's ...

I think Rubin sees things that way, too, all the time, but for him it's a source of strength. He lives in other people's garbage, and everything he drags home must have been new and shiny once, must have meant something, however briefly, to someone. So he sweeps it all up into his crazy-looking truck and hauls it back to his place and lets it compost there until he thinks of something new to do with it. Once he was showing me a book of twentieth-century art he liked, and there was a picture of an automated sculpture called *Dead Birds Fly Again,* a thing that whirled real dead birds around and around on a string, and he smiled and nodded, and I could see he felt the artist was a spiritual ancestor of some kind. But what could Rubin do with my framed posters and my Mexican futon from the Bay and my temper-foam bed from IKEA? Well, I thought, taking a first chilly sip, he'd be able to think of something, which was why he was a famous artist and I wasn't.

I went and pressed my forehead against the plate glass window, as cold as the glass in my hand. Time to go, I said to myself. You are exhibiting symptoms of urban singles angst. There are cures for this. Drink up. Go.

I didn't attain a state of partytime that night. Neither did I exhibit adult common sense and give up, go home, watch some ancient movie, and fall asleep on my futon. The tension those three weeks had built up in me drove me like the mainspring of a mechanical watch, and I went ticking off through nighttown, lubricating my more or less random progress with more drinks. It was one of those nights, I quickly decided, when you slip into an alternate continuum, a city that looks exactly like the one where you live, except for the peculiar difference that it contains not one person you love or know or have even spoken to before. Nights like that, you can go into a familiar bar and find that the staff has just been replaced; then you understand that your real motive in going there was simply to see a familiar face, on a waitress or a bartender, whoever ... This sort of thing has been known to mediate against partytime.

I kept it rolling, though, through six or eight places, and eventually it rolled me into a West End club that looked as if it hadn't been redecorated since the nineties. A lot of peeling chrome over plastic, blurry holograms that gave you a headache if you tried to make them out. I think Barry had told me about the place, but I can't imagine why. I looked around and grinned. If I was looking to be depressed, I'd come to the right place. Yes, I told myself as I took a corner stool at the bar, this was genuinely sad, really the pits. Dreadful enough to halt the momentum of my shitty evening, which was undoubtedly a good thing. I'd have one more for the road, admire the grot, and then cab it on home.

And then I saw Lise.

She hadn't seen me, not yet, and I still had my coat on, tweed collar up against the weather. She was down the bar and around the corner with a couple of empty drinks in front of her, big ones, the kind that come with little Hong Kong parasols or plastic mermaids in them, and as she looked up at the boy beside her, I saw the wizz flash in her eyes and knew that those drinks had never contained alcohol, because the levels of drug she was running couldn't tolerate the mix. The kid, though, was gone, numb grinning drunk and about ready to slide off his stool, and running on about something as he made repeated attempts to focus his eyes and get a better look at Lise, who sat there with her wardrobe team's black leather blouson zipped to her chin and her skull about to burn through her white face like a thousand-watt bulb. And seeing that, seeing her there, I knew a whole lot of things at once.

That she really was dying, either from the wizz or her disease or the combination of the two. That she damned well knew it. That the boy beside her was too drunk to have picked up on the exoskeleton, but not too drunk to register the expensive jacket and the money she had for drinks. And that what I was seeing was exactly what it looked like.

But I couldn't add it up, right away, couldn't compute. Something in me cringed.

And she was smiling, or anyway doing a thing she must have thought was like a smile, the expression she knew was appropriate to the situation, and nodding in time to the kid's slurred inanities, and that awful line of hers came back to me, the one about liking to watch.

And I know something now. I know that if I hadn't happened in there, hadn't seen them, I'd have been able to accept all that came later. Might even have found a way to rejoice on her behalf, or found a way to trust in whatever it is that she's since become, or had built in her image, a program that pretends to be Lise to the extent that it believes it's her. I could have believed what Rubin believes, that she was so truly past it, our hi-tech Saint Joan burning for union with that hardwired godhead in Hollywood, that nothing mattered to her except the hour of her departure. That she threw away that poor sad body with a cry of release, free of the bonds of polycarbon and hated flesh. Well, maybe, after all, she did. Maybe it was that way. I'm sure that's the way she expected it to be.

But seeing her there, that drunken kid's hand in hers, that hand she couldn't even feel, I knew, once and for all, that no human motive is ever entirely pure. Even Lise, with that corrosive, crazy drive to stardom and cybernetic immortality, had weaknesses. Was human in a way I hated myself for admitting.

She'd gone out that night, I knew, to kiss herself goodbye. To find someone drunk enough to do it for her. Because, I knew then, it was true: She did like to watch.

I think she saw me, as I left. I was practically running. If she did, I suppose she hated me worse than ever, for the horror and the pity in my face.

I never saw her again.

Someday I'll ask Rubin why Wild Turkey sours are the only drink he knows how to make. Industrial-strength, Rubin's sours. He passes me the dented aluminum cup, while his place ticks and stirs around us with the furtive activity of his smaller creations.

"You ought to come to Frankfurt," he says again.

"Why, Rubin?"

"Because pretty soon she's going to call you up. And I think maybe you aren't ready for it. You're still screwed up about this, and it'll sound like her and think like her, and you'll get too weird behind it. Come over to Frankfurt with me and you can get a little breathing space. She won't know you're there —"

"I told you," I say, remembering her at the bar in that club, "lots of work. Max —"

"Stuff Max. Max you just made rich. Max can sit on his hands. You're rich yourself, from your royalty cut on *Kings*, if you weren't too stubborn to dial up your bank account. You can afford a vacation."

I look at him and wonder when I'll tell him the story of that final glimpse. "Rubin, I appreciate it, man, but I just —"

He sighs, drinks. "But what?"

"Rubin, if she calls me, is it *her?*"

He looks at me a long time. "God only knows." His cup clicks on the table. "I mean, Casey, the technology is there, so who, man, really who, is to say?"

"And you think I should come with you to Frankfurt?"

He takes off his steel-rimmed glasses and polishes them inefficiently on the front of his plaid flannel shirt. "Yeah, I do.

You need the rest. Maybe you don't need it now, but you're going to later."

"How's that?"

"When you have to edit her next release. Which will almost certainly be soon, because she needs money bad. She's taking up a lot of ROM on some corporate mainframe, and her share of *Kings* won't come close to paying for what they had to do to put her there. And you're her editor, Casey. I mean, who else?"

And I just stare at him as he puts the glasses back on, like I can't move at all.

"Who else, man?"

And one of his constructs clicks right then, just a clear and tiny sound, and it comes to me, he's right.

POLKA PARTNERS, UPTOWN INDIANS AND WHITE FOLKS

Lee Maracle

When I was a petulant youth, it never ceased to amaze me how we could turn the largest cities into small towns. Wherever we went we seemed to take the country with us. Downtown — the skids for white folks — was for us just another village, not really part of Vancouver. We never saw the myriads of Saturday shoppers battling for bargains, and the traffic went by largely unnoticed except that we had to watch out not to get hit when crossing against the light. Drunk or sober, we amble along the three square blocks that make up the area as though it were a village stuck in the middle of nowhere.

I was part of the crowd sliding along the street toward the park. A hint of wind laced the air. Six leaves curled around crazily just above the sidewalk. Ol' Mose was leaning against the mailbox chuckling at the same leaves. It was fall. Ol' Mose had that wistful look on his face — he was thinking about home, missing it. The colour of earth death, the scent of harvest amidst the riot of fire colours, like a glorious party just before it's all over — earth's last supper is hard to deal with in the middle of the tired old grey buildings of the downtown periphery. I can see the mountains of my home through the cracks between the buildings that aren't butted one up against the other. It seems a little hokey to take a bus across the bridge and haul ass through nature's bounty, so I don't do it any more.

"Say," Mose almost straightened up in a subtle show of courtesy meant for me. I laughed before he said anything funny.

"You still holding up that ol' mailbox? I thought I left you here yesterday leaning on the same box." Mose laughed and told me he was just keeping it company till Tony came out of the store.

"What's he doing at the tailor's? Don't believe I ever saw one of us going in there before."

"His sister is getting married. He's buying a new shirt."

"Well, hell, must be his favourite sister. Turning the old one inside out was good enough for the last one who got foolish like that." Tony comes out of the store grinning from ear to ear, proudly displaying a brand new bag.

"First time I ever bought something no one ever wore before." We examine his new clothes without taking anything out of the bag and head in the direction of the café. Every urban reserve has its café. In Vancouver it was the 4-Star, but it could have been the Silver Grill in Kamloops or any small, Chinese-Canadian café in any other city that was clean, plain, a little worn-looking and with food about the same. Jimmy the waiter likes us and the manager doesn't like anybody.

We don't go there to eat much more than a plate of fries, a cup of tea or some wonton soup. We talk, laugh and behave like we were visiting our neighbours rather than dining out. When the bill comes we all dig in and put our collective cash on the table hoping it adds up. Once we were a few cents short. The manager was about to give it to us and Jimmy slipped in the nickel. We gave it back to him about six months down the road. Jimmy tried to make a joke about "interest" but we didn't get it, which made him laugh all the harder and like us even more.

"Oh shit." In the park across from the café some guy was bent over another guy, cleaning out his wallet. Tony and I broke into a run.

"Hay-ay." The roller tried to bolt but I ran him down and thoughtlessly scolded the purveyor of the passed-out man's purse before I relieved him of his catch. Tony standing behind me must have geared up my mouth. I peeked inside the wallet — there was a whack of cash in there. I looked at the victim: a pricey leather jacket, wool slacks, gloves, Italian shoes and long black hair. He was an uptown Native, slumming, I guessed. Without feeling anything about what I was thinking, I wondered where all these uptown Natives are coming from, and pulled out a couple of twenties and handed it to the thief. He thanked me and took off.

Tony looked askance at me and asked if we should wake him up, like he thought it would be a good idea to just leave him. Mose grunted something about how he looked like your regular tourist. I gave them one of my *c'mon you guys, he's one of us* looks and moved to the bench he almost sat on. A few slaps and a pinch on the sensitive part of the neck brought him around. He grunted like a bear coming out of hibernation and sat up on one elbow, nearly falling off with the effort. I didn't recognize the booze he was drinking; must be some kind of fancy liquor I didn't know about. I leaned into his face to identify his tribe.

"My, Granny, what big teeth you have," he said, squinting up at me between glances to the left and right. His hand reached for his hip.

"It ain't there," and he sighed without swearing. I handed him his wallet.

"You didn't steal my wallet just to shame me, so someone else must have taken it and you retrieved it — correct?" Every syllable fell out of his mouth clear and accentless.

"Where are you from?"

"Isn't it customary in Vancouver to begin with hello and how are you, maybe what's your name, before collecting vital statistics?" The arrogance I recognized, but I couldn't put together the words to answer his question. Vancouver had become a collector of Natives from all over. Where you were from determined how we treated you in some way I couldn't explain, so I ignored what he said.

"You're bigger than most but you don't look prairie, so you must be from Ontario."

"That too. Where am I?"

"Pigeon Park. Where are your glasses?"

"Huh?" and the blast of unfresh booze made me step back.

"Your glasses."

"Now that is twice in a row you have identified a fact of my life without ever having seen me before. You are a clever little girl, did you know that?" He was upright and looking at me different, studiously, I think. A small crowd gathered behind me.

"Wrong two out of three. I am clever, but I am not little or a girl. This must be the first time you been here." Titters from the crowd.

"Bingo." His mouth formed a perfect smile, white teeth even and well cared for. He is beginning to look like a polka partner from the other side of the tracks that form my colour bar. As I walk away, Tony is wearing a smug grin and Mose is chuckling. Polka Boy knows he's been told off. He's European enough to imagine he was getting somewhere, but Indian enough to know he's blown it. He doesn't look all that confused.

Mose jumps into small talk like there hadn't been any interruption in our conversation. "So Frankie bought a new car." We laugh. Frankie has owned and junked a perpetual run of cars but none of them could ever have passed for new. We get all caught up in laughing about the aging symptoms of all the cars he ever bought. Polka Boy recedes into the train of Frankie's cars and their missing parts that grew in Frankie's yard like a graveyard. I am already slipping away from the laughter and dreaming of Frankie and home and thinking he stays on our little reserve just so he can keep the train of wrecks coming, or else he'd have joined us on this side long ago.

Frankie is inside the café surrounded by the regulars and bragging about his Salish Cadillac. "Not a damn thing wrong with it, talked him into lettin' it go for twenty-five bucks."

"Did the chauffeur come with it?" and everyone cracks up. The conversation rolls around the parameters of our village and the odd or funny stories about the people in it. I stop listening and think about polkas and Prince George and the only Indian conference I ever went to. Everyone there had been uptown, dressed in the Sunday best of white folks. It surprised me at the time. The music was the same, but the people were like the man in the square. They pinched out their words, pronouncing every single letter and whistling out their s's as though they were all terrified about saying fis' instead of fish. The polka music brought out the risqué side of me and despite my better judgement, I had opted for a mattress thrash with some guy.

It was like tying on a good one. The morning after sharpened the loneliness. I guess loneliness is the mother of all promiscuity, because here I was thinking of doing it again — only now the body had the face of the man in the park. It shook me a little. I reached into my pocket, calculated my share of the food costs and wondered if I had a free quarter. The banter at the table took on a slippery quality. I couldn't focus on the faces. My hand toyed with the quarter and of its own accord put it to rest in the folds of my pocket.

Time crawled by all winter. I spent most of it staring at my mountains just across the water, watching snow woman dress them up in white and wishing I was lost there. Every now and then I'd venture out to the old café, but Polka Boy seemed to spend a lot of time there. His dress code and language never changed, but he did learn to turn the volume of his arrogance down enough to grow on everyone. He was at the 4-Star talking up this "centre" he wanted to create. He captivated the imaginations of the regulars. I am not sure whether it was him that scared me or his centre. No one here dreamed dreams like that. Life here is raw, wine is drunk not because it is genteel, but because it blurs, dulls the need for dreams, knocks your sense of future back into the neighbourhoods of the people it's meant for — white folks.

I stared out of my window at the street below as though somehow my eyes would screw out from the sidewalks the words to describe my feelings. Why the hell did anyone want a centre, an office? We had the café. It was a hangout for those of us not quite cognizant of the largesse of the city, but aware we were not truly alone. Bridge Indians. Not village, not urban. An office is urban. Somehow Jimmy the waiter, the cranky manager and their café kept us just a little village. It was a place where we could locate our own in any city. Like an urban trail to the local downtown village. This guy wanted to sever the trail.

I scribbled little notes to myself: "*the Silver Grill in Kamloops, the 4-Star in Vancouver, Ken's Café somewhere else ... An office is not a hangout.*" Scribbling didn't help and I took to the wine bottle. In those days I didn't have much respect for my private words. The blur of the wine and the rhythm of country music and Patsy Cline crying in my living room didn't do much either. After a while the blur became stark, the pictures stayed real. What got blurry was my capacity to think about it, to see my way out, and that got unbearable too, so I left it behind. I was feeling like I needed to see my way out, even if it was only a dream, when I stumbled into the café.

I had been holed up for a while. I joined Frankie's table. Aside from his penchant for buying old cars he also served up his own kind of journalism. He ran down the news ... Rufus had sobered up in great anticipation of the centre and making the village more respectable ... Polka Boy was soon to rent an office and some Métis woman was going to be the secretary. I tried not to encourage such talk. You don't need hope to cloud your life either. I stayed long enough for Tony to tease me about how I looked as though my best friend had died, and everyone chided me for being a stuck-up hermit.

Outside spring had sneaked up on my world. Spiky slivers of earth-milk squeezed from her voluptuous breasts streaked across my face. I imagined the crocus flowers of home forcing their way through these sidewalks and trees, buds upturned, lining the dingy street. A frightful clatter of bumping, grunting and laughter from a group of villagers and my almost-polka-partner right there in the thick of it all broke my reverie. They were actually moving into a little storefront on the drag. I followed the racket inside. Everyone who had a sense of stability for our sorry little half-village was there, save Tony and Frankie. It was Polka Boy's community centre/street patrol come to life.

I could barely stay on my feet. The room pulsed with movement and the people receded. My imagination ran on about the reality of it, arguing with the impossibility of it surviving. I saw the street, its frail dark citizenry rushing pell-mell toward this dream and imploding at the end of the dream's arrest. For arrest it would. No one would allow the total transformation of this end of town into a real community. Its attraction, its magic, lay in remaining a peripheral half-village that could accommodate sentinels — not people, but sentinels, alone on a bridge, guarding nothing.

My smile hardened itself onto the line of my face while my insides cried in silence. My words, empty of content, fell in broken shards to the floor before they reached the faces they were aimed at. Nonsense greetings, mumbles of "how are you," dropped unanswered. They were busy. Every lousy piece of furniture — the old black telephone, file cabinets, coffee makers and cups — was carefully hauled in as though it was the finest possession these poor folks had ever seen.

I pretended to be caught in the wonder of it all. "Here, put the desk over there, no, here, plug the phone in, couches over there," and soon I was in the centre of it, as though it had been my idea all along. It was a star-quality performance for an Indian who would never see Hollywood. I kept it up all through the move. At home later, Tony and Frankie's faces haunted me. It occurred to me that they had been sitting at the back of the café alone for the first time. Tony didn't buy the dream and Frankie had no interest in dreaming for the folks down here. He had never left our reserve.

I stopped dropping by Tony's place for the regular tea and laughter while I wrestled with joining the gang at the centre or stubbornly clinging to the old café. It took a couple of months, but I did join the ranks of staff and volunteers who manned the office and conducted the street patrol. The office: it never struck anyone as hilarious at the time, at least no one laughed out loud, but the office was about as unofficial as it could be. One dingy little storefront on the drag, with its unwashed windows, worn linoleum and walls that sorely wanted finishing. The desk we had was not quite old enough to be antique but worn enough to be a joke, and the file cabinet needed a wrestler's touch to use. It had all been furnished by people who had bought their furniture second hand and had made a good deal of rugged use of it before handing it to us. But it was ours and we had never had a storefront that we could enter, have coffee and get treated like real customers.

We had a real secretary who hauled our butts across the fields of office life in the other world. She was appalled by our office and the nature of our work, but by and by she got used to it. Her first day would have been a major disaster had we noticed anything amiss, but naive as we were we didn't pay attention to her wool suit and high-heeled shoes or the cloying scent of her perfume. She coached us in filing, telephone reception and office politeness, though she could never get us to stop asking people if they were related to so-and-so from such-and-such if the name sounded familiar.

She came in one day full of her office etiquette and told us the mayor was coming. A hubbub of questions sprang up — "Who is the mayor anyway? What does he do? Why is he coming here? When?" — without regard to answers. She shut us all up, then told us what to say to sound smart without giving anything away. She ended the lesson with "and don't ask him about his relatives."

Old Rufus was best at it. He had had a lot of experience as a kid with tourists in his West Coast island home. He and the other kids had learned to small-talk while they fleeced them of whatever quarters they could get. The mayor loved him. Edmonds came in shortly after the mayor's arrival. The press was there and the place was a general zoo. I was squeezed up in the corner. I knew enough about who the mayor was to stay in my corner. He was head of police and that was enough for me to have nothing to say. Edmonds puffed up his chest, asked the mayor if he liked Edmonds' clean suit. The mayor said a constipated-sounding "why, yes," and Edmonds was on a roll.

"How is your grandmother?"

"She's dead."

"Too bad, mine too ... mmm, mm ... and where are you from?"

"I am from Kitsilano," and Edmonds corrected him, "I mean, where are your grandmothers from, what part of Europe?" ... and the secretary grabbed the mayor and pointed to the statistical breakdown of newly employed youth, etc.

Ol' Edmonds didn't catch on to the coaching, and the secretary had a few laughs about that later. "How is your grandmother?" and she would bust up. Defensively, Rufus pointed out that it must have cost Ol' Edmonds five bucks to clean his suit. It was the first time I ever saw an Indian laugh at how we are and Rufus felt it too. I couldn't put my finger on it then, but it occurs to me now that Edmonds was something like our unelected chief. He was the one we all went to to settle disputes or claim the dead. She shouldn't have laughed.

Polka Boy was our boss and he spent more time at a place called head office than he did down at the storefront. Everything was going so fast. I got to be friends with the secretary, who took me uptown every now and then, showed me other places she had worked. Great anonymous buildings, filled with women who sat behind desks in assembly line-style, banging out pieces of paper with weird words on them like "accounts receivable," "correspondence," "budget reports" and such. A couple of times we went in. She chatted with the women about everything from the new technology to new hairdos. When they laughed they seemed to hold the laughter in the way a kid squeezes air out of a balloon so as to make just a little squeaking sound. It all felt so bizarre.

Then I was beginning to feel weepy, like there was something being born inside and growing of its own will — a strange kind of yearning. The tears began to possess a beginning, an end and a reason for their growth. Although I didn't really want to know, it came anyway, flash flood-style. As the mystery of office work fell away from these women, the common bond of survival was replacing my former hostility. The sea of white faces began to take on names with characters.

It was around this time that the doctor came. She wanted to start this clinic and was asking us to help. Us? Help a doctor? I plugged my laughter with "What do you want us to do?"

"First, I am a lesbian feminist."

"Is that a special kind of doctor?" The secretary and Polka Boy both laughed. I wished I had gone to school past seventh grade.

"She's gay," the secretary translated.

Thick silence followed. We didn't quite know what to do with the information. Some hung their heads like they'd rather not know. I wasn't sure what this had to do with the question ... did she want us to help her find a woman? ... change her mind? I knew better than to ask. I looked at the boss, the guy who gathered us here in the first place. He was studying me intently. He slowly repositioned himself before speaking. I had the feeling that he had set this up. She didn't need us to help, she needed him, and he wouldn't move without all of us and somehow he thought I was the key to getting everyone else's co-operation.

He went into a monologue about the number of accidents, the deaths of our people on their way to the hospital or in the emergency room, and patiently painted a picture of racist negligence for us. A clinic with a friendly doctor would assure proper, immediate care. Where the hell is all this going? I didn't say that, I just looked away like the rest. I guess he decided to gamble on our assent because at the end he just said, "We can't promise you won't get abuse from some of the street people, if that is what you are asking. We can guarantee the staff here won't bother you. We don't care who sleeps with who."

Oh Gawd, this is going to be a mess. We all knew one of the guys was gay. We also knew he had to hide this fact from some of our lovely clientele. We further knew that he had never publicly admitted it to any of us. It was an open secret. We all side-glanced him. He stared catatonically off into space.

The meeting was over, chairs were put away and I got ready to go out the door. A hand tapped my shoulder and the boss called me aside. In the little walled-in space behind the storefront he asked me what I thought.

"That you're about the densest Indian I ever met."

"Why?"

It was too hard to tell him that white people cannot deal with the beauty in some of us and the crass ugliness in others. They can't know why we are silent about serious truth and so noisy about nonsense. Difference among us, and our silence, frightens them. They run around the world collecting us like artifacts. If they manage to find some Native who has escaped all the crap and behaves like their ancestors, they expect the rest of us to be the same. The reality that some of us are rotters is too much for them.

"Don't ask me, I don't know who your mother was." Pretty low. He sat bolt upright in his chair and then waved me out the door. We were never close. Until then, he treated me in the same distant and friendly way he treated everyone else. At times he had been disgustingly condescending, even arrogant. After that remark he got real cold. At night I looked out my window, screwing my eyes into the sidewalk, and cudgelled myself for saying anything about his mother.

I could hear the rich laughter of Tony and his family next door. Probably Frankie was there cutting up the rug and laying out the laughs. I missed them.

I knocked. They didn't answer. I wondered why my feet just didn't walk in as usual. Shit. I must have stood for a couple of minutes arguing with myself. For the first time in my life it didn't feel right to just walk in on Tony. I made up mind to go home and then the door swung.

"Jeez, Sis. You scared me. I thought you must be a cop or something." I backed up and he came out with me. We were both leaning on the porch and Tony started rolling a smoke. I handed him a tailor-made. His eyebrows went up.

"And do you have a savings account too?"

"With or without money in it?"

He laughed. "Well, now, you tell me."

"With."

He turned to face the dark, pulling hard on his cigarette. My hand holding the extra tailor-made dropped uselessly to my side. That, too, was different. Nothing was usual any more.

Tony's voice purred on, gentle and slow. He told me they were dredging and filling False Creek again, making it smaller. Pretty soon we wouldn't be able to tell we had ever been here. I knew he was talking about me, us, changing our ways until we were just like them. I didn't say a word and he never got any closer to really telling me off than that. I left as soon as the story was over. Back in my room it dawned on me: he hadn't invited me inside. And the weeping began again.

The doctor worked out. We fell in love with her. She was soft spoken, thoughtful, and enjoyed a good laugh when things looked their worst — just like us. She could hear every word you said and understand where they were coming from. She put up with no end of junk from some of her customers — patients she called them — and never laid their stuff on us. I got so caught up in the wonder of it all that autumn came and went without me thinking about the beauty of the colours of impending earth death or yearning for my mountains. Already, a slushy abysmal snow was trying to cover the sidewalks with some dignity. My mind was wandering around the endless days and nights of laughter that brightened the office down here. I had not thought of Tony or Frankie for a long time and the weeping got lost somewhere in the joy of our work.

I scraped all the tops of the mailboxes on the way to work, trying to get enough snow to toss in the boss's direction. He seemed like he wanted to break the ice between us and laugh again. This would do it. The door squeaked when I opened it. *Doggone, now he'll see me.* I slipped my hand with the snowball behind my back and peeked inside, softly giggling. There he was, holding the weeping doctor, a faraway, angry look on his face. My insides started to shake. I tried not to think about anything. The snow was melting and my hand started to freeze. I tossed what hadn't melted outside while I urged the door shut as though reverent silence would fix things. I took a quick glance out first, so as not to hit anyone with my snowball. It had started to rain and I just closed my eyes. "Here it comes, here comes the night" was squeezing itself out on the radio.

"The clinic didn't get its funding and we are moving uptown." The words came out measured and flat.

"Why?"

"The city said they could not justify funding a racially segregated clinic."

"I meant the moving," bit words through clenched teeth. How could he possibly think I cared more about the clinic, her white do-gooding conscience work. The office, that was ours. He squeezed her, she mumbled that it was all right. I didn't look at her. He started in about how the Indians uptown were getting themselves into hot water fighting each other in the bars and the city ...

"I don't give a shit about a horde of uptown Indians with too much money and not enough sense not to kill each other. This ..." I never finished. I bolted, slammed the door so hard the glass broke. I reeled on home, thinking about winter, polka partners and this dirty town. Visions of assembly line women office workers still going about their jobs and white women doctors setting up shingles in other parts of town crowded between the sight of him moving despite his better judgement. My knees felt knobby, my legs too long, my hair lashed coarse at my face and the tawny brown of my skin became a stain, a stigma, like the street. Hope. Expectations. Great expectations I had never had. An office. A simple gawdamned office where we could breathe community into our souls was all we hoped for, and it had been too much. I staggered down the street trying to hold onto little trivial bits of life that might help stabilize the rage. Old sidewalks are the only things in the world that age without getting dingy and dirty looking. The older they get, the whiter they look. Appropriate. And I am mad all over again. My feet play an old childhood game, "don't step on the crack or break your mother's back." Funny, I never thought about the significance of the ditty before. "Break your mother's back," and the first day the doctor came rolled into focus ... "Don't ask me 'who is your mother?'"

All the games I ever played came back. Rough games, games which hurt the participants, filled my memory. "Let's hide on Ruby," and little Ruby standing there in the middle of the sidewalk, silently weeping. Old Grandma warning us, "Whatever you throw out will come back to haunt you." She never said it with any particular tone of voice — just kind of let it go, matter-of-fact. The old mailbox is turned over again. I set it right and lean on it and think about deserting Ruby like Polka Boy is deserting us.

Grandma, I wanted to say, you don't know the half of it. How was I supposed to know that the things I threw out would come back on the whole kit and caboodle of us? The liquor store to the left is calling me. I answer. Overproof rum, that'll shut the nagging little woman whispering conscience material into my ear. Some old geezer wants a quarter. I am pissed enough to tell him to shut the fuck up. I look, open my mouth and then change my mind and move toward home.

Tony must have been watching me from his window on the old worn balcony of our project apartment house. I wasn't inside but a minute and a knock brought him through the door. He sits across from me just about where the slash of the curtain cuts a little sunlight onto his face. The rest of the room is semi-light. The trail of sunlight against his northern features makes him seem prettier than us from down here. No fat cheeks, just neatly chiselled high cheekbones, flesh stretching over them tight. His jaw is square and the hollow of his cheeks darker, sharpening his perfectly straight nose. He knows I am looking at him. He lets me despite his embarrassment, maybe sadness. I've known him nearly all my life and this is the first time I've ever thought about how he looks.

"Can see the liquor store from here ... looked like you were considering going in."

"Well, I never."

"Saw that too. But it don't stop me from wondering why. It's been a while for you, hasn't it?"

"I guess I don't feel so young any more."

A healthy "mnhmnh," and silence. In the still quiet I remembered Tony and Mose outside the tailor's before all this. I didn't go to the wedding, didn't even ask how it was. I was really scraping around inside my head trying to think about all the changes that had happened inside of me, trying to place snippets of new knowledge I'd gained and old habits I'd broken and make some sense of them. They whirled too fast. Memory after memory chasing each other in no particular order. It made me dizzy. The weeping is filling my gut, then Tony's voice tears up all the images.

"Saw Frankie today. Crazy guy. He ain't supposed to be driving. You know Frankie — talk a salesman into buying his own dictionary." My face wants to grin. "Cop stops him. He forgot to signal. Right away, Frankie jumps out of the car, lifts up his hood and pulls the plug out of the cap and tells me 'try her now.'" I'm smiling, nearly chuckling.

"Dumb cop says, 'what seems to be the problem?' and Frankie says, 'I do not know, officer, it just won't start.' He says it kind of condescendingly, but the cop, he don't notice. 'Let's have a look,' the cop says. Pretty soon, Frankie's in the car trying to start her while this cop is out there trying to fix what Frankie broke." The thought of Frankie and a serious young cop fussing over a half-dead Chevy in the middle of downtown traffic cracks me up. "Cop finally figures it out, all kinda proud, Frankie is no end to thanks, even puts the hood down. They say their howdy-dos and off we go."

"Cops can be extraordinarily stupid."

"Now, now," Tony says, "you know they hire only the smartest morons. Now, you going to tell me what the problem is? I didn't come here to entertain you for nothing, you know." He is serious. It dawns on me that Tony hasn't been serious since he was a kid. Was it seventh grade? Yeah, in seventh grade Tony walked out the doors of that school and never went back. Why the hell did he leave? His question is still hanging on his face. I don't think I can answer him. Every time I try to think about that place too many thoughts get all crowded up together and none of them ever sits still long enough for me to figure anything.

"You really liked the place, didn't you?" I nod. "Yeah, that boss of yours, pretty smart guy. Just breezed into town from Harvard or Yale or whatever university he come from, set it up and now he's breezing out again." He waits for this to sink in. "Come on outside, want to show you something." On the balcony he lights a smoke and leans into his own conversation. "See down there, Stace, just over there by the water. One time, Ol' Marta tells me, the shore come forward on the inlet — maybe a quarter mile or more. These people filled it up and put a sugar refinery on it. Yeah. Sugar is sweet, but you eat too much, you want more and pretty soon you're like Joey, forty and crippled with arthritis. You know what I mean, Stace. One day water, next day sugar, next day pain."

"Shuddup." I lean against the wall. He tosses his cigarette over the balcony, tips his imaginary hat and strolls off. My bleary mind begins working away, trying to get a hold of the significance of the story. It repeats it as though to memorize it so I can run it by me one more time on some other occasion, when all my parts are working. The sun is sinking under a pall of dirty blue-grey haze. What was it? One day sweet, next day water. No. Shit. I lost it. The phone rings. Shit.

"Are you all right?" It's Polka Boy. I consider slapping the phone on the table and then hanging up. The image makes me smile. Childish.

"Yeah. Shouldn't I be?" Someone should have kicked my butt a long time ago for letting the acid leak into my mouth and burn holes in my speech like that.

"You didn't look so good this morning." He is purring. That voice I recognize. Bastard, I think. I can see him leaning back in his chair, teeth flashing and voice curling up out of his lips, confident and self-assured. He doesn't remember that I have seen him have seductive conversations with almost every other woman he talked to over that old black phone. He just can't help it; his sympathy begins and ends as a sultry invite. My tongue freezes. I stop helping him with the conversation.

"Look, I would like to talk to you about this. I did what I could. Maybe not enough, but I ran out of words. The boys at head office ..." Uncomfortable for him, these pauses — he can't handle dead air space. He fills it up with more bullshit. Then, "Can we meet and talk? There are some things you could help with." I see clearly for just a moment. That look he gave me when the doctor came. I could feel his look through the phone. Get the lead street girl on your side and the rest will follow. I could help him bring the downtown folks uptown.

"I can't haul furniture." My voice is as dead as I can make it. He doesn't notice. Maybe he can't hear. I laugh to myself. The bugger just can't stand losing. One last kick at the street. Pluck the rose left behind by tragedy. I want to play him. Hurt him, the way he hurt us. *Don't be a fool, guys like him got little tin badges and water pumps for hearts. They aren't made of flesh and blood.*

I can hear the tail end of his last line, "I didn't mean that." It sounds like a salesman who thinks he has his foot in the door. A wispy goodbye I was sure he didn't hear and I gently put down the receiver. Without bothering to turn out the lights I slept. Slept the sleep of the dead. Dreamless. Lifeless sleep. I didn't ever want to wake.

Sunshine plays softly with the colours of my dusty lamps. The radio is playing old tunes. It must be noon. "You are my sunshine" cranks out, tinny and ridiculous. I have heard that tune till I could just puke. Whoever she was, she did not live here, did not harbour futile dreams of dingy offices, and she never had to wrap up in a blanket in the dark without any hydro. She didn't know how it feels to crack cornball jokes about no hydro as though it was the best damned bit of fun you had had in a long time.

Hydro. Today's the last day.

I walk downtown. The office is just a deserted hole now. A dead office looks smaller, more confining than one alive with busy people. Memories of the people float about, wafting to the corners of my mind. I look away and stare hard in the direction of the hydro office. The sound of the street, the roar of cars grows louder. The murmur of hundreds of voices drowns the voices of my memory. I'm walking, not staggering. I can't resist peeking in at the 4-Star. Jimmy is still there. He is drumming the counter. Bored. One lone old white man sits in front of him eating his soup. Jimmy doesn't bother looking at him at all. "Nobody I know," and I laugh at the remark he always whispered to me whenever a white man entered. I decide to stop by on my way back.

I pass through uptown Granville on the way to the hydro office. There they all are, a new crew, fixing up the building, and in the middle of the crowd is my smiling Polka Boy. He sees me, lets his lips form a smile just like nothing happened. One day water, next day sugar, next day pain. Must have been the Pepsodent smile that reminded me, and I smile too. My eyes face his, but the whole of me is not looking at him any more. The light changes and I turn, one last wave, and cross. Everything after that is mechanical and unmemorable. I pay the hydro bill, experience rudeness from some prissy white girl and tell her that I understand. She works in an office. She looks as confused as Polka Boy when I leave.

OUT ON MAIN STREET

Shani Mootoo

I.

Janet and me? We does go Main Street to see pretty pretty sari and bangle, and to eat we belly full a burfi and gulub jamoon, but we doh go too often because, yuh see, is dem sweets self what does give people like we a presupposition for untameable hip and thigh.

Another reason we shy to frequent dere is dat we is watered-down Indians — we ain't good grade A Indians. We skin brown, is true, but we doh even think 'bout India unless something happen over dere and it come on de news. Mih family remain Hindu ever since mih ancestors leave India behind, but nowadays dey doh believe in praying unless things real bad, because, as mih father always singing, like if is a mantra: "Do good and good will be bestowed unto you." So he is a veritable saint cause he always doing good by his women friends and dey chilren. I sure some a dem must be mih half sister and brother, oui!

Mostly, back home, we is kitchen Indians: some kind a Indian food every day, at least once a day, but we doh get cardamom and other fancy spice down dere so de food not spicy like Indian food I eat in restaurants up here. But it have one thing we doh make joke 'bout down dere: we like we meethai and sweetrice too much, and it remain overly authentic, like de day Naana and Naani step off de boat in Port of Spain harbour over a hundred and sixty years ago. Check out dese hips here nah, dey is pure sugar and condensed milk, pure sweetness!

But Janet family different. In de ole days when Canadian missionaries land in Trinidad dey used to make a bee-line straight for Indians from down South. And Janet great grandparents is one a de first South families dat exchange over from Indian to Presbyterian. Dat was a long time ago.

When Janet born, she father, one Mr. John Mahase, insist on asking de Reverend MacDougal from Trace Settlement Church, a leftover from de Canadian Mission, to name de baby girl. De good Reverend choose de name Constance cause dat was his mother name. But de mother a de child, Mrs. Savitri Mahase, wanted to name de child sheself. Ever since Savitri was a lil girl she like de yellow hair, fair skin and pretty pretty clothes Janet and John used to wear in de primary school reader — since she lil she want to change she name from Savitri to Janet but she own father get vex and say how Savitri was his mother name and how she will insult his mother if she gone and change it. So

Savitri get she own way once by marrying this fella name John, and she do a encore, by calling she daughter Janet, even doh husband John upset for days at she for insulting de good Reverend by throwing out de name a de Reverend mother.

So dat is how my girlfriend, a darkskin Indian girl with thick black hair (pretty fuh so!) get a name like Janet.

She come from a long line a Presbyterian school teacher, headmaster and headmistress. Savitri still teaching from de same Janet and John reader in a primary school in San Fernando, and John, getting more and more obtuse in his ole age, is headmaster more dan twenty years now in Princes Town Boys' Presbyterian High School. Everybody back home know dat family good good. Dat is why Janet leave in two twos. Soon as A Level finish she pack up and take off like a jet plane so she could live without people only shoo-shooing behind she back ... "But A A! Yuh ain't hear de goods 'bout John Mahase daughter, gyul! How yuh mean yuh ain't hear? Is a big thing! Everybody talking 'bout she. Hear dis, nah! Yuh ever see she wear a dress? Yes! Doh look at mih so. Yuh reading mih right!"

Is only recentish I realize Mahase is a Hindu last name. In de ole days every Mahase in de country turn Presbyterian and now de name doh have no association with Hindu or Indian whatso-ever. I used to think of it as a Presbyterian Church name until some days ago when we meet a Hindu fella fresh from India name Yogdesh Mahase who never even hear of Presbyterian.

De other day I ask Janet what she know 'bout Divali. She say, "It's the Hindu festival of lights, isn't it?" like a line straight out a dictionary. Yuh think she know anything 'bout how lord Rama get himself exile in a forest for fourteen years, and how when it come time for him to go back home his followers light up a pathway to help him make his way out, and dat is what Divali lights is all about? All Janet know is 'bout going for drive in de country to see light, and she could remember looking forward, around Divali time, to the lil brown paper-bag packages full a burfi and parasad that she father Hindu students used to bring for him.

One time in a Indian restaurant she ask for parasad for dessert. Well! Since den I never go back in dat restaurant, I embarrass fuh so!

I used to think I was a Hindu par excellence until I come up here and see real flesh and blood Indian from India. Up here, I learning 'bout all kind a custom and food and music and clothes dat we never see or hear 'bout in good ole Trinidad. Is de next best thing to going to India, in truth, oui! But Indian store clerk on Main Street doh have no patience with us, specially when we talking English to dem. Yuh ask dem a question in English and dey insist on giving de answer in Hindi or Punjabi or Urdu or Gujarati. How I suppose to know de difference even! And den dey look at yuh disdainful disdainful — like yuh disloyal, like yuh is a traitor.

But yuh know, it have one other reason I real reluctant to go Main Street. Yuh see, Janet pretty fuh so! And I doh like de way men does look at she, as if because she wearing jeans and T-shirt and high-heel shoe and makeup and have long hair loose and flying about like she is a walking-talking shampoo ad, dat she easy. And de women always looking at she beady eye, like she loose and going to thief dey man. Dat kind a thing always make me want to put mih arm round she waist like, she is my woman, take yuh eyes off she! and shock de false teeth right out dey mouth. And den is a whole other story when dey see me with mih crew cut and mih blue jeans tuck inside mih jim-boots. Walking next to Janet, who so femme dat she redundant, tend to make me look like a gender dey forget to classify. Before going Main Street I does parade in front de mirror practising a jiggly-wiggly kind a walk. But if I ain't walking like a strong-man monkey I doh exactly feel right and I always revert back to mih true colours. De men dem does look at me like if dey is exactly what I need a taste of to cure me good and proper. I could see dey eyes watching Janet and me, dey face growing dark as dey imagining all kind a situation and position. And de women dem embarrass fuh so to watch me in mih eye, like dey fraid I will jump up and try to kiss dem, or make pass at dem. Yuh know, sometimes I wonder if I ain't mad enough to do it just for a little bacchanal, nah!

Going for a outing with mih Janet on Main Street ain't easy! If only it wasn't for burfi and gulub jamoon! If only I had a learned how to cook dem kind a thing before I leave home and come up here to live!

2.

In large deep-orange Sanskrit-style letters, de sign on de saffron-colour awning above de door read *Kush Valley Sweets*. Underneath in smaller red letters it had *Desserts Fit For The Gods*. It was a corner building. The front and side was one big glass wall. Inside was big. Big like a gymnasium. Yuh could see in through de brown tint windows: dark brown plastic chair, and brown table, each one de length of a door, line up stiff and straight in row after row like if is a school room.

Before entering de restaurant I ask Janet to wait one minute outside with me while I rumfle up mih memory, pulling out all de sweet names I know from home, besides burfi and gulub jamoon: meethai, jilebi, sweetrice (but dey call dat kheer up here), and ladhoo. By now, of course, mih mouth watering fuh so! When I feel confident enough dat I wouldn't make a fool a mih Brown self by asking what dis one name? and what dat one name? we went in de restaurant. In two twos all de spice in de place take a flying leap in our direction and give us one big welcome hug up, tight fuh so! Since den dey take up permanent residence in de jacket I wear dat day!

Mostly it had women customers sitting at de tables, chatting and laughing, eating sweets and sipping masala tea. De only men in de place was de waiters, and all six waiters was men. I figure dat dey was brothers, not too hard to conclude, because all a dem had de same full round chin, round as if de chin stretch tight over a ping-pong ball, and dey had de same big roving eyes. I know better dan to think dey was mere waiters in de employ of a owner who chook up in a office in de back. I sure dat dat was dey own family business, dey stomach proudly preceding dem and dey shoulders throw back in de confidence of dey ownership.

It ain't dat I paranoid, yuh understand, but from de moment we enter de fellas dem get over-animated, even amorously agitated. Janet again! All six pair a eyes land up on she, following she every move and body part. Dat in itself is something dat does madden me, oui! but also a kind a irrational envy have a tendency to manifest in me. It was like I didn't exist. Sometimes it could be a real problem going out with a good-looker, yes! While I ain't remotely interested in having a squeak of a flirtation with a man, it doh hurt a ego to have a man notice yuh once in a very long while. But with Janet at mih side, I doh have de chance of a penny shave-ice in de hot sun. I tuck mih elbows in as close to mih sides as I could so I wouldn't look like a strong man next to she, and over to de l-o-n-g glass case jam up with sweets I jiggle and wiggle in mih best imitation a some a dem gay fellas dat I see downtown Vancouver, de ones who more femme dan even Janet. I tell she not to pay de brothers no attention, because if any a dem flirt with she I could start a fight right dere and den. And I didn't feel to mess up mih crew cut in a fight.

De case had sweets in every nuance of colour in a rainbow. Sweets I never before see and doh know de names of. But dat was all right because I wasn't going to order dose ones anyway.

Since before we leave home Janet have she mind set on a nice thick syrupy curl a jilebi and a piece a plain burfi so I order dose for she and den I ask de waiter-fella, resplendent with thick thick bright-yellow gold chain and ID bracelet, for a stick a meethai for mihself. I stand up waiting by de glass case for it but de waiter/ owner lean up on de back wall behind de counter watching me like he ain't hear me. So I say loud enough for him, and every body else in de room to hear, "I would like to have one piece a meethai please," and den he smile and lift up his hands, palms open-out motioning across de vast expanse a glass case, and he say, "Your choice! Whichever you want, Miss." But he still lean up against de back wall grinning. So I stick mih head out and up like a turtle and say louder, and slowly, "One piece a meethai — dis one!" and I point sharp to de stick a flour mix with ghee, deep fry and den roll up in sugar. He say, "That is koorma, Miss. One piece only?"

Mih voice drop low all by itself. "Oh ho! Yes, one piece. Where I come from we does call dat meethai." And den I add, but only loud enough for Janet to hear, "And mih name ain't 'Miss.'"

He open his palms out and indicate de entire panorama a sweets and he say, "These are all meethai, Miss. Meethai is Sweets. Where are you from?"

I ignore his question and to show him I undaunted, I point to a round pink ball and say, "I'll have one a dese sugarcakes too please." He start grinning broad broad like if he half-pitying, half-laughing at dis Indian-in-skin-colour-only, and den he tell me, "That is called chum-chum, Miss." I snap back at him, "Yeh, well back home we does call dat sugarcake, Mr. Chum-chum."

At de table Janet say, "You know, Pud (Pud, short for Pudding; is dat she does call me when she feeling close to me, or sorry for me), it's true that we call that 'meethai' back home. Just like how we call 'siu mai' 'tim sam.' As if 'dim sum' is just one little piece a food. What did he call that sweet again?"

"Cultural bastards, Janet, cultural bastards. Dat is what we is.

Yuh know, one time a fella from India who living up here call me a bastardized Indian because I didn't know Hindi. And now look at dis, nah! De thing is: all a we in Trinidad is cultural bastards, Janet, all a we. *Toutes bagailles!* Chinese people. Black people. White people. Syrian. Lebanese. I looking forward to de day I find out dat place inside me where I am nothing else but Trinidadian, whatever dat could turn out to be."

I take a bite a de chum-chum, de texture was like grind-up coconut but it had no coconut, not even a hint a coconut taste in it. De thing was juicy with sweet rose water oozing out a it. De rose water perfume enter mih nose and get trap in mih cranium. Ah drink two cup a masala tea and a lassi and still de rose water perfume was on mih tongue like if I had a overdosed on Butchart Gardens.

Suddenly de door a de restaurant spring open wide with a strong force and two big burly fellas stumble in, almost rolling over on to de ground. Dey get up, eyes red and slow and dey skin burning pink with booze. Dey straighten up so much to overcompensate for falling forward, dat dey find deyself leaning backward. Everybody stop talking and was watching dem. De guy in front put his hand up to his forehead and take a deep Walter Raleigh bow, bringing de hand down to his waist in a rolling circular movement. Out loud he greet everybody with *"Alarm o salay koom."* A part a me wanted to bust out laughing. Another part make mih jaw drop open in disbelief. De calm in de place get rumfle up. De two fellas dem, feeling chupid now because nobody reply to dey greeting, gone up to de counter to

Chum-chum trying to make a little conversation with him. De same booze-pink *alarm-o-salay-koom*-fella say to Chum-chum, "Hey, howaryah?"

Chum-Chum give a lil nod and de fella carry right on, "Are you Sikh?"

Chum-chum brothers converge near de counter, busying dey-selves in de vicinity. Chum-chum look at his brothers kind a quizzical, and he touch his cheek and feel his forehead with de back a his palm. He say, "No, I think I am fine, thank you. But I am sorry if I look sick, Sir."

De burly fella confuse now, so he try again.

"Where are you from?"

Chum-chum say, "Fiji, Sir."

"Oh! Fiji, eh! Lotsa palm trees and beautiful women, eh! Is it true that you guys can have more than one wife?"

De exchange make mih blood rise up in a boiling froth. De restaurant suddenly get a gruff quietness 'bout it except for a woman I hear whispering angrily to another woman at de table behind us, "I hate this! I just hate it! I can't stand to see our men humiliated by them, right in front of us. He should refuse to serve them, he should throw them out. Who on earth do they think they are? The awful fools!" And de friend whisper back, "If he throws them out all of us will suffer in the long run."

I could discern de hair on de back a de neck a Chum-chum brothers standing up, annoyed, and at de same time de brothers look like dey was shrinking in stature. Chum-chum get serious, and he politely say, "What can I get for you?"

Pinko get de message and he point to a few items in de case

and say, "One of each, to go please."

Holding de white takeout box in one hand he extend de other to Chum-chum and say, "How do you say 'Excuse me, I'm sorry' in Fiji?"

Chum-chum shake his head and say, "It's okay. Have a good day."

Pinko insist, "No, tell me please. I think I just behaved badly, and I want to apologize. How do you say 'I'm sorry' in Fiji?"

Chum-chum say, "Your apology is accepted. Everything is okay." And he discreetly turn away to serve a person who had just entered de restaurant. De fellas take de hint dat was broad like daylight, and back out de restaurant like two little mouse.

Everybody was feeling sorry for Chum-chum and Brothers. One a dem come up to de table across from us to take a order from a woman with a giraffe-long neck who say, "Brother, we mustn't accept how these people think they can treat us. You men really put up with too many insults and abuse over here. I really felt for you."

Another woman gone up to de counter to converse with Chum-chum in she language. She reach out and touch his hand, sympathy-like. Chum-chum hold the one hand in his two and make a verbose speech to her as she nod she head in agreement generously. To italicize her support, she buy a takeout box a two burfi, or rather, dat's what I think dey was.

De door a de restaurant open again, and a bevy of Indian-looking women saunter in, dress up to weaken a person's decorum. De Miss Universe pageant traipse across de room to a table. Chum-chum and Brothers start smoothing dey hair back, and pushing de front a dey shirts neatly into dey pants. One brother take out a pack a Dentyne from his shirt pocket and pop one in his mouth. One take out a comb from his back pocket and smooth down his hair. All a dem den converge on dat single table to take orders. Dey begin to behave like young pups in mating season. Only, de women dem wasn't impress by all this tra-la-la at all and ignore dem except to make dey order, straight to de point. Well, it look like Brothers' egos were having a rough day and dey start roving 'bout de room, dey egos and de crotch a dey pants leading far in front dem. One brother gone over to Giraffebai to see if she want anything more. He call she "dear" and put his hand on she back. Giraffebai straighten she back in surprise and reply in a not-too-friendly way. When he gone to write up de bill she see me looking at she and she say to me, "Whoever does he think he is! Calling me dear and touching me like that! Why do these men always think that they have permission to touch whatever and wherever they want! And you can't make a fuss about it in public, because it is exactly what those people out there want to hear about so that they can say how sexist and uncivilized our culture is."

I shake mih head in understanding and say, "Yeah. I know. Yuh right!"

De atmosphere in de room take a hairpin turn, and it was man aggressing on woman, woman warding off a herd a man who just had dey pride publicly cut up a couple a times in just a few minutes.

One brother walk over to Janet and me and he stand up facing me with his hands clasp in front a his crotch, like if he protecting it. Stiff stiff, looking at me, he say, "Will that be all?"

Mih crew cut start to tingle, so I put on mih femmest smile and say, "Yes, that's it, thank you. Just the bill please." De smartass turn to face Janet and he remove his hands from in front a his crotch and slip his thumbs inside his pants like a cowboy 'bout to do a square dance. He smile, looking down at her attentive fuh so, and he say, "Can I do anything for you?"

I didn't give Janet time fuh his intent to even register before I bulldoze in mih most un-femmest manner, "She have everything she need, man, thank you. The bill please." Yuh think he hear me? It was like I was talking to thin air. He remain smiling at Janet, but she, looking at me, not at him, say, "You heard her. The bill please."

Before he could even leave de table proper, I start mih tirade. "But A A! Yuh see dat? Yuh could believe dat! De effing so-and-so! One minute yuh feel sorry fuh dem and next minute dey harassing de heck out a you. Janet, he crazy to mess with my woman, yes!" Janet get vex with me and say I overreacting, and is not fuh me to be vex, but fuh she to be vex. Is she he insult, and she could take good enough care a sheself.

I tell she I don't know why she don't cut off all dat long hair, and stop wearing lipstick and eyeliner. Well, who tell me to say dat! She get real vex and say dat nobody will tell she how to dress and how not to dress, not me and not any man. Well I could see de potential dat dis fight had coming, and when Janet get fighting vex, watch out! It hard to get a word in edgewise, yes! And she does bring up incidents from years back dat have no bearing on de current situation. So I draw back quick quick but she don't waste time; she was already off to a good start. It was best to leave right dere and den.

Just when I stand up to leave, de doors dem open up and in walk Sandy and Lise, coming for dey weekly hit a Indian sweets. Well, with Sandy and Lise is a dead giveaway dat dey not dressing fuh any man, it have no place in dey life fuh man-vibes, and dat in fact dey have a blatant penchant fuh women. Soon as dey enter de room yuh could see de brothers and de couple men customers dat had come in minutes before stare dem down from head to Birkenstocks, dey eyes bulging with disgust. And de women in de room start shoo-shooing, and putting dey hand in front dey mouth to stop dey surprise, and false teeth, too, from falling out. Sandy and Lise spot us instantly and dey call out to us, shameless, loud and affectionate. Dey leap over to us, eager to hug up and kiss like if dey hadn't seen us for years, but it was really only since two nights aback when we went out to dey favourite Indian restaurant for dinner. I figure dat de display was a genuine happiness to be seen wit us in dat place. While we stand up dere chatting, Sandy insist on rubbing she hand up and down Janet back — wit friendly intent, mind you, and same time Lise have she arm round Sandy waist. Well, all cover get blown. If it was even remotely possible dat I wasn't noticeable before, now Janet and I were over-exposed. We could a easily suffer from hypothermia, specially since it suddenly get cold cold in dere. We say goodbye, not soon enough, and as we were leaving I turn to acknowlege Giraffebai, but instead a any recognition of our buddiness against de fresh brothers, I get a face dat look like it was in de presence of a very foul smell.

De good thing, doh, is dat Janet had become so incensed 'bout how we get scorned, dat she forgot I tell she to cut she hair and to ease up on de makeup, and so I get save from hearing 'bout how I too jealous, and how much I inhibit she, and how she would prefer if I would grow my hair, and wear lipstick and put on a dress sometimes. I so glad, oui! dat I didn't have to go through hearing how I too demanding a she, like de time, she say, I prevent she from seeing a ole boyfriend when he was in town for a couple hours en route to live in Australia with his new bride (because, she say, I was jealous dat ten years ago dey sleep together). Well, look at mih crosses, nah! Like if I really so possessive and jealous!

So tell me, what yuh think 'bout dis nah, girl?

FIRE AT THE ATIVAN FACTORY

Douglas Coupland

Wyatt has worked overtime in the latex room, carefully sculpting the skin texture of an alien needed for shooting after the weekend. His hands, of which he is inordinately proud — long-fingered and hairless after years of chemical exposure — are poxed with resins and paints, his fingernails irretrievably pitted and scratched. These are the scars of his unusual work as creative director in the prosthesis division of a local special effects production company named Flesh. This week, a quickie low-budget movie-of-the-week for a U.S. cable network is being squeezed through the production mill like so much meat byproduct through a sausage maker. "Everything but the *oink*," as Wyatt had said just to the staff that afternoon which raised smiles among his Flesh coworkers, all of whom have become virtuoso moulders, flensers and painters of latex and fibreglass bodies over the past five years. Crime shoots are a specialty with Flesh — the creation of dozens of tortellini and ravioli of fake blood embedded within torso moulds, all of which is electrically wired to explode in synch once the cameras roll. Lately Flesh has moved heavily into the production of aliens. Aliens, in their own way, are easier craft than humans because aliens, like the future, don't really exist; any blank or difficult spots can be easily filled in with flights of fancy.

Wyatt glances at the window: the sun has already gone down. Through the walls Wyatt can hear the thrums and parps of vehicles rushing home, gleefully preparing to celebrate the passing of 1999 into 2000. Earlier in the afternoon when Wyatt had made an emergency epoxy run to London Drugs up on Lonsdale, he could sense the lifting of a large weight of concern off the shoulders of North Vancouver's citizenry. It felt to Wyatt as though an enormous asteroid had been floating over the city for at least the past month, threatening to clomp down like a sack of potatoes at any minute. This sensation had made this year's Christmas an oddly dour event. "The last Christmas of the century," Wyatt's family members kept on saying — for whatever that was worth.

Wyatt's wife, Kathleen (no kids), had sat through an agonizingly long ritual gift-opening ceremony at his parents' house — nieces and nephews and in-laws squawking and cooing, sending subtle signals to Wyatt and Kathleen: *why no kids?*

But now the impending asteroid has tumbled away. The city is popping upward like newly sprouting seeds twisting up to the sun and Wyatt feels slightly martyred for staying to work late while everybody else packed it in early to go home and prepare for midnight.

Wyatt thinks of the movie plot around which his current alien — now flopped across his left knee as he pokes it and texturizes it — revolves. Honey-blond aliens, disguised as real-estate agents, lure prospective human beings to houses secretly equipped for biological experimentation. The only Earth food the alien real-estate agents are able to eat is birth-control pills. At night they rampage the city's drugstores foraging and killing for their needs.

Needless to say, the hero and heroine link the pill thefts to the housing sales and arrive in the nick of time to prevent two adorable tots (in real life cell-toting vain-at-thirteen monsters) from being vivisected. The final scene involves a Pontiac Sunfire convertible full of starving alien agents which is surrounded by guns and flashing police cruisers. The trapped aliens pop out of their false human bodies and reveal themselves in full, gluey millipedal horror, and are then promptly shot by local police (whose bodies are embedded with bloody ravioli) but not before the neighbourhood lies in ruins.

The End.

The cable network is getting a true bargain. Aside from special effects, the whole film can be shot in under twelve working days with only a minimum of exterior shots and the Canadian dollar hasn't been worth less against the American in years. Fully a third of the budget is going into the final scene, and this is a testament, Wyatt feels, to the studio's high evaluation of his skills.

Wyatt has been quiet the past few days — and so has been, basically, everybody in the shop — cutting latex, mixing aniline dyes and testing glass eyeball sizes as they mulled over history's impending magnificent odometer turn. But Wyatt has more on his mind to be concerned with than mere numbers. Since September he and Kathleen have been seeing fertility specialists both down in Seattle and up in Vancouver and the results, now in, have been, after endless pap tests, forced ejaculations, pH checks, blood samples and endlessly rehashed personal histories ... *inconclusive.*

"What do you mean you don't *know?*" Wyatt had spat out at Dr. Arkasian. "You *must* know." Through the windows Vancouver had looked grey and overcast, as though the entire city had been manufactured rather than built.

"Sorry Wyatt, there's no real answer."

"Is it my sperm? My fault?"

"Not — particularly."

"Kathleen then — no eggs? Bad eggs? Damaged eggs?"

Dr. Arkasian tried to cool Wyatt down. There was no clear answer. In Wyatt's mind he saw his sperm rushing toward Kathleen's egg only to slow down as they approach and then one by one fall asleep or die. Wyatt sees Kathleen's eggs as though they were chicken eggs, all yolk and no white — eggs that exude a spermisomnolent spray. Can eggs sleep? Can sperms sleep and dream? They're only half a creature, really — yet how can they be alive — how can they dream?

Kathleen has no brothers and sisters and wanted nothing more with her marriage to Wyatt than to have fifteen children.

Wyatt's enormous family was to Kathleen, as it can so often be with single children, a great aphrodisiac. The two of them certainly give it every try they can but —

But *what?*

"There has to be a single cause," Wyatt said, thinking aloud to Dr. Arkasian back at the office just before Christmas. "Something I ate, maybe. Something Kathleen once breathed. A medicine we took as children —"

"That *could* well be the case," Dr. Arkasian replied in a platitudinous way, visibly anxious to hustle the childless couple from his office in the absence of any clear explanation for their infertility.

And so now Wyatt has been mulling over his and Kathleen's position within the world. For the past week he's been rerunning memories in his head — memories of the things his body has ingested and absorbed since being born in 1964: vaccinations as a child; antibiotics, sulfa drugs and antifungals as a teenager; the car exhausts breathed the two years he worked as a mechanic; food additives, recreational cannabis, cocaine, amphetamines and recently (and just once) ecstasy and ... and what *else?* That strange smell that pervaded the outdoor cafe in Rome back in 1986? Spraying the house's yard with pesticides? Pesticides! Jesus — not even *God* knows what they put into those. And then there's Kathleen with her birth-control pills which, although Kathleen declaims against it, must surely have been sapping away at least a fraction of her reproductive capacity.

Wyatt puts down his alien and holds his body tightly around his chests and whoops in a gulp of air. *Shit: the chemicals he uses for his models.* He's using cleaner chemicals now but for years his days were rife with toluene, xylene, resins and —

Wyatt feels sick.

Wyatt wasn't always a body maker. He ended up there by way of building miniatures for TV and films. It had been a hoot and he hadn't quite wanted to leave miniatures, but Kathleen and he had just married and they needed the extra money because they wanted to have a ... *kid.*

Part of the reason for Wyatt's initial success model-building was that he could build alien spacecraft that looked genuinely *alien.* Most other alien-craft designers would glance through a book on insects, choose one that they liked and then just build a modified version of that insect in metal. Not Wyatt. Instead he went to the library and scanned the books on pharmaceutical and plastics molecules — forms that had no need to respond to the mundanities of gravity, light or biology.

"Honestly, Wyatt," said Marv, his boss, years ago, "where do you get these ideas from? They're so — *new. Fresh.*"

To Wyatt the real architecture of the twentieth century was at the microscopic level: cloned proteins, superconductors, branch-chained detergents, prescription medicines ... Why, the molecular shape of the anti-depressant Venlafaxine (a.k.a. Wellbutrin) alone had paid for the house's down payment — by way of its becoming the overall blueprint of an alien space cruiser in a B film that did lousily in theatrical release but which cleaned up on video and overseas. Now *there* was a molecule that looked like something that only the meanest and scariest aliens would design. Good for them. Good for Venlafaxine.

Wyatt would have actually liked to have *tried* Venlafaxine. Over the past two years his childlessness has given him an increasing whack of anxiety and depression — yet he balked at taking Venlafaxine for reasons of jinx. In the end he wound up with an unshakeable addiction to Ativan, innocuous tiny white pills chemically related to all the other sedatives such as Xanax, Darvon, Valium. Miss one pill and Wyatt's brain felt as though it had been epoxied solid. Titred reductions proved doomed. His twice-daily dose was finite and loathed. He hated his addiction but saw no way around it. Wyatt was happy that nobody except Kathleen knew about it.

Kathleen, on the other hand, had tried a host of space-cruiser anti-depressants, finally settling for an old stand-by, Elavil, a drug once given to shell-shocked WWII British pilots to get them back into their planes and back into the fight. She flowed through her days more peacefully now (if a little spacey) and she endured the holiday season, which was more than she had hoped for.

And now Kathleen was in Saskatchewan tending to her father, laid low with alcoholism and touting a liver as soft and puffy as a water balloon. Wyatt, back in Vancouver, had an invitation to attend Donny and Christine's New Year's party but doubted he would attend. Donny and Christine's New Year's party was *not* the place where he had always envisioned himself at century's end. Since childhood he had pictured himself ... where, on that special midnight? Eating champagne Jell-O cubes with Diana Ross at the top of the Empire State Building? Copulating in zero-G on a Space Shuttle? Swimming with bilingual dolphins in the Sea of Japan? No, Wyatt had never seen himself at 11:59:59, December 31, 1999 at *Donny and Christine's place*, sixty-percent drunk on a microbrew-of-the-week, remembering to take his meds shortly after the stroke of twelve, and ringing in the New Year with U2's "New Year's Day," a song Christine chose each year with a numbing repetition that she had successfully elevated into a cherished personality quirk.

And then the idea hits him: it's not Kathleen and it's not himself that's to blame — it's the whole bloody *century*. A hundred years of extremes. A hundred years of molecules never before seen in the universe. A century of action and progress and activity and destiny. A century that has slowly infiltrated Wyatt's system — the fat cells in his brain, the neurons of his spine; the flesh of his palm and eyeballs — his liver and kidneys and heart and his sleepy little sperms — a century now pulsing within him — a century with which he is unable to detach himself. Or can he?

Wyatt reaches for a paper cup from the Dixie-cup dispenser, the cups used for mixing fibreglass resins, not for the drinking of water.

Wyatt fills the cup from the cafeteria tap and looks at its contents — clear and harmless. Or maybe not. Copper. Chlorine. Bacteria. Viruses. He leaves the cup on the counter and walks out the back door, turning out the lights and alarming the building.

The traffic is quite heavy for that part of town for that time of day — 5:30, and everybody is excitedly preparing for the night. The rain is also heavy but the rain comes as no surprise at that time of year. There's a bit of a traffic slowdown on the highway near Lonsdale but minutes later, Wyatt arrives home to the small house up in Edgemont Village. In the house there are two messages on his machine. Kathleen calling to say she'll be phoning just before midnight and one from Donny asking if he can bring ice to the party. Wyatt erases both messages and stands in the front doorway area of the house: some bills, a throw rug with a kink in one corner, some boots and an unread newspaper.

I want every damn bit of that hellish century out of my system. I want it clean. Whatever the twenty-first century brings me, that's fine, but I want the twentieth century out of my system now.

This idea takes him with a jolt. It is a *real* idea, not a confabulated whiff of impulse. It is instantly clear to Wyatt that he must fully cleanse his system.

Very well then.

From the bedroom he retrieves a pair of handcuffs, remnants of an earlier sexual era when he and Kathleen could have sex without sweet darkness. From there he goes to the front hall where he puts on three coats overtop each other and then he walks through the sliding glass upper balcony door, into the dark and onto the wood balcony. There, he sits down on a $9.95 white plastic stool — a chintzy stackable drecky chair of a type that appeared one summer a few years ago, and erased all other patio chairs in the world. "A category killer," the salesman had called it.

He sits on this category-killing chair and handcuffs himself to the metal railing beside him. Before allowing himself time to reflect, he throws the key through the bushes and down into an adjoining creek running at a full alpine swoosh.

And it is then, while there is the noise of the creek and the rain, that there is also the silence. Great silence. Rain slopping down onto the yellow hat attached to the outermost jacket layer.

It's jarring at first, the clash between the cold wet outdoors and the warm dry indoors. But then his eyes adjust to the foggy wet dark, his skin to the dank, and his ears to the weather and the landscape.

This is how I want the twentieth century to end, he thinks. Personally — alone — in contemplation — during an act of purification.

He looks at his watch. The time is 10:45 — where did the hours go? And then he becomes aware that he has been looking at his watch. He removes it and throws it down into the creek along with the handcuff keys.

He shivers and then shivers some more. His fingers feel rubbery and chilled. His core temperature is falling. He can hear cars roaring around the suburb. He hears a few bangs — premature fireworks lit by the overeager.

Shortly Wyatt's teeth begin to chatter and he wonders if he's made a dreadful mistake. He stands up and tries to yank at the railing and in so doing slips and sends his chair flying toward the balcony's other end, banging his knee in the process, forcing him to sit on the wet planks. And it is at this point where his phone rings and he curses himself and the world. It rings ten times and dies. And half a minute later party-goers across the city bang and carouse and ignite, welcoming three fresh new zeros into their world.

Goodbye, 1999.

And after an hour the kerfuffle ends. It is still the world. Not much has changed, or has it? Wyatt is unable to sleep — and won't be able to sleep for days; within his body the idea of sleep and Ativan are one and the same.

His core temperature lowers still further and he shouts for his neighbours to come retrieve him from this stupid idea but the creek and the rain are too loud, drowning out his voice so that even to himself his words seem smothered before they can get away from his ever-chilling body. His efforts at uprooting the steel railing from the porch have merely sapped his energy. He is truly stuck.

Around 3:00 a.m. his brain begins to revolt against him. His eyes flutter and soon he will go into seizure. A bony hand clenches his scalp's top. His breathing shortens and becomes non-automatic. He is aware of every breath but increasingly removed from this awareness at the same time.

I am cold, he thinks. *I am cold and this is how I'll be ending — cold.* His three coats are soaked through. He thinks he hears the phone ring again, but can't tell if he's imagining it. All he wants is for the cold to end and as he wishes for this, he remembers the first time he tried Ativan and he remembers how much he loved it. And he remembers joking with his GP about possible addiction. "What if I get hooked on this stuff?"

"You won't get hooked."

"What if I do get hooked and what if the Ativan factory burns down — what would I do then?" They both had a forced laugh over that one.

And now, somewhere across the Pacific, somewhere west of Honolulu, the century ends absolutely. The International Dateline is crossed and as it does so, Wyatt pictures the burning factory and he imagines he is standing next to it, warming his hands, warming his body and warming his core as he leaves the twentieth century and the twentieth century leaves him.

CITY OF MY DREAMS

Zsuzsi Gartner

Sooner or later, everyone in the country came to this city by the mountains and the sea. Some just to ogle, many to stay. People here liked it with something that bordered on religious fervour. They acted as if they should be heartily congratulated for where they lived, much the same way the contestants on *Jeopardy!* are applauded when they pick the Daily Double even though they haven't really done anything yet. Their enthusiam made Lewis feel small and mean. How could she hate paradise? "It gets caught in my teeth," she told her friend Lila, "like spinach."

All around her, people did things for kicks that to Lewis seemed nothing short of death-defying. Trooping into the wilderness with foil packets of dehydrated food, like astronauts, determined to ride the rapids, scale icefalls, bounce down mountain faces with their feet bound to fibreglass boards, Dr. Seuss hats on their heads. She shook her head and hung onto her coffee mug with both hands. Caffeine, that was her wild ride.

She who had looked into the face of death with its tired living room eyes and laughed.

The little green-haired girl was back in the store, lingering over the soaps, dipping her fingers into the pots of face masks and hair creams. She had been in almost every day this week, but never bought anything.

Lewis worked in a place that looked like a cheese shop but sold soap. It was a cosmetic deli. She cut wedges of soaps like Guava Nun and Rabbit Cool from huge slabs with a thing very much like a cheese cutter, weighed them, wrapped them, and stuck on the little price per gram sticker the machine spit out. The face masks and creams and shampoos were scooped into little plastic tubs like coleslaw, mashed down, weighed and priced. There were also massage bars that looked and smelled like chocolate, and shampoo bars that looked and smelled like oatcakes with raisins. The customers all said the same thing (over and over and over again) — "MMMmmm, this smells good enough to eat!" — but Lewis kept smiling. It was all stupidly expensive and the customers were mostly pleasant — clean, pleasant people with lots of money. No deranged artists threatening to set themselves on fire.

The green-haired girl dragged three fingers through the vat of apple-mint face mask and then, looking right at Lewis through a cluster of very blond private school students in hiked-up kilts, she pulled her fingers down her right cheek and then her left. As she turned to leave the store, Lewis felt a little tribal beat in the vicinity of her heart. Something deeply carnivorous and sinewy. Something to do with meat and flames. A clue to her secret city? Or heartburn from the onion flan from Meinhardt's she'd had for lunch?

Lewis wished she had said something. Later that night lying in bed, it came to her, what she should have said.

"Don't smile or it'll crack."

For a brief, shining moment several months back, Lewis had had what most people would consider a great job. She was one of the programmers at the film festival the city hosted each fall and all of her friends envied her — *imagine getting paid to watch movies!*

But it wasn't long before earnest student filmmakers from the city's four (four!) film schools started descending on the festival office, like infant spiders parachuting out of their pods, demanding to know why she had rejected their mini-mockumentaries or Tarantino rip-offs. At least half of their films were about people who go through a whole bunch of bad shit and then wake up to find out it's all just a dream. If only life were like that, Lewis often found herself thinking.

One guy even tried to bribe her with a descrambler. He had a little goatee and long fingernails. He snapped a *TV Times* open and shook it at her, "Look at all these channels," he said, "All these channels could be yours." She moved down the hall and he followed, flapping the TV listings at her and wailing, "My movie's only three minutes long!" Three minutes too long, Lewis thought. She tried picturing him as someone's son, the cream in some doting mother's coffee. She tried feeling sorry for him because he was already growing jowls. Too late. Her heart was forming a thin, but impenetrable crust like the one that covered the earth while it was still young and fragile and lava bubbled just below the surface. When she asked him to leave, he started crying.

Then there was the fidgety young man who showed up on his skateboard. He whooshed right through her office door, then braked abruptly. The skateboard, an orange goat painted on it with X's for eyes, shot straight up into the air. He caught it in one meaty paw and stuffed it under his armpit.

"You didn't answer my phone calls," he said. She thought the stud drilled through his tongue should have caused a slight lisp, but it didn't.

"And you are?"

"Justin."

"Justin what?" They all seemed to be named Justin.

"I made the film about the dude who goes through all this bad shit and then wakes up and finds out it was all just a dream."

Lewis sighed.

"Watch it backwards," Justin hissed, his eyes startlingly like Charles Manson's.

"What?"

"Just watch it backwards." And he was gone, wheels grinding down the corridor.

Paul is dead? Lewis thought.

"Shouldn't we get a security guard," she asked the festival director, "or a Doberman or something?"

But nothing could have prepared Lewis for the woman who showed up on her doorstep at home on that Saturday morning. She wasn't a kid, either. She was about Lewis's age, early thirties, but with this real lived-in look in her eyes. Her eyes were a living room of despair, full of mismatched furniture and candles stuck in Chianti bottles, dripping all over the place, a syringe under the wicker chair, a Ouija board on the coffee table. She held a tin can with a plastic nozzle in one hand and a Bic lighter in the other. Her neck was dishpan-hand red and streaked with sweat. Tiny neighbour kids trundled back and forth across the common area on their trikes, oblivious to what was going on, ringing their little bells feebly with inexperienced thumbs and veering into the cedar hedges. The woman stood there on the step of Lewis's co-op and threatened to douse herself with gasoline and set herself on fire if Lewis didn't program her film.

There were those students in South Korea who had set themselves on fire recently to protest unfair labour practices, and there was that Quaker who had immolated himself in front of the Pentagon in a statement against the war in Vietnam. To Lewis, although they seemed insane, they were also somewhat noble. But to be willing to die for a bad, really bad, eleven-minute film in which a naked Barbie sat spinning on an old record turntable? The woman could not be serious. Besides, it wasn't even technically a film; it was shot on video. Rules, Lewis had always believed, were rules. She wouldn't be forced into compromising her aesthetics, and she wasn't about to let herself be blackmailed. But that didn't mean she couldn't be polite.

"Would you like some coffee?" Lewis asked. "I could make a fresh pot."

"Ten, nine, eight," the woman chanted, dropping to her knees on the bristly welcome mat and holding the can above her head.

Lewis hesitated, then tried to call her bluff. "Maybe you'd prefer herbal tea?" she asked with her best hostessy smile, which she hoped wasn't twitching.

"Seven, six, five." The little kids joined in. *Ding, ding, ding.*

Lewis found herself inexplicably laughing as the woman flicked her Bic. She looked around, as if expecting someone to step from the shadows of an upstairs balcony, aim a video camera down into the courtyard and announce, "Smile, you're on —"

After all the emergency crews had come and gone, a police officer took down her name. "And your first name?" he said, holding his pen above his little notepad. "That is my first name," Lewis told him. Her mother had listened to a lot of Johnny Cash before she was born. As a little girl, Lewis had pretended her name was Louise. She later went through a phase in university during which, after a several beers in the student pub, she'd greet strangers by standing on a chair and bellowing, "How do you *Do-is*, my name is *Lew-is!*" No one ever got it except a pudgy, down-to-earth girl named Lila from Hundred Mile House up north and so they became friends.

The policeman had asked if she wanted to make a statement. When she didn't answer, he assured her that she had nothing to worry about, that people like this always single someone out, wanting an accomplice. "My brother was driving along Marine Drive and a guy jumped out from behind a mailbox and threw himself in front of his car," he told her, "Just like that — boom."

Then the policeman left, and the neighbours disappeared inside, and Lewis stood alone on her steps. There were clumps of dried fire retardant on the door jamb, on the charred welcome mat, and on the cedar hedges on both sides of the steps. It was an optimistic pink, like fibreglass insulation. Like cotton candy. She went inside and in the hall mirror she saw that there was a fleck of the dried pink foam on the tip of her nose.

She had phoned Lila and got her answering machine. "I just killed somebody," Lewis said, collapsing into the corner of the couch, the spent fire extinguisher nestled in her lap like a small, cherry-red dachshund.

Lewis had a cousin who lived in the only residential building in the entire city that was earthquake-ready. He travelled a lot as a buyer for a swimsuit import company and had found a lover in Seoul (and in Hong Kong, and in Manila), so he was often away and let Lewis stay at his place whenever she wanted.

The building balanced on a fat stick, like half a popsicle, and wobbled slightly when there was high wind. It had a complex suspension system and was said to be able to withstand tremors of up to 7.8 on the Richter scale. The city lay at the very edge of a fault line and scientists said that it was due for "the big one" any time now, the earth cracking painfully open, the ocean rearing up in towering sheets. The scientists wrung their hands and prophesied death and destruction unless the government, the citizens, didn't do something, didn't build more popsicle buildings and popsicle schools and batten down the hatches. They didn't say wrath of God — they were people of science, after all — but you could see it in their eyes. More of these buildings had been planned, but it was decided they were too expensive. And, besides, those who could afford to live in them wanted things like swimming pools, and you couldn't put a swimming pool in an earthquake-ready building. Lewis did like the idea of doing endless lengths on her back while down below the city crumbled, although it was a thought best kept to herself.

One of the best things about the building was the sign by the front door. Entercom, it said. Lewis would slink through the lobby to the elevator chanting to herself, "Enter calm, enter calm, enter calm."

She was worried her cousin would move on a whim. Then she'd be banished from this earthquake-ready building with its Entercom. And she would miss it fiercely. She would miss the large, ten-gallon plastic kegs of water stored in all the available closets. He even had a couple stacked in the bedroom closet, behind the box containing the bench press he never used. There were emergency candles. Matches. Lots of AA batteries and a transister radio. Canned food. Oodles of canned tuna and fruit leather. This was the place to be if Armageddon ever threatened. A wrath-of-God-proof dwelling, with a view.

After a week or so of her cumin-smelling, cat-infested, spider plant-ridden co-op full of overly friendly Sesame Street-style neighbours, Lewis loved to slip into the expensive, scentless lobby of the Enter Calm building with its David Hockney Exhibition poster on the wall and speed up to the seventeenth floor in the almost silent elevator, the apartment key tight in her hand. Once, she found she was gripping it so hard that it left the imprint of a fish in her palm — a fat, archetypal fish, like a third eye. The God-fish. She pressed her hand flat against the big living room window and showed it the enormous, fog-shrouded tankers in the inlet. "All this could be yours," she told the fish.

Lila, who was on the housing co-op board and had helped Lewis get a subsidized unit by vouching for her character even though the rest of the board suspected she wasn't a true co-op type at heart, couldn't understand what she liked about the Entercom building. "It's so sterile," she'd said, standing near the big window, but not touching it. "I'd get nosebleeds living up this high. You can't even see any grass."

Lewis had brought her old boyfriend there, just once, hoping some altitude would revive her waning interest in this pleasant, sturdy man who wore good-quality T-shirts and had dropped a lack-lustre freelance magazine career to manage a mutual fund. He even laughed when she said, intending to be nasty, "The Dow Jones Average, so they play '70s power rock or what?" But lying in bed with him up there, she felt her sense of calm threatened, her sacred space violated. The relationship was like a woman standing on her front steps threatening to set herself on fire — something Lewis couldn't consider seriously until it was too late. "What if I took tap-dancing lessons and got a little sailor suit?" she asked him while twisting the corner of the duvet cover until it looked like the spire of a gingerbread church in the Black

Forest. Her boyfriend had turned from leafing through one of her cousin's body-building magazines and looked at Lewis. "Are you trying to tell me something?"

What she really loved was being up there by herself, ready for anything. It was the only time she didn't feel the urge to flee to that place she combed her tangled mind for while she cut and measured soap and swept the sweet-smelling flakes into shimmery mounds.

She imagined saying nonchalantly to interested strangers while dragging a tea bag — Russian Caravan, luxuriously caffeinated — back and forth in a china cup, as if dredging a river for a body, the tea spreading like a rust stain through the water. "The city of my dreams, oh, it's equal parts whimsy and rot." The interested strangers nodded their heads and murmured encouragement in faintly foreign accents.

The trouble was, Lewis had no idea where this city was. It couldn't be a place as well-worn as Paris or New York with their centuries of ghosts. Besides, she had been to both and found them lacking. The most wonderful thing about Paris had been the multitude of public washrooms. There were ancient, subterranean ones, moist like caves, and modern, nuclear age-looking cylinders set along the boulevards with doors that slid open when you dropped a franc into a slot. Once inside, music played — old David Bowie, "Let's Dance," a Paul McCartney/ Michael Jackson duet, "The Doggone Girl is Mine" (whatever *were* they thinking?) — and the toilet automatically washed and dried you. But you couldn't move somewhere just for the public washrooms. And in New York she had felt needy, as if the city continually dangled baubles in her face that she couldn't have. And that was after only three days. If she lived there she would grow frenzied with desires and most likely end up at Grand Central aggressively shaking a Dean & Deluca paper cup with lipstick marks around the rim, yelling, "Money for baubles, not booze. Must have a Hermés handbag!" while at her elbow a Vietnam vet with one leg and a Welsh terrier in his lap whistled "The Star Spangled Banner" while the dog yipped crossly.

What she wanted was a place to love that was hers, and hers alone. An oasis with good taxi takeout. A contemporary Xanadu.

The soap shop was always bright and cheerful. The colours were primary, the packaging minimal and ecologically sound. Just being in there made you feel like you were a better person — at least that was the effect the owners, represented by a numbered holding company somewhere in England, appeared to be gunning for. When was the last time buying soap made you feel like Mother Teresa?

Selling soap was an occupation, Lewis told herself, that was a balm to her besieged senses. She forced herself to count her blessings — small, fuzzy blessings with hard centres, like little lint-covered candies you'd find wedged between car seats — to have a job at all. Look at the little green-haired girl, who wasn't really a girl, Lewis now realized, but a very small, almost wraith-like person, maybe in her late teens or early twenties. It was obvious she didn't have a job. And what did she do? She came in and ate the oatmeal and avocado face masks when she thought Lewis wasn't looking. Spooned them into her mouth with the wooden paddles that were used to mush the stuff into containers. Lewis wondered if she'd come across her in some back alley, stiffened into a board, her insides smooth and poreless and glowing with health, while flies buzzed in and out of her algae-coloured dreadlocks. But she didn't say anything. She never looked at her kindly and said, "It'll crack if you smile."

The little green-haired person never smiled.

And Lewis, who certainly wasn't a girl any more, became a girl again the moment she stepped behind the counter at the shop. "Ask the soap girl," people would say to each other. "The soap girl will know."

A handsome man came into the soap shop and leaned smiling against the counter, drumming his fingers lightly on its surface. His cufflinks clinked against the chrome trim, tiny garnets flashing in the light. "Do you have any asiago?" Lewis laughed, and then wondered why she was laughing at the uninspired jokes of self-consciously handsome men who wore cufflinks.

What was happening to her? What had happened to her brain? It was as if she was here, while her brain was back at home soaking in a bucket of ammonia-based solution. It was this city, she decided, this city with its aggressive mellowness like chicory coffee. Too many people told her to relax when they were going off the rails themselves. Cyclists clashed with drivers, and although she had once seen a guy jump from his Isuzu Trooper in front of the Pocky Store on Cambie hefting something that might have been a crowbar, it was the bicycle people who were generally nastier. Coming out of the liquor store by the IGA on Broadway the week before she had watched a long, lean cyclist with bulging calves and an exhaust mask across his face, righteously shaking a fist at the sky. "It's assholes like you who are ruining the planet," he yelled at no one in particular as cars tried to nose around him and out of the parking lot.

In the city of her dreams, only small children rode bicycles.

In the city of her dreams, soap made you clean but not holy.

It had been a strange spring. People both grumbled about it and made jokes, but underneath it all was a distinct layer of worry. The media speculated about the causes: global warning, el Niño, the next ice age, weather patterns manipulated by the Russians (postulated by those who weren't yet aware the Cold War had ended and the only Commie Pinkos to be found were the vodka and beet juice martinis at an after hours club called Gouzenko's in Yaletown), cattle hormones, keloid earth, growth fatigue, mutant minerals, a Coca-Cola/Nike/Disney™ conspiracy, wormholes in space, every expert — right-wing, left-wing, or just regular-wing nut — had a theory. Lewis found it interesting that no one wanted to admit that it was just plain weird and they didn't have a clue what was going on. They wanted someone or something to blame.

Crocuses usually thrust themselves out of the cold ground in late January, while the rest of the country was still covered in snow. Magnolia blossoms, thick and fleshy, and cherry blossoms, frilly, pungent, were not uncommon in February, but here it was May already, and the only glorious things sprang from the cracks in the sidewalks and in empty lots full of ground glass and tired earth. Purple-headed thistle, wild dill, six feet tall, bolting, and dandelions ran rampant through the crabgrass. Nothing wanted to grow in the fertilized, compost-and-mushroom manure-rich, well-tended public and private gardens. Not even weeds.

And the squirrels. Everyone agreed that there were more of them than usual. They zigzagged back and forth across the streets in a frenzy, peanuts (Lewis had no idea where they got all those peanuts) clamped in their little jaws. Someone used the word *infestation* and suddenly that's what it was. The trees rustled with squabbling squirrels and dried squirrel shit rattled down the rooftops and clogged the eavestroughs. A child in her co-op had been attacked. A red squirrel ran right up the front of his body, leaving mean claw marks, and snatched a granola bar out of his hand as he was about to put it into his mouth. The parents' council was divided between teaching their children survival skills for the urban wilderness or just poisoning the buggers. Tempers flared.

The beaches seemed dirtier, too. E-coli counts rose and people went into the water at their own risk. A swimmer who ignored the warnings had created a wave of near hysteria that lasted almost two weeks after she came out of the water at Spanish Banks with a lesion on her stomach that resembled Salman Rushdie's profile. The fact that this happened on Valentine's Day, on the eighth anniversary of the *fatwa*, was hard to overlook. No one asked, why would anyone go swimming in the ocean in February? People did that kind of thing here. People had the right.

Of course the cyclists blamed the drivers and the drivers blamed the government.

No one noticed the clean-shaven man wrapped in a sheet who

stood in the middle of the Burrard Street Bridge, day after day, with a sign that read: DESERTS & WASTELANDS WILL BECOME FERTILE AND BEAUTIFUL.

And, every day, during that week in mid-May, Lewis continued to watch the little green-haired girl feed at the colourful vats in the soap store, mechanically trowelling the stuff in as if she was filling a very large, growing crack in the walls of San Simeon.

Lewis picked at crabgrass while the local historian made his speech, Lila beaming beside him in front of the dilapidated house. Lila had a heart like a monster truck — a V8 engine that roared and seldom needed retooling, huge wheels that could drive over anything, fat pistons pumping for victory, a gas tank of biblical porportions, and was rust-proof to boot. Compared to Lila's, Lewis's heart was like something that had only been driven by a little old member of the Christian right in Kelowna on Sundays.

Lila spent much of her time saving things. Murrelets, forests, even lives. She volunteered one night a week for the Suicide Hotline, talking people out of their valleys of despair, telling them they could beat the bastards, whoever the bastards were — those ninjas of the heart who struck swiftly in the dark, or battalions of voices telling the person she was a worthless shit. Of course it was all anonymous and Lila never knew if she had really done any good. Lewis thought not knowing would drive her crazy. But Lila just shrugged her shoulders and said, "Well, you just gotta try."

Lila didn't understand earthquake-proof, though. The things she loved were sprawling and messy and about to fall apart. Like this old house. The front porch sagged, all the paint had long ago flaked off and a section of the roof was missing. It had been brought to its knees but was still grinning, its charred filigree trim like teeth spread wide.

Children trailing black balloons ran around screaming, mouths smeared with black icing from Lila's enormous coffin cake. She had organized this Black Birthday Party to protest the fact that the city was hedging on its promise to declare the eighty-year-old house a heritage property. Without that designation, the owner was free to tear it down and build yet another salmon-stucco sixplex. There had already been evidence of squatters and two fires had been set within the past month. The firefighters had barely arrived in time, the historian told them.

"This Edwardian lady," the historian said, the mike popping and sound system hissing, "is one of the last of her generation. Just as indicative of her time as an Erickson or an Henriquez is of ours."

Now Lila was at the microphone, gripping its stem with emotion. "This is our past. This house is us. *Ich bin ein* Edwardian house!!" The small crowd of about two dozen people costumed like ghouls clapped and cheered. The light drizzle stopped as suddenly as it had begun. Lewis felt twitchy. She wouldn't have been surprised if the owner pulled up in a tan Eldorado and swooped down on them with legal firearms to assert his rights. And really, what was his crime? That he failed to see the value of the past? Maybe he was onto something.

The protesters looked like older, more jovial versions of the

Marilyn Manson fans who had accidentally heaved in the huge plate glass window at A&B Sound the other night while trying to get a glimpse of their idol. Lewis had watched them on the news and thought they looked weirdly cowed as they were dispersed down Seymour Street by the police, as if really shaken by the unexpected violence of their numbers. After all, these weren't hockey fans out for blood, bladders bursting with Molson's, but chubby suburban teenagers who just wanted the new Antichrist to autograph their freshly shaved heads with a black Sharpie. But watching them, Lewis thought she could understand their rumbling hunger for something authentic, something beyond garage bands, 7-Eleven parking lots, and a disembodied future. "Excuse, excuse me," one white-faced, black-lipped, elaborately pierced young woman had said, elbowing her way through the crowd toward a TV camera. "Excuse me, but can I say something? To all you people who have recently jumped on the Marilyn Manson bandwagon" — she paused dramatically — "I just want to say: Go back to your lives of conformity."

She looked like someone who wrote intense graffiti on toilet stall doors. She looked like someone who might one day try to set herself on fire.

Behind her wavered a sea of young people, all white-faced, black-lipped, and elaborately pierced.

"This cake is so good!" A middle-aged woman in black sweat-pants, black flip-flops, and black toenail polish beside Lewis licked her fingers with gusto and then stuck her tongue out. "Is my tongue blue?"

It was. And so were her teeth, which still had bits of cake stuck between them and something orange as well that the woman must have eaten earlier.

"Let me see yours." The woman was one of those aggressively sociable types that often showed up at Lila's causes. The kind that bullied people into participating.

"Come on, open up." Lewis opened her mouth and stuck out her tongue, but only because she was afraid the woman would actually try to pry her tongue out with a saliva-coated finger if she didn't play along.

"Yours is blue, too!" The woman seemed genuinely delighted. Now they were sisters. Now they were of a tribe. All around them, people were sticking their tongues out at each other, blue tongues glistening in the sudden sunshine, and laughing loosely. What would be appropriate now, Lewis thought, would be to feel a surge of love for all these playful, well-meaning people. People who believed in saving things. Or at least in attending lawn parties with total strangers.

Lila appeared at her side and squeezed her shoulder. "I'm so glad you could come." She made two little fists and danced around, jabbing at the air. "I think we're really going to do it this time. I think we're really going to beat the bastards."

Unlike Lila, Lewis didn't think you ever could really beat the bastards. You just got a chance to do some fancy footwork, get in a few punches, before you got KO'd. The problem was that you never really knew who the bastards were. Mostly you just fooled yourself into thinking they were over there somewhere. But Lewis suspected they were closer to home. *Ich bin ein*

Bastard. Weren't they all? A bunch of little bastards pretending everything rotten was someone else's fault.

"Come on, open up, let's see your tongue," the flip-flop woman commanded Lila.

Lewis was distracted by the flash of something green and familiar behind a broken basement window at the side of the house, beside the loose drainpipe. She turned her head so fast her neck burned viciously. Dry heat rose in waves off her skin. She was sure that if someone looked at her now, really *looked* at her, they would see the flames rising from her collarbone and licking her right ear.

A dragonfly zipped by, bottle blue and fat. The flip-flop woman said something about it sewing her lips shut, clapping her hand over her mouth and giggling that maybe there was really something to old wives' tales. "Don't I wish," Lewis thought, looking right at her. She didn't realize she'd said it out loud until the woman turned abruptly and stomped away, plastic sandals thwacking against her moist, pink heels, sending dandelion fluff spinning into the air.

The little green-haired girl ate slowly and with intense concentration. She had been at it since midmorning, licking each flat wooden paddle clean before moving on to the next vat. A few customers drifted through the store, lifting samples to their noses, dipping their pinkies into the face masks and creams. Raspberry Buffalo, a new one, seemed to be a particular favourite. But when they saw what the green-haired girl was doing, they made a big show of giving her a wide berth, as if her weird hunger was contagious, or that in her dreadlocked rapaciousness she might actually take a bite of their own clean, lightly perfumed flesh. They glanced to see if Lewis was looking and narrowed their eyes, inviting her censure. They wanted her to *do* something.

One older woman, with the blunt grey bangs and well-knit Cowichan sweater of a Point Grey matron — the kind of woman who could, no doubt, identify all the birds that arrived at the feeder on her back patio and had a handsome son studying geophysics at UBC, and a husband, faithful or not, who built their fireplace mantle by hand on weekends from granite they had quarried themselves *en famille* from Nelson Island, a place you could only arrive at by private boat — came up to Lewis at the counter.

"That young woman," she motioned toward the green-haired girl, "is going to make herself sick."

"You ate some." Lewis made sure she smiled as she said this, a bravado smile flush with truth. And it was true. The woman had tried the Raspberry Buffalo. She had dunked her middle finger in quickly and then popped it into her mouth. And then went off into a reverie as if the taste reminded her of something but she wasn't quite sure what. Happier times certainly.

"I *tasted* it. Even a little bit of Lysol won't kill you."

"She's hungry."

"Well, I'll go get her a sandwich. I'll get her something from the Bread Garden." She was already reaching into her canvas shoulderbag and pulling out her wallet. Lewis didn't want to argue with this woman who seemed so well-intentioned, but it struck her, as though through layers of cold air, that the green-haired girl was hers. Hers to save or not to save. She was the bird at Lewis's feeder, and this woman couldn't have her.

"She seems to prefer personal hygiene products."

"I'd like to use your phone, please. I'd like to call an ambulance." Lewis admired how matter-of-factly the woman said this. The veins in her neck didn't tighten and she didn't sound the least bit testy. There was something very Lila-like about her and Lewis felt like crawling up onto the counter and resting her flaming forehead against the woman's thick-knit bosom, which would no doubt have the sweet hand-washed smell of Woolite or Zero. This was the thing you did when there was a problem you couldn't handle. You picked up a telephone and you dialled 911. You didn't make jokes. You didn't laugh. You didn't pick up used syringes from the ground while you waited for the bus and jab them into the grublike blue veins under your tongue.

Lewis reached for the phone and was about to push it across the counter toward the woman. Then she pictured the green-haired girl in the stainless steel bathroom of a hospital ward desperately gulping generic shampoo from a litre bottle while she showered, or gnawing on bars of soap under the thin covers of her cot while the anorexic in the next bed quietly wept in her sleep, jerking at her IV so that the stand rattled against the floor. The shadow of the little man who thought he was a vacuum cleaner passed back and forth across the doorway of the room all night as he went up and down the hallway on his hands and knees, hoovering up any small debris the cleaner might have left behind, a cellophane candy wrapper catching in his throat and crackling loudly, like the loose corrugated metal sides of the shacks at a deserted research station on the tip of the Antarctic crackled incessantly in the wind, although there was no one there to hear them.

Lewis kept her hand on the receiver. "I'll take care of it. She's my friend."

She liked the sound of that. *My little green-haired friend.* As if she had a pal from Mars.

Everyone knew that too little oxygen could be dangerous. When you were oxygen-deprived your nose bled and when you reached dizzying altitudes the blood vessels in your eyes started to pop. But what about too much oxygen? Maybe at a certain point the health benefits peaked and began to tip into the red. At sea level, surrounded by so many trees, maybe they were all overdosing, Lewis thought. She felt heavier and heavier every day. She had this obscene sense of gravity.

Up in the Entercom building, though, she felt lighter, as if the air was truly thinner seventeen storeys above sea level. If she pressed herself flat against the big living room window, naked except for a pair of boxer shorts, so flat that her breasts pancaked out like during a mammogram, so flat that her eyeballs were almost touching the glass and her breath fogged the surface in a wreath around her head, it seemed as if she was actually floating in the air over the inlet, over the Taiwanese tankers filled with Polish sailors, over the glowing heaps of slag and lime and sawdust, over the whole twinkling mess down there where everyone seemed to be trying so hard to prove they could be something if only someone else would give them a chance.

If she pressed herself flat like that, when the nine o'clock gun went off in Stanley Park she could feel the cannon shot reverberate through her body. And after that, she could sleep. In clean, white sheets, surrounded by gallons and gallons of filtered, mineralized water, the fire extinguisher on the wall in the kitchen a sentinel over her dreams, its nozzle, in shadow, like a little beak.

McSpadden Park was almost empty. Two guys in jeans and rubber boots played hockey on the cracked asphalt tennis court in the distance, having a very good time too, it seemed, throwing themselves against the wire fencing to see how far they would bounce back and hooting every time the puck tore another hole in the already tattered net or almost nailed a squirrel. Lewis sat on a bench, drilling the tips of her shoes into the dirt, waiting for Lila who wanted to show her something at the old house. Lewis watched a few dog men, as she had come to call them, circle the park picking up after their pets. They were nondescript men, neither young nor old, who could be spotted here in the early evenings, eyes to the ground, used bread bags in their hands. There seemed to be more and more of them lately. Lonely men circling the park with their plastic bags of steaming turds, their dogs romping off ahead of them, and then looking back as if to say, *Don't worry, I won't desert you.* Lewis tried envisioning the stories of their lives and gave up, deciding she couldn't give them the benefit of the doubt, that their lives, at best, would have the makings of an Anita Brookner novel, an exquisitely wrought — but banal — tale of loneliness, false hopes, and inevitable failure.

They wouldn't even try to dodge the sucker punch, wouldn't see it coming.

"Lewis!"

In front of her stood Guy Gregory, the golden boy of her film school class. Even now, after almost ten years, he seemed to radiate that same weird glow that had made everyone want to throw themselves at his feet. People carried his lighting kits, gave up their editing suites for him, offered him free drugs, threw off their clothes. Even when he indulged these favours, he cultivated an air of ascetism that allowed him to hover slightly above the fray. When he looked right at a person, beamed his light on them, he could make them feel they were the most important person in the world. People basked in that glow. Then, just as abruptly, he would turn away and they'd be left in the shade, shivering. Lewis shivered now, remembering that although she had never belonged to his inner sanctum of groupies, she had once washed his feet.

Guy Gregory was the kind of person who was always called by both his first and last names. "Guy Gregory," Lewis said, and then wondered what else there was to say.

"Lewis, Lewis," he said, standing in front of her, blocking the last remnants of the evening sun. She noticed that she felt cold, and was surprised. Where was the warmth? There Guy Gregory was, beaming his light on her, and she sat on a bench in McSpadden Park shivering while a couple of morons played slash hockey in the distance and the dog men shuffled along, dejected but ever conscientious. She wished he would either sit down or leave, but he just stood there.

"So," she said, "I heard you're down in L.A. now. Doing TV."

"Yeah, well," Guy Gregory said, and then looked toward the hockey-playing hosers. He watched them for a few seconds and then sighed. "I miss that kind of thing down there."

"What kind of thing?"

"Real people."

Lewis almost snorted.

Guy Gregory looked down on her like he wanted to pat the top of her head. As if she were a Pekingese with an unfortunate face and a bandaged paw or a cripple auditioning for the chorus-line of *Chicago*. "I heard about what happened to you. Jesus Christ. Or, HeyZeus, as they say at Taco Bell."

"Yeah, well," she said, trying his studied nonchalance on for size, her rising panic a large insect in her throat, a scarab twitching.

"Could happen to anyone," Guy Gregory said. "You know, I think I slept with her once, but I really can't remember for sure."

Lewis looked hard at the ground between Guy Gregory's feet. There was a small fissure, a crack, a seam in the earth. Maybe if she wished hard enough it would open up to swallow him whole like a python would a goat. Suck him in and spit out his bones and hooves for organic fertilizer.

He crouched down, tugging at the knees of his khakis, until they were face to face. "What did it smell like, if don't mind me asking? All that hair on fire, that burning flesh."

Her hand swung out before she even realized what she was doing, propelled by a thick, sulfurous laugh that came from deep in her throat. A laugh edged in blue flame that should have melted the flesh right off his face. Lewis hit Guy Gregory hard in the nose with the heel of her hand, knocking him out of his crouch, and ran. She slammed into one of the dog men, wheeling him around, sending his bag of freshly gathered shit into the air. The man's chocolate Lab chased her up the street, yelping indignantly, but stopped obediently at the curb as Lewis jumped into the intersection, dodging a cyclist who was pumping hard, running a red. He shot her the finger. An aging vw microbus, dragging its back bumper, red long johns for curtains in the back windows and bumper stickers all over it (*Hemp!* — SUBVERT THE DOMINANT PARADIGM — *Hey, Magic Happens*) slammed on the brakes. The driver stuck his head out the window and yelled in a reedy voice, "Move to Toronto if you're in such a hurry, bitch!"

Several blocks away Lewis finally stopped. She rested against a fence, wiped her hair away from her face and saw that there was blood on her hand.

"Did you feel it?" Lila asked. Lewis lay on the bed, the telephone receiver cold against her ear, trying to figure out whose voice she was listening to. "You weren't at home or work so I figured I'd find you there."

"Lila?"

"Did you feel it?"

"What?"

"The earthquake. You didn't feel it?"

"Maybe it was the nine o'clock gun."

"It just happened this morning. You're not still in bed? It's after ten."

Lewis didn't answer. She couldn't remember how long she'd

been sleeping. Days, hours, weeks. The sheets were damp. She had come straight to the Entercom building after running from the park. She showered for a long time, until the water ran like ice pellets down her back and the man downstairs cranked his Rachmaninoff No. 3 — London Symphony Orchestra, André Previn conducting — up to full volume to show his displeasure, and then she crawled into bed without even towelling off, without looking out the window, without waiting for the nine o'clock gun, and plunged into a sleep of desert rest, a parched sleep during which someone tried to teach her how to milk a cactus, plunging a dull kitchen knife in again and again. Now her tongue felt like a suede shoe, a Hush Puppy rammed to the roof of her mouth.

"It was only preshock," Lila said. "It's all over the radio. The CBC had this guy on who said there'll likely be another one. He sounded excited, like he was talking about hockey playoffs or something. They say to stay in a basement if you can. You know, sleep in a door jamb. Oh Lewis, I'm so worried about the old house."

"Why?" Lewis heard voices in the hallway. A nanny collecting the children of the couple in number 1732, her usually laid-back Jamaican patois strained to a terse, urgent staccato.

"I went by yesterday, after I went to look for you at the park."

"Sorry." Lewis wondered why Lila hadn't called the flip-flop woman or one of the tribe of other jolly blue-tongued do-gooders.

"I saw that someone was living in the basement, just as I thought. If a candle tips over, you know, that's it. This, this person wouldn't come out. I saw her flatten herself against the wall

when I looked in with my flashlight. I yelled through the basement window, but she wouldn't answer. I understand about
squatters' rights, you know, but this house, it's so fragile. And the
smell in there, it's weird. Sweet and sour. I didn't want to go in,
not by myself. I don't want a confrontation. I think I have to call
the police."

She felt Lila drifting away, like a helium balloon that slips
from your hand when you're not paying attention and tumbles
end over end on a breeze over rooftops, growing ever smaller.

"It's not even your house," Lewis said.

The children at the school for the deaf are the first to sense
something's happening. It's recess and they're out in the
playground when they all stiffen for several seconds, even the girl
hanging upside down on the monkey bars, her braids dragging in
the sand. Then they start signing rapidly, little fingers fluttering,
small fists smacking into palms. The birds rise up and darken the
sky all over the city.

Carnivores and lacto-vegans cling to each other as tectonic
plates shift and groan beneath them. Chum salmon leap through
the massive cracks in the concrete at the foot of the Cambie
Street Bridge, chum that haven't been seen here since the 1920s,
chum the size of raccoons and grinning like gargoyles. The old
polar bear, the only animal left in the zoo, left waiting there
to die, scrambles for purchase as the warm slab of concrete
underneath his nicotine-tipped fur buckles, and he slides into
the churning moat, wailing as only polar bears can. The ocean
spits deadheads, sending logs rocketing through the city like

battering rams to crack open the massive walls of the new library, the Bay, GM Place, St. Paul's Hospital, splitting heads as they whistle by like heat-seeking missiles. All over the Lower Mainland film sets collapse as the earth heaves and honey wagons shoot into the sky, their contents raining down like some stinking vengeance for a long-forgotten crime.

Piles of baby skulls, smooth as china cups, heave out of vaults below Shaughnessy mansions that once housed convents. Nudists scramble madly up the cliff face from their beach, clutching at branches and swollen arbutus roots, brambles tearing at their pubic hair and genitals, as the ocean roars behind them, a towering inferno of water swallowing pan pipes, arthritic dogs and coolers of dope and sangrias. They're shocked, not because the end has come, but because it's so Old Testament when they had thought it would be man-made — a cold, clinical apocalypse so that they could say, *We told you so.*

Suddenly, there's no cliff and they're all clutching at the air.

Lewis hurries along the street looking for the green-haired girl.

When she finds her, she knows the thing to do would be to make their way together, as quickly and calmly as possible, back to the apartment in the Entercom building.

Then the thing to do would be to lock the door and wait for the city to crumble.

THE CANVASBACK

Timothy Taylor

Excerpt from the novel *Stanley Park*

They arranged to meet at Lost Lagoon. It was an in-between place, the city on one side, Stanley Park on the other. Ten years of rare contact and they had sought each other out. Surprised each other, created expectations.

Now the Professor was late.

Jeremy Papier found a bench up the hill from the lagoon and opened a section of newspaper across the wet boards. The bench was between two old cherry trees, the pink blossoms of which met high over his head forming an arch, a doorway. It wasn't precisely the spot they'd discussed — the Professor had suggested the boathouse — but it was within eyesight, within shouting distance. It was close enough. If he had to wait, Jeremy thought, settling onto the paper and blowing out a long breath, he was going to sit. He crossed one long, aching leg over the other. He fingered the tooling on a favourite pair of cowboy boots, ran long fingers through tangled black hair.

He sat because he was tired, certainly. Jeremy accepted that being a chef, even a relatively young chef, meant being exhausted most of the time. But there had also been a family portrait taken here, on this bench, years before. Also early spring, he remembered; the three of them sat here under the cherry blossoms. Jeremy on the one side, seven years old. His mother, Hélène, on the other. The Professor had his arms around them both, feet flat on the grass. He looked extremely pleased. Jeremy's mother was less obviously so, her expression typically guarded, although she made dozens of copies of the photo and sent these off to relatives spread across Europe from Ireland to Spain, from the Czech Republic as far east as Bulgaria. Documenting settlement. He wondered if his father, who had no relations other than those in the photo, would remember this detail.

Now Jeremy lit a cigarette and watched an erratic stream of homeless people making their way into the forest for the night. When he arrived there had been seawall walkers and hotdog eaters, birdwatchers, rollerbladers, chess players returning from the picnic tables over by bowling greens. Then lagoon traffic changed direction like a freak tide. The flow of those returning to their warm apartments in the West End tapered to nothing and the paths were filled with the delusional, the alcoholic, the paranoid, the bipolar. The Professor's subjects, his obsession. The inbound. Four hundred hectares of Stanley Park, offering its bleak, anonymous shelter to those without other options.

Of course, Jeremy didn't have to remind himself, the Professor had other options.

They had discussed meeting on the phone earlier in the week. When Jeremy picked up — expecting a late reservation, maybe his black-cod supplier, who was due into Vancouver the next morning — he heard wind and trees rustling at the other end of the line. Normally reticent, the Professor was animated about his most recent research.

"... following on from everything that I have done," he said, "culminating with this work." From his end, standing at a pay phone on the far side of the lagoon, the Professor could hear the dishwasher hammering away in the background behind his son's tired response.

"*Participatory* anthropology. Is that what you call it now?" Jeremy was saying. "I thought it was *immersive.*"

"Like everything," the Professor answered carefully, "my work has evolved."

He needed help with something, the said Professor said. He wanted to meet.

"How unusual," Jeremy said.

"And what advice can I give on running a restaurant?" the Professor shot back.

"None," Jeremy answered. "I just said there was something I wanted to talk to you about. Something that had to do with the restaurant."

"Strange times," the Professor said, looking around into the darkness near the pay phone. Checking instinctively.

Very strange. The stream of those inbound had slowed to a trickle. A trio of men passed, bent behind shopping carts that were draped and hung with plastic, heaped to the height of pack horses, bags full of other bags. Jeremy could only wonder at the purpose of them all, although the Professor could have told him that the bag itself captured the imagination. It held emblematic power. For its ability to hold, certainly. To secure contents, to carry belongings from place to place. But even the smell of the plastic, its oily permanence, suggested the resilience of things discarded.

Jeremy watched the three men make their way around the lagoon and disappear into the trails. He glanced at his watch, sighed. Lifted his chin and breathed in the saline breeze. It brought to mind the ocean beyond the park, sockeye salmon schooling in the deep, waiting for the DNA-encoded signal to turn in their millions and rush the mouth of the Fraser, the tributary offshoot, the rivulet of water and the gravel-bed spawning grounds beyond. Mate, complete the cycle, die. And then, punctuating this thought, the rhododendron bushes across the lawn boiled briefly and disgorged Caruzo, the Professor's manic vanguard.

"Hey, hey," Caruzo said, approaching the bench. "Chef Papier." He exhaled the words in a blast.

He dressed for the mobile outdoor life, Caruzo. Three or four sweaters, a torn corduroy jacket, a heavy coat, then a raincoat over all of that. It made the big man even bigger, the size of a lineman, six foot five, although stooped a little with the years. Those being of an indeterminate number; Jeremy imagined only that it must be between fifty and ninety. Caruzo had a white garbage bag tied on over one shoe, although it was only threatening to rain, and pants wrapped at the knees in electrical tape. His ageless, wind-beaten face was protected by a blunt beard that fell to his chest. Exposed skin had darkened, blackened as a chameleon might against the same forest backdrop.

"The Professor," Caruzo announced, "is waiting."

Jeremy followed Caruzo between the cherry trees and around the lagoon. They passed down an alley of oak trees that stirred another memory of his mother. When they were alone — the Professor was often in the field on other projects, never explained — Jeremy and his mother would spend weekends here, feeding the animals. Bread for the swans, nuts for the squirrels. The raccoons would take eggs from your hand and climb up into these same bent trees, crack their prize gingerly and suck clean the interior. Once a raccoon bobbed its head in silent thanks before eating. His mother laughed for a long time at that. It was as happy as he remembered her being, ever. From his earliest memories right up to the day in October 1987 when Hélène Papier died, not long after his twentieth birthday. His father was again in the field. Jeremy had been seeking his own petulant distance, living on campus, playing in a bad rockabilly band called The Decoders and failing economics. When Jeremy thought of it now — ten years separating him from the events that had so tragically, so quickly, unfolded — it sometimes felt as if she had given up on both of them, all at once. In the middle of dream turned left, not right. Taken her leave. The suddenness of it sent Jeremy and his father flying across the world in different directions.

Caruzo marched ahead. He was chanting, as he would from time to time.

> *"October 5, 1947,*
> *The date of their demise,*
> *When the things I saw in the trees and the sky*
> *made me finally realise,*
> *It's the fir and the arbutus*
> *Whose leaves will fall to meet ye,*
> *And touching the soil mark the morning of toil*
> *When the light it fails to greet ye.*
>
> *"And now I singe, any food, any feeding,*
> *Feeding, drink or clothing,*
> *Come dame or maid,*
> *Be not afraid, poor Tom will injure nothing."*

When he reached the end of the chorus, Caruzo stopped on the path, held his hands out as if soliciting critical commentary.

"Food, drink or clothing?" Jeremy asked.

"How about a toonie?" Caruzo said.

Jeremy produced the two-dollar coin and they walked another fifty yards, over a small arched bridge and up to a trail mouth that entered the forest proper. A pay phone stood there. And since the Professor was still nowhere to be seen, Jeremy phoned Jules at the restaurant.

"How are you making out?" she asked him. She had the cordless phone tucked under her chin while she walked across the kitchen of The Monkey's Paw Bistro.

"It's all extremely strange," he said by way of an answer.

"Strange itself is not bad," Jules said. "All my father ever talks about are husbands and mutual funds. Turns out the evaluation criteria are similar."

She was trying to cheer him up, which he appreciated as always. "What are the numbers tonight?" he asked her.

"Twenty-six covers early. We have a six-top late. A few tentatives."

"Thursday," he said, exasperated.

"Walk-in Thursday," Jules said. Jeremy deduced from the steady scraping sound he heard that she was stirring the roasted carrot-ginger soup he had prepped earlier.

"I was going to use a bit of cinnamon in that soup," he said. "Is Zeena in?"

"Zeena, of course, is in," Jules said, and then, knowing he was trying to think about work as an alternative to what lay before him, she prodded, "Talk to me, sugar. How's he doing?"

Well, he's living in a park, for one. But Jeremy knew what she was really asking. "I can't be sure," he said to Jules. "He's not here yet."

"He'll show," Jules said. "Take the evening. I'll manage."

"Everything else prepped up?"

"Puh-lease."

"I made a demi from those duck bones. I was going to use that in the sauce for the duck breast with an apricot preserve ..."

Sous-chef Jules Capelli met these instructions with long-suffering silence.

"Sorry."

"I got the notes," Jules said. "Now take the night and I'll see you tomorrow."

Caruzo had become the messenger. He could still cover great distances quickly on his long legs, and so he had been sent to set up this meeting, loping all the way across town to The Monkey's Paw to secure Jeremy's commitment in person. He returned with the good news, and a complimentary plate of lamb sausage and new-potato ragout inside him, retracing his steps through favourite back alleys, forest paths and finally to the Professor's camp.

"Yo hey," Caruzo called from the darkness, adhering to the protocol they had developed: Call from a short, respectful distance away. If there is no answer, come back later. "Hi, Professor," he called.

The Professor cracked the fly with two fingertips. He was sitting cross-legged in the middle of the little tent, sorting through piles of yellow foolscap pages. Each legal-sized sheet covered on both sides with handwritten notes, scrawled in pencil.

"Yo hey," Caruzo said. "Chef says yes. Jay-Jay is coming."

The Professor leaned out of the tent a little ways to catch the words. He was pleased.

"Five o'clock tomorrow," Caruzo said, nodding vigorously. "But hey," he continued, then stalled. The Professor waited while the big man squinted and relaxed his eyes repeatedly, milking out the thought.

"It's good," Caruzo said. "Jay-Jay coming."

"Jeremy coming is good," the Professor said, nodding reassurance.

"I'll meet him at the boathouse," Caruzo said. "Meet him, bring him in?"

"Fine," the Professor agreed. "I'll meet you both at the bulrushes."

"Right," Caruzo nodded. "Right." But he made no move to disappear into the dark, no move to find his way through the blackness to his own camp, so skilfully hidden for all these years. Instead he waited, a little nervously. "Do you want to talk?" the Professor asked, sensing Caruzo's mood. He quickly confirmed the presence of a pencil behind his ear, then felt around himself for one of his yellow legal pads.

He made a small fire. Then, as he had done so many nights since he discovered this place and the people in it, the Professor leaned back in the grass around the fire and only listened.

Caruzo spoke in the tongues of angels, although the fire of his words licked around the ideas he worked to express and often consumed them. Tonight again, he spoke of the children. "Their death pulled," Caruzo said, rocking. "The boy, the girl. Killed as they were. It pulled me and it sent me. Pulled others too. We were like the dry leaves, and their death was a puff of black air. For years I searched for them, and when I found them it all began." He gestured around himself at the park, the darkness. "From a leaf to a lifer," he went on. "That's me. A lifer to a leaf."

He burned himself out eventually and left as he typically did: without offering firm solutions to his riddles and without saying goodnight. He rose from his haunches, turned in the soft grass and vanished into the shadows.

The Professor read over his notes, then put the yellow legal pad back in the tent. He returned to the fire to watch it as the flames died. Since their last series of meetings, Caruzo had not untangled. So their deaths had drawn him here, the Professor thought, trying to work it through. The leaf blown by the evil event, the black wind. The leaf becoming a lifer, permanent. The lifer anticipating how he would one day, again, become a leaf. Was that it?

The Professor put his hands behind his head and stared up through the canopy of trees to find those pieces of the night sky that were visible. The fragments of constellations that, for those who could believe such things, would provide direction. He remembered how Hélène had disdained astrology, indeed most forms of the mystical. There was a certain cliché about the gypsy fortune teller with which she could not bear association. He learned this quickly after they first met. Nineteen fifty-six, Lyon. Hélène was living with her father and uncles, aunts and cousins, trying out city life after generations on the road. The Professor (not yet a professor) was over from Canada with his yellow pads and sharp pencils, observing. The first case study of a professional lifetime under way. His thesis named with some of the romance by which it had been electrified: *Romani Alighted: Remembering the Vardo*. Work from which all else had grown, the Professor thought now, branches sifting air above him. Their marriage, certainly. Hélène had been drawn to his interest in her. To his own unknowable history too, perhaps. Before his own father, now dead, there was only an expanse of unknown. A book of blank pages.

But the work with Hélène's family had also given birth to all his other work. Launched him across the anthropological landscape. Squatters in the Delta. Russian stowaways. The earliest Vancouver panhandlers who had peopled his successful book, *Will Work for Food.* Hélène might not always have appreciated her role at the root of things. And neither of them could have known how Stanley Park itself lay sleeping in their future.

The fire was out. The Professor climbed into his tent to sleep. He didn't dream of Caruzo. Didn't lie unconscious under images of Hélène's beauty, the unfolding of their years or even the October morning when he had awoken in the field with a very particular hollow feeling. The morning he had phoned Hélène, and the phone had rung and rung.

A welcome relief, this dreamless sleep.

In the morning he climbed down from the forest to the men's room by Second Beach. Familiar steps. He removed the pane of glass at the back of the locked building, as Caruzo had shown him long ago. He climbed in, washed, shaved. Then he spent the day on his favourite cliff, high above the sea in a salty breeze, thinking of how it might all be finally finished. Ten years later than expected, but one could not schedule tragedy or the irregular dawn of understanding.

When it was time to meet his son, the Professor pulled the fly-fishing net from his pack and walked down through the forest to the lagoon. At the trail mouth he stood in the shelter of a salal bush, eyes on the path. It was just before five. Caruzo appeared when he promised, leading Jeremy over the arched stone bridge and toward him. The Professor watched, but did not step from the bushes immediately, and the boy did as he would. He grew exasperated. His eyes found a pay phone nearby, a distraction. He stabbed the keypad with a finger, his back to Caruzo. Wishing, no doubt, to be anywhere but here. When he hung up, the Professor stepped from his hiding place, and Caruzo disappeared into the trees as agreed. The Professor enjoyed noting how the densely overlapping branches did not move as he entered the green face of the forest. Caruzo was merely absorbed.

"I can't stay long." These were the first words his son found.

"I thought maybe dinner."

"It's Thursday. I can't leave Jules alone."

His restaurant did not come up without mention of this name. "Oh, I'll bet you can," the Professor said.

They stood face to face in the falling light, the Professor's head just a degree to one side. The boy wasn't sleeping well, he thought. There were dark circles under his eyes. Black hair strawing this way and that. Was I wiry back then, like he is now? A little pale? They were still around the same six-foot height, the Professor observed, looking steadily into his son's eyes and thinking: I have not yet begun to shrink.

Jeremy thought only that his father looked better than he might under the circumstances. His eyes were bright, his brows pranced upward with good humour. True, his hair was dirty and his fingernails were black, and he was carrying an old wooden fly-fishing net pinched under one elbow for no evident reason.

"Perhaps you'll stay long enough to see me catch my dinner then," the Professor said. One needed darkness, he went on to explain. And so they sat on the bench and talked, circling but not meeting the matter at hand. Demand nothing, the Professor thought. And so they talked about the Stanley Park game-bird population, instead. A point of mutual interest, the Professor imagined.

"You eat duck?" Jeremy asked. A passer-by might have assumed he was about to provide cooking tips. Sear off the breast on a medium grill, skin side down. Render the fat. Finish skin side up, just a couple minutes. Sauce it and you're good to go.

But to which the Professor answered: "I've been here quite a few months and I didn't bring groceries. Have you eaten starlings?" He was aware that it sounded like a challenge. "Delicious, although you'll need two or three per person."

"I've eaten ortolan," Jeremy said, and then was irritable with himself for being drawn into the conversation on that level.

"Now, the mallard is a fantastically light sleeper," the Professor informed him.

Jeremy looked away.

"The canvasback even more so, fiendishly difficult to catch. The important thing is to learn a little each day here. Just a little. I spent a week trying to catch my first bird. A week. Do you know what I mean?"

"I have no idea what you mean," Jeremy answered. "I buy my ducks direct from a guy named Bertrand who lives on a farm up the valley."

"Although presumably someone catches them for Bertrand.

Say though, I've been reading about you. Anya Dickie's review of The Monkey's Foot. Brilliant job."

"The Monkey's Paw Bistro."

"Purple prose but a nice conclusion. How did the Dickie woman say it again?"

Jeremy sighed and looked out over the lagoon. The dynamic between them, he thought, didn't change much with the years, the location or their relative mental health.

"'Crosstown Celebrates Local Beverages and Bounty,'" Jeremy finally said, reciting the headline, which was also the lead line and the closing line of a typically enthusiastic Dickie restaurant review. She had been quite taken with the way Jules and he shared a passion for local meat, produce, cheese and wine.

"I could use that," the Professor said. "'Local bounty' is rather good. I think we share this passion, you and I."

Jeremy considered a retort along the lines of: "You and I share nothing but blood." But he imagined this approach would end the conversation. He would get no advice and have who knows what other effect on his father, and so he sat there and listened as the Professor elaborated on their supposed professional overlap, describing what he called "the stories of the residents." There was great deference in his voice. There had always been people here, the Professor said, solemn. There had been a First Nation, of course. Squatters later. Men who lived in trees. But this generation was the homeless, the new Stanley Park people. This was the story — collected lives and anecdotes, assorted obsessions and misfortunes — the Professor would now stitch together. The great Work-In-Progress.

"Is Sopwith Hill taking it?" Jeremy asked. A prestigious if aging textbook house, Sopwith had done the Professor's other books, some of these approaching mainstream popularity. Jeremy actually read one before the disastrous fall of 1987, before he fled to the culinary institute in Dijon. He couldn't remember the title, but he thought the Professor had spent three months in the downtown east side, interviewing panhandlers. Panhandling himself and living in a range of unsafe outdoor places, including under parked cars left overnight in a downtown parkade. Jeremy heard this story after the fact, his mother's bitter version. At one point (she had fumed) somebody had returned early to retrieve their car and had nearly run him over. He moved into an unused culvert behind the SeaBus Terminal at that point. "To be run over, that would maybe be the best to understand these people. These 'no-homes,'" she had said to Jeremy. "Only in dying like them, you can no longer write about them."

The Professor looked briefly away before answering the question. His son's tone registered doubt, incredulity. "They'll take it eventually." But his voice was a little tight.

So Jeremy sat back on the bench they had found, ran his fingers through his hair, which was in worse disarray than usual, a manic bristle. It was only appropriate that it started to rain lightly just then, fine drops hissing into the foliage around them.

"Fires," said the Professor, attempting to illustrate his point about learning a little each day. "Now there's something I knew nothing about. Thank God for Caruzo."

It was, for a moment, the single most unexpected revelation of the evening: the Professor could light fires.

They talked for over an hour this way, holding one another at a familiar arm's-length, both in their own way reflecting that Hélène was all the distance between them. Alive, she provided the bridge. Gone, she was the chasm itself. They might not yet have filled any of that emptiness, but a silver distance opened between them and the city. They sat, at the very least, in the same descending darkness, looking across the lagoon to the now gleaming towers of the West End, a parallel universe separated from them by the surface of the water on which slept hundreds of ducks.

"You stand watch," the Professor instructed quietly, when he deemed the time was right.

"For what?"

It was only his first visit. "Others."

Jeremy looked distinctly concerned.

"Not militant vegetarians precisely. More like the police."

"Oh, just that," the chef said. "Well, then: Charge."

Jeremy took shelter under a cedar. The Professor got down on his hands and knees and began to creep across the walkway. He held the old fly-fishing net in front of himself as he approached the clutch of rushes on the far side of the path. He rose to his knees and parted the papery stalks silently, the net aloft. Jeremy could make out several ducks within range. As he watched, all movement ceased.

And then the Professor merely fell forward, arm outstretched, pitching across the water. It was like a silent movie until a quarter second before his impact, when every duck within sixty yards burst from sleep and the lagoon simultaneously, and all previous tranquility, all silver thoughtfulness and reflection, drained out of the water in a spray of violent splashing. The air filled with black thudding shapes. Several birds left the water in a confused tangle and collided with one another, falling back into the lagoon. One fell onto the path in front of Jeremy, where it skidded, spun, seemed to glance at him in reproach before launching into flight again.

The one snared in the net, meanwhile, flew briefly in desperation, powerful wings holding it above water despite the Professor's full weight. Fighting. Flailing. Sinking suddenly. His father's head and upper body disappeared into the lagoon. He lay there, half-submerged, like he'd been shot. And then there was a gasping re-emergence, the duck now held by its neck, quivering, nearly drowned. The Professor breathing heavily. Water plastering down his hair, running down his face, his body blackened with it. He set the net aside, took the duck firmly in both his hands. He snapped his wrists sharply, cracking the neck. The bird was instantly still.

The Professor raised a finger to his lips. They waited. No celebration was permitted yet. The circling survivors reflocked above them, then homed in stupidly on another not distant part of the lagoon. As they swished to their new sleeping place the stillness slowly returned to the water.

Still no movement from the Professor, except a slight cocking of his head to the breeze. Listening to some small sound, measuring an intangible indicator that he knew from experience must either dissipate or return before he dared move. And when the Professor's variable fell (or rose) into the green zone, only then did they quietly scramble away from the lagoon, up through the grassy passageway to the Park Drive. Pausing just seconds at the edge of the new blacktop with its bright yellow markings for the angle parkers, then across this surface and into the cool forest. Even here they walked a distance without speaking.

When the city was almost inaudible, replaced with the sound of clacking cedars and moaning wind, the Professor stopped. "Ha ha," he said. Beaming again. He held his hands apart, in one the duck dangling by the neck, dripping water, beak and eyes serenely closed. "Look at that, would you? It never stops pleasing me to pluck from this forest the things that I need. Carefully and craftily I make my way."

He looked from his son to the bird and back again.

"And you are off to work now, I suppose," the Professor said, hoping he had stirred something. Guilt might do for now, although curiosity would be better.

"It's a nice bird," Jeremy heard himself say calmly, although his heart was pounding. Against his own better judgement he reached for the duck, thinking of cooking school and of France, of the ducks he himself had been taught to kill. Here, as the trees rattled against one another above them, Jeremy reached across his father to touch this duck, wanting to hold it while he knew it was still warm.

"Look at that. A nice redhead."

"Canvasback," the Professor corrected.

"Redhead," he said again, more emphatically.

"Oh no," the Professor said. "Definitely a canvasback."

"This duck," Jeremy said, irritated at their disagreement during this brief moment he had been enjoying, "is a redhead."

"This duck," answered the Professor, wincing now at the error, "is no redhead. With all due respect to your culinary education, Chef, I fear it has failed you here. There are pheasants, there are guinea hens and ortolans. Then there are park ducks. If you want to know about park ducks, I am, as they say, your man."

"Chestnut head —" Jeremy began.

"Cripes, Jeremy, shut the yawp just for a minute. Your red has a pronounced high forehead, a grey body and a much blacker tail. They are also a good deal less common around here, rare even. You see, my boy, I wouldn't have taken a redhead had there been a redhead to take. Which there wasn't, *ergo* this duck isn't."

At which point he took the bird back and slid it into a plastic shopping bag he produced from under his sweater. And without warning to Jeremy, he peeled off to the left and disappeared into the black forest between a towering stump and a half-fallen maple.

"This is ludicrous," Jeremy said, stopping and speaking emphatically to the empty pine-needle path. "I mean ... shit," he said. Here they were again, firing at each other in the blackness.

He looked up the path, down it, then into the still darker forest listening to the Professor moving away from him through the underbrush, the soft sound floating back. This moment would be the time to come to one's senses, Jeremy thought. To get the hell back into the city, to The Monkey's Paw, where twenty-six covers would be seated, conversation rising. Jules was probably now riding a wave of incoming appetizer orders, beginning to slam, the sound-track urging everything and everybody onward into the night.

Or he could wait here. Thirty seconds from now the Professor would be gone. He might still be able to hear him, but he'd never find him. Not in that. In the darkness and the trees and the bramble. And the Professor wouldn't even notice, or he'd notice, maybe, but not be particularly surprised. He would forge ahead through this forest to his hidden spot. (Perhaps he doesn't want me to see his spot, thought Jeremy.) Either way, he'd be fine. Just listen to him.

Somewhere up in the woods, the Professor was reciting a poem quietly. Jeremy had to hold himself very still to pick out the words.

> *"With an hoste of furious fancies,*
> *Whereof I am commander,*
> *With a burning speare, and a horse of air,*
> *To the wildernesse, I wander."*

A challenge, of course, and it didn't get any quieter; the poem now came floating out of the swaying blackness from a single spot where the Professor stood, smiling and reciting, leaning his head back and looking toward the crack of black sky visible at the tops of the trees.

Jeremy crashed into the forest toward him. And when he found his father, they stood for a moment and looked at each other. Jeremy's favourite cowboy boots were past wet, the branches now reaching to soak his back and neck.

"Is this it?" he said. Through the trees Jeremy could make out campfires spread in the darkness around them.

"Not quite yet," the Professor said, motioning with his head that they should continue. He turned and hoisted a leg up to a foothold on a large root-covered rock, gripped the gnarled wood with his fingertips and disappeared over the top.

It was the root end of a gigantic tree, Jeremy realized. Torn from the soil by a gust of wind, torn up along with the huge boulder to which the roots had been clinging. Jeremy clambered inexpertly after his father and stood at the base of the broad trunk. It stretched out in front of them like a bridge, 150 feet long, silver in the moonlight. As they walked it bowed slightly beneath them. It surprised Jeremy, this slight bending of the massive trunk. He would have thought their weight was not enough to move such a great thing, a thing that vaulted them through the brush to a completely different part of the park. A denser part. A part that had no relation to anything that he had previously known.

"What we want is a fire," the Professor said from ahead of him, as they descended a slope.

And he lit good fires too, Jeremy discovered. After half an hour tramping through the damp and the dark, the Professor made a small hot fire in just a few minutes. Built with few words spoken, in a trench at the centre of his camp.

While the Professor changed into dry clothes, Jeremy squatted back-assed to the heat and considered that if he were abandoned here, he would be lost until morning. Perhaps even then. So busy a park, thousands of visitors a day. Never once had he felt lost in it, as he was now.

A map and a global positioning system would have revealed

to him that he was not far from things that he knew. Just a couple of hundred yards off the Park Drive, near Prospect Point, in fact. Here a densely forested slope fell from the road, down to the top of a cliff that towered a hundred feet above the seawall and the ocean below. The Professor had found a clearing between the trees at the very edge of this cliff. There were tamped-down ferns and a tent built against the trunk of a cedar, a space big enough for one very still, very accomplished sleeper. And through the branches of this tree, and the others that umbrella-ed over the small clearing, one had a view of the harbour, freighters silent at their moorage, well lit. At the bottom of the cliffs and to the left stood Siwash Rock, which pillared fifty feet out of the water near the shore. A rock that was once a bather, legend had it, a bather honoured by the gods with this permanent place at the lip of forest that had been his home.

The Professor plucked the canvasback and drew it smoothly. He buried the entrails some distance away. He washed his hands and the bird with water from a plastic juice container. "Did you bring salt by any chance?" he asked, returning to the fire. "No matter, I have a packet left."

"How about string?" Jeremy asked. You might as well do it right, he thought. And when the Professor produced his string, Jeremy trussed the bird, tying it into the fork of a blackened Y-shaped stick. He buried the other end of the stick in the soft earth, supported it across a large stone and cantilevered the bird above the flames. By sliding the stone back and forth, the bird's height and roasting temperature could be very roughly adjusted.

He sat back in the dry area of fern nearest the flames and folded his arms across his knees.

There was silence for some time. The bird began to glisten, then hiss gently. Finally the aroma was released: smoky, fatty, rich with oil. He twisted the stick a quarter turn.

"This is all quite illegal, of course," Jeremy said finally, aware that the comment was softened by his own complicity. But the Professor only looked at him as if he were a little slow for just getting this point. "All right," Jeremy went on, failing to resist a small smile. The duck smelled good. "How do you catch a starling?"

"Caruzo showed me," the Professor said, re-energized. "Peanut butter spread on top of a good strong epoxy from any hardware store. On a stick or a low branch in a relatively clear area, not too far into the forest. You can watch from quite close by; they are not a shy bird. Or scarce, for that matter. It works nicely, although you'll want to remove the feet before you cook them."

Jeremy rocked gently back and forth. Shook his head as if to clear it. "You clean them up, like that?" he asked, nodding toward the juice container full of water.

"I take the starlings down to the men's room by the beach," the Professor said, "where I can spread out and do a good job." Now he was rummaging through his leather case, which he had slung up in the low branches of the nearby cedar. "Same place I charge my notebook." He re-emerged from the branches carrying a bottle of wine. "I bought this for you. A Rioja. You like Spain, don't you?"

"Never been."

"Right. France, was it?"

"France," Jeremy said.

The Professor uncorked the wine. Then he unsnapped a collapsible field cup from inside its pouch, telescoped it out, poured some of the red wine and handed it across the fire to Jeremy. He had a plastic cup for himself.

When they both had wine, Jeremy still did not sip. The Professor felt the pause and looked at his son.

"Participatory anthropology —" Jeremy began.

"Quite beyond immersion," the Professor said. "The next step, really."

Jeremy chose his words carefully. "I thought you had given this up."

"I had," the Professor said. "But I left something unfinished. Something I thought should be put to rest."

Jeremy wasn't sure he understood.

"My own celebration of 'local bounty,'" the Professor said, nodding toward the duck and smiling.

"Not funny," Jeremy answered.

"You don't like that we might be working on parallel projects."

Jeremy sighed and lifted the silver cup in the orange light that flickered around them. "*Santé*," he said. "To your health."

"*A la vôtre*," said the Professor, before drinking. "To yours too."

They charred the bird a bit on the back and the legs. It was tough to cook directly over such a low flame. Still, it wasn't badly done. The breast was crispy, meat the texture of medium steak. The professor cut them off pieces in turn, which they ate with their hands, sitting cross-legged next to one another in the dry ferns near the fire.

"It's not really cooking, I realize," said the Professor. "Perhaps with a salal-berry cream sauce we could tart it up to your customer's level of sophistication."

"Sure." Although: salal-berry cream sauce. Not bad.

"Salt?" the Professor dangled the packet at eye level.

Jeremy took the paper envelope of precious salt and sprinkled some across the piece of canvasback breast in his fingers. He chewed and swallowed. Then took a breath.

"I'm just a cook."

The Professor glanced up. "Oh yes?"

"That's all," Jeremy said. "So I like local produce. So I like local rabbits. Whatever."

"Whatever? Meaning: no reason for this preference? No larger significance?"

"Of course it has significance. There just isn't any big —"

"Any big reason for it?" the Professor said.

Maybe not, Jeremy thought. He swallowed another mouthful of duck and held a greasy finger up in front of himself. "If somebody asked me, 'What are you trying to accomplish?'" he started, "I would answer that I was trying to remind people of something. Of what the soil under their feet has to offer. Of a time when they would have known only the food that their own soil could offer."

"Sort of a nostalgia thing," the Professor said.

"Make fun," Jeremy said, "but how would you answer the same question?"

"I would say," the Professor answered, "that I am here allowing the words of this wilderness to penetrate me, to understand what is being said by these people. Because I believe it is something that concerns us all, some more than most. You and I, for example. Or perhaps we are just ready to hear these words. You and I."

Jeremy looked away. Part of this answer was pleasing, the inclusion. The remainder was exasperating. "And what are those words exactly?"

"In aggregate, something along these lines:

> 'With an hoste of furious fancies,
> Whereof I am commander,
> With a burning speare, and a horse of air,
> To the wildernesse, I wander.'

Jeremy shook his head and sat back. "And to think Sopwith Hill won't commit to that."

"The stories don't come all at once, shrink-wrapped with a complimentary bookmark."

"Give me one. Just one to get a sense —"

"Well, there is this Siwash character," the Professor said. "He sits in the forest — a few hundred yards that way, near Siwash Rock — counting." Counting people, the Professor went on to explain. Nobody knew why, and the Professor had only spoken with him twice since arriving. Siwash made him tea both times, their dialogue polite, cagey. He had arrived, he explained, like so many others had arrived. "I am blown here," Siwash had said, running a hand over a waxy scalp, then pulling on an ear that appeared to have two lobes. "I was washed up on the beach like all the others. Crawled free from the wreckage of an imperfect landscape onto these perfect shores. I will never leave."

He liked maps. The Professor described how dozens had been Scotch-taped to the walls of the concrete bunker that the man called home. National Geographic maps of the earth's polar regions. A black starlight globe. Various cylindrical and conical projections. All these hung in the relative darkness of the concrete room, glowering obscurely from the shadows in a bunker that had once been a pillbox, an armed outpost on a rock outcropping above Siwash Rock. A vantage point from which the authorities once thought they could repel Japanese invaders during the dark and paranoid days of Vancouver's World War II.

But what about this counting? "Is there a number?" At their second meeting, the Professor tried to press down on this issue. He had decided the tea was China Black. "Is it a number you're waiting to reach? Like a thousand, or ten thousand?"

No number, Siwash told him, and became elusive.

"Maybe a head count of some kind," Jeremy offered, intrigued by the idea. The map-lined pillbox in a public park was richly eccentric, but it sounded cosier that his father's set-up.

"Caruzo thinks it is a tally, yes. But even he doesn't know," the Professor said, nodding. In fact, Caruzo did not speak of Siwash often, and the Professor had never seen them together. He imagined it would be like having two evangelists in the same room. They could talk, but they already had views on everything, and their words were better directed at others.

"Caruzo," Jeremy said. "I suppose he is another story."

"I would think so, perhaps even the first chapter of a longer story. I understand you see him from time to time at the restaurant around breakfast."

"Yes, thank you. He's been a Friday regular for the past month. If you have any more people living around here who want free coffee and cigarettes and maybe a snack in the morning, you just send them along."

"Those volumes you couldn't handle," the Professor pointed out.

"I suppose you sent him to see how I was doing?" Jeremy said.

"And you also sent him back with word that you wanted to see me," the Professor responded. "So we have both used him as a messenger, haven't we?"

They drifted into silence for a moment, the fire dropped to coals.

"I remember a photograph. The three of us at the lagoon," the Professor said eventually.

Jeremy looked up sharply at the mention of it. "Under the cherry trees."

"That's the one," the Professor said, smiling. He cut off some more duck. "You see how there is also a great deal of us held in this wilderness."

Jeremy didn't know what to think of that comment. They were silent for a few minutes.

"You wanted to see me. To ask me something, I suspect," the Professor said finally. "But I sense you are suddenly shy. Perhaps I can balance the scale by asking my favour of you first."

Jeremy nodded in agreement.

"I need someone in the city. Someone to do some research."

It surprised him. "Why not Caruzo?" he heard himself say.

"Well, Caruzo can't read, for one."

"Why not you?"

"Fine then."

"Sorry. Tell me."

The Professor took a moment before continuing. "Babes in the Wood," he said finally.

Jeremy waited for more, and when nothing came said: "Who are —"

"Who *were* murdered in Stanley Park, not far from here. Two children, conventionally understood to be brothers, although there have been different views on this over the years. In any case, two children, unsolved murder. Still, this story is not a murder mystery, understand. I am interested in the myths surrounding their death, about their bodies still being buried here in the park. About related matters."

"And when exactly?" Jeremy said, growing faintly nervous.

"Oh," the Professor said. "A long time ago. Fifty years. It was in all the papers at the time. Two little kids, murdered with a small hatchet in this park. Not half a mile from where we're sitting, in fact. The killer, never found. The reason, inexplicable. The repercussions —" And here the Professor leaned forward and looked at his son very closely. "The repercussions still spilling down through the years."

There was a second of silence.

"All right," Jeremy said. "What can I do?"

"I need details," the Professor said. "You could try the library."
Jeremy thought for a second.

"Yes?" the Professor pressed, canting a bit forward.

"Sure," Jeremy said. "I promise."

"There are stories, you understand?" The Professor was looking again directly at his son. "There is Siwash and there are others. There are individual stories written in code. Say mental illness, say what you like. But I have come to understand recently, very recently, that in these stories there are threads that weave together into a single chord. A single story lives at the centre of it all, and by this story the others might be interpreted."

"These kids," Jeremy said, voice flat.

"Their death. Perhaps."

Jeremy nodded, feeling helpless. A promise to do some research didn't sound like a lot coming out. Released into the dark air between them, it gained volume and weight, instantly.

"Well then?" the Professor said, thinking they should move on before the boy reconsidered. "Do tell." And with this comment, he lay back in the ferns, his head outside of the pool of firelight, supported in his two interlocked hands, elbows flaring out and framing his darkened face. A coal sparked and threw an instant of reflection into his black pupils.

"The Monkey's Paw is everything I want to do," said Jeremy, by way of introduction. "Jules and I work exceptionally well together. We understand each other precisely."

"Jules Capelli, yes. Plus, the alliterative Anya Dickie likes you," the Professor said.

Jeremy nodded. "That review helped us, I can tell you. We were in deep trouble there for a while," he said. Even thinking about it made him nervous.

The Professor waited.

"Money trouble," Jeremy explained.

"Ah, yes," his father said. He was not overly familiar with this kind of trouble.

"No matter how good people say we are, the downtown east side makes some people uncomfortable. That is, some of the foodies we would otherwise be attracting won't go there. Plus, what we do is not always cheap to begin with. A prawn raised in a vat in the basement of a factory in Singapore is about half the price of a fresh prawn from the Queen Charlotte Islands. Not as good, clearly, but cheaper."

"Fascinating," said the Professor, who was enjoying the ideological drama captured in the story. "It is inefficient, perhaps, to have your passion for local ingredients."

"Maybe that's it," Jeremy said. "In any case, I almost crashed the whole thing. It was close. Debts, credit cards, cheques. I'm bad with that stuff. And even now, it would be misleading to say we're hugely profitable."

"I see," the Professor said. "Now you feel pressure from the moneylenders, and it is distracting you from what you love to do, is that it?"

"Sure. Partly."

"And despite these pressures, you have little control over increasing your own business. So you simply cook well, remain devoted to your culinary principles, and hope that a lot of people will eventually come to appreciate your efforts and come to your restaurant and spend money, et cetera, et cetera."

Jeremy nodded wearily. "Basically. The strain of which brings me to the question."

The Professor sat up and poked the coals. "I'm listening."

"Dante Beale."

His father stopped poking the coals and looked at him. "What about Dante?"

"He's offered to invest. He likes the restaurant. He knows I'm struggling. He believes in what I'm doing."

"The barista boy," the Professor said.

"He *employs* baristas," Jeremy said. "Thousands of them too. Inferno International Coffee is huge — you have to give him credit for that."

"Credit," said the Professor, thinking back. "Isn't that what he gave you?"

"He guaranteed my bank loan. This arrangement would be quite different."

"I'm sure."

"This would be an opportunity to let someone else worry about the money for a change."

The Professor was skeptical.

"I know this is unusual," Jeremy said, "but I'm asking for advice here. You know him."

"I don't trust him."

"And you've been neighbours, friends, for what ... twenty years?"

"I didn't say, 'I don't like him.' I said, 'I don't trust him.'"

"Explain."

"He's wrong for you," the Professor said, not quite explaining.

"It's a bad situation. Did I mention the bank is not happy?"

"You didn't, no."

"And Inferno is powerful. Big and getting bigger."

"I've heard. How many of those awful coffee shops are there now?"

"Hundreds. All over North America. He could really help."

"Dante will not help you do what you want to do," the Professor stated bluntly. "Dante is only one thing. He has always been the same thing in the many years I have known him. At one time I admired his focus, but now I see the man for what he is and what his worldview implies. Dante is a price. Dante is a sale. Dante abhors anything that is not a commodity. You, on the other hand ... well, 'local bounty.' That's pretty good, actually. That's a pretty good idea."

"I agree but —"

"He is about only one thing, Jeremy. Mammon. The almighty dollar."

"Well," Jeremy said. "In those terms Dante is about $230,000 to me."

"Which means what exactly?" the Professor asked.

"The amount of my debt, more or less."

The Professor winced. "That's a lot, isn't it?"

Jeremy looked away into the darkness. It certainly was a lot.

"And the price for this timely assistance?" the Professor asked.

"Majority ownership. I work the rest off."

"I see. He then owns you."

"I may not be worth much without him."

"Bankrupt or not, I am under the impression you are exceptionally good at what you do," the Professor said, giving an atypical compliment, back-handed or otherwise.

"So, how should I respond to this offer?"

"*Turn him down,*" the Professor said, articulating each word very clearly.

They were staring across the embers at each other. For reasons Jeremy could not yet explain, this answer was suddenly what he had expected all along. And he saw himself as a fool for having asked, for having thought that silence could be fruitfully ended between them. "That's it?" he said.

The Professor raised his eyebrows and shrugged.

"That's all I get after slogging through the forest to talk to you? Coming here in the middle of the evening?" Jeremy gestured angrily at the duck carcass, still hanging on the roasting stick, which toppled on cue into the fire pit.

The Professor responded calmly. "Did you want more advice or just different advice?"

The silence bristled.

"Why not talk to Jules about this?" the Professor asked.

"It's complicated," Jeremy said, but this reminder swamped his anger with different feelings. There would be problems here, he knew. And Jules was a little bit like the Professor in her commitment to the things she believed. "Me going broke wouldn't be doing her any favours either," he said finally, shaking his head.

"Even so," the Professor continued, "you would have held onto the one thing that provides you with stability and roots."

At which point Jeremy had to lie back in the ferns and laugh out loud. "Roots? Listen to you."

"All right, all right, keep it down," said the Professor. "I realize my present work puts at risk my credibility on the matter of stability, but if you just understood how important —"

Jeremy sat up straight. "Are you the voice crying in the wilderness?" he said. "I mean *the* voice." Then he lay back and let himself laugh some more. His father now allowed a small smile.

"You know, quiet is normally a good policy around here," the Professor said. "The attention one attracts is not always good attention."

Tell me about it, thought Jeremy.

A MAP OF THE CITY

Madeleine Thien

Excerpt from the short story
"A Map of the City"

In the years after I left home, I used to glimpse my parents in unexpected places. I would see the two of them in the Safeway, my mother standing patiently by while my father weighed oranges in his hands, feeling for signs of imperfection. I would see them on the opposite sidewalk, blurred and old, traffic streaming between us. During these sightings, I never felt the urge to join them. I only wanted to remain where I was and watch while they negotiated their way through the aisles, their bodies slow with old age.

Of course, it was never them. By this time, my father had returned from Indonesia and my mother was living alone in an apartment outside of the city. I had not seen my parents side by side in almost a decade. It would be some other couple, vague and kindly looking, who would catch my eye, remind me of things I thought I had long forgotten.

My husband Will once said that longing manifests itself in sight. In therapy groups, people tell of seeing their loved ones long after they have passed away — a father, sitting in his usual armchair, a sister in the garden.

To Will, I said that longing was not the point. In any case, my parents were still alive.

Will said, "Death isn't what I meant exactly. And don't be so sure about the longing."

"Why not?"

"Because it's plain. You miss them all the time."

I let this sit for a moment, then I broke into a smile. Will was unfailingly patient. He let me dance around a topic but never come to rest on it. He forgave all my inabilities, first and foremost my unwillingness to speak with him about my family.

At first, this allowed me to put all my energy into the here and now, our present life. In hindsight, I see it also freed me to walk away, at least for a period of time, from certain obligations. I asked myself, does my family have any hold on me? For a long time, I tried to say *no*. We would remain separate from each other until the end. But then Will and I married, and when I thought about my own future, the possibility of children, I saw how the tables had turned. *Yes*, I realized. Their hold would never diminish. For the first time I was struck by the disarray of my life. Walking away had not saved me as I had hoped it would.

My father used to own a furniture store.

That is a sentence I might have said to Will, but I can't recall now exactly which details I gave him.

My father used to own a furniture store and the store was named Bargain Mart. The front was made entirely of glass. A big white awning sheltered the entrance. I still remember that, when I was a child, my grade 1 teacher singled me out. "Oh, yes," she said. "It's your father who owns that store, isn't it? The furniture store on Hastings Street."

I nodded proudly. Even to me, at that age, the idea of owner-ship meant something. Along Hastings Street was the bakery, the deli, the children's clothing store, the light shop. My father's furniture store was one among these and it had its place in the accepted order of things.

On weekends, I assisted my father. I turned over the CLOSED sign. Together, we sprayed Windex on the front windows. The couches were used, or sold on consignment, so you could find an armchair for ten or fifteen dollars, a sofa for thirty. When my father made a sale, he let me deliver the receipt and change to the customer, which I did proudly.

I was six years old then, and I dreamed commercials. In my mind, my father was the owner of an exciting retail outlet. Soon the furniture store would be a household word: *Bargain Mart*. Parents would announce to their children that this weekend's excursion would be to *Bargain Mart*, and children across the city would look up from their Cream of Wheat and cheer. From where we lived in Burnaby, in the spill of houses beneath the mountain, to Maple Ridge and Vancouver, people would flock to my father's store, carting away sofas on their shoulders, tables in their arms. My father standing at the front, hands on his hips, young.

My parents were thirty when they emigrated from Indonesia. The first business they owned in Vancouver was a restaurant, The All Day Grill. My father cooked up steak and eggs, sweet and sour pork on rice and beef dip sandwiches.

I was born shortly after they arrived in Canada. When I was five months old, the doctors diagnosed me with kidney failure. This is what my mother told me — after twelve hours of cooking at the restaurant, my father would drive to the hospital. He would sweep into the nursery and gather me in his arms, careful of all my intravenous tubes. We paced the hallway, my father rolling the iv cart ahead of us. My mother says I recognized him. In his arms, I was peaceful, but when he returned me to my bed, I wailed and fought. The nurses complained that each time my father left, I threw tantrums, then shredded my cotton blanket with my tiny hands. I lost a kidney, but came out of the hospital when I was one. The restaurant went under.

Perhaps because of this, my father would often say that I had ruined his life. This was never said in a malicious manner, or one meant to wound me. It was matter-of-fact, the way one might speak of a change in the weather or an accident far away. If something was troubling him, my father would give a slow shake of his head. "Ever since you were born, Miriam, my life has been terrible." The smallest hint of a smile.

When I tell people this, laughing, they shake their heads in disbelief. I suppose I can understand how these words might sound to a stranger. Insensitive. Cruel. But this is not so. Between my father and me there was always a tacit understanding. Despite the teasing, he had an unwavering faith in me. "My daughter, Miriam," he said to everyone. "When she grows up, she is going to buy her parents a big house."

I would hold onto his hand when he said this, my face glowing with pride.

Of course my father never expected such things from me. It was only a joke, a laughing aside to tell me that his faith in me was abundant. Still, in the years after I left home, I wanted it to be true. I wanted to present my father with a house, hand him the key to his perfect life. By that time, he was living alone. The years had taken their toll on my family and he was estranged from my mother and me.

I needed to ask him, *Have I disappointed you?* but the question itself seemed too simple. What kind of answer could he give? We had failed each other in so many unintended ways and then we had drifted apart. My father seemed lost in the past and I did not trust myself to guide him into the present. So I kept my distance and thought from time to time how things might have turned out differently. If I had been the kind of daughter I never was, faithful and capable, who could hold a family together through all its small tragedies.

Bargain Mart, with its hall of couches, is now a restaurant. The floor-to-ceiling glass nicely curtained. Ethiopian, my mother thinks, or is it Japanese? Some mornings I wake up remembering the store, not how it looked inside but how it looked when you stood at the front, at the glass, the view of the street and the stores across. It is not the kind of place you can find so easily now, a neighbourhood furniture store, family-owned.

As a child, I faked illness in order to be taken there. Once, I tiptoed into the bathroom and held the blow-dryer up to my face. Then I stood at my parents' bedside. Two hands pressed to my stomach, I whispered, "Ache." A pause. Then, "*Ache.*" My mother eyed me suspiciously. But my father, somehow, believed me. He held the palm of his hand to my forehead and his face filled with worry.

While I lounged in bed, my father brought me Eggo waffles, a glass of milk, and one tablet of aspirin crushed soft as sand. Then he called my grade 1 teacher to tell her I was sick again. Instead of school, he would take me with him to the furniture store.

Together, we walked across the front lawn, the cold grass crunching like snow under our shoes. I held both hands over my stomach and watched my breath unroll ahead of me, a white windsock. My father scraped ice off the windshield in scratchy lines, he leaned his body far across the car, arms out like a swimmer. After he was done, we sat in silence, watching the ice melt in little triangles off the windshield. When the car was warm enough, my father said, "Okay," and I replied, "Okay." We rolled forward on the grass. He turned down the alley, exhaust lifting like a plume behind us. The car lumbered down Hastings Street, past the bakery and the deli and the light shop.

In front of the store, we stood shivering on the sidewalk while my father fit the key into the lock. When the door jingled open, the lemony smell of cleanser wafted out. My father mopped the floors every night before closing and the scent stayed trapped inside until morning. In the store, all the couches seemed to call to me — the creaky recliner, the velvet love seat. I ran ahead of him into the maze of sofas.

Along one wall there was a closet storage room. It had no door and my father had hung a shower curtain there instead. On my sick days, I slept inside the closet. My bed was a plastic lawn chair. When customers began to arrive, my father pulled the shower curtain closed so that I could sleep.

"Dad," I said once, unable to see around the corner to where he was sitting. "What are you doing right now?"

"Right now? I'm trying to imagine what other people see when they come into the store."

"How come?"

He paused thoughtfully. "I'm the salesman. I must understand the buying patterns. Then I can find some way to convince them that they need this couch or that chair."

"Oh," I said. "It's like an argument."

"A bit like one. Only there's no fighting. Just persuasion. That's the beauty of my job. The best salesmen do that, they convince you to see their point of view."

There was a radio he kept on his desk at the back, and he sang along to the John Denver song "Take Me Home, Country Roads," his voice filled with gusto. "You look a little like him," my father joked. "With those ears on you."

I climbed out of the lawn chair. Walking in my bare feet, I

took my father by the hand, pointing out the pieces I liked. "Don't sell this one while I'm at school," I told him. "Or this one. I put my name on it." He looked at the scrawl in blue crayon on the upholstery: *Miriam*. No anger. Too tired, maybe, like the time I begged him to let me mow the lawn and I promptly ran over the electrical cord, severing it in two. No anger there, either.

In the closet, I could always get a feel for the way things were going in the store. Rarely was business brisk. My father was not the type to push anyone into a purchase. "Big commitment to buy a couch," he said to one person. "It's important to be sure."

To someone else, he said, "This piece here? Oh, yes. See the way it reclines. Very smoothly. Just like new. Yes, a very good price."

On the other side of the shower curtain, a pair of shoes stopped and waited. A low whistle. The man talked about inflation, the way a dollar just didn't go as far as it used to.

"Yes," my father replied, his voice filled with sympathy. "That is very true."

The shower curtain opened suddenly and I was blinded by light. "Jesus Christ," the man said, stepping backwards, his hand dropping the curtain.

My father hurried forward. "My daughter, she is resting."

The man stared at me, aghast. I smiled helpfully.

"No problem, no problem." My father nodded at me and yanked the shower curtain closed.

"I'm very sorry. I didn't realize," his voice trailed off.

"No problem," my father said again, boisterously. "She is resting only."

Their feet disappeared from sight, the door jingling soon after.

That afternoon, I watched my father read the newspaper, cover to cover, retaining names and news for his casual conversation. "Trudeau," he said to one customer, then shrugged his shoulders, or "Bill Bennett," or "Thatcherism," the word hanging disturbingly in the air.

Outside, rain poured down in thin streams off the white awning, splashing the sidewalk. There was a lull and my father reached into his desk and pulled out a handful of photographs. I had seen them before, Indonesian plantations spread out under wide skies. He tapped his index finger down, pointing out the house where my parents lived before coming to Vancouver. Stilts like legs holding it off the ground. My father ran his hands over the trees in the backdrop, told me about the fruit, strange and exotic things, rambutan and durians. From memory, he sketched a map of Irian Jaya — the shape like a half-torso, one arm waving — where my parents had lived for a short time. "Do you miss it?" I asked him.

"What's to miss?" he said, smiling gently.

I didn't know.

"I only miss the fruit," he said, putting the photos away. "The country, I've almost forgotten."

My father and I played tic-tac-toe until six o'clock, and then my father closed the store. While he counted the cash, I washed the floor, dragging the mop behind me as I paced back and forth. Eventually, my father took the mop from me and scrubbed diligently at the scuff marks and water stains. Then he turned the lights down and locked the door behind us. We drove home in the Buick, past the Knight and Day Restaurant that had burned down three times in the last two years. My father pointed through the windshield. "See that restaurant?" he said. "That restaurant's burning down *night and day*." He laughed almost hysterically.

At home, my father washed the vegetables for dinner. I set the table so that everything was ready by the time my mother came home at seven, exhausted from her job at the tire store.

Over dinner, my parents inquired after each other's day. My mother spooned some liver onto my plate, wondering aloud why I might be sick. "Did you eat something bad?" she asked.

"Here," my father said, lifting his chopsticks toward me. "Eat more vegetables."

Afterward, as he was clearing the dishes, they worried over the day's receipts. Only two small sales. "January is like this," my father said. "It's to be expected."

"December was like this too," my mother replied.

"It will pick up."

My mother sighed. "It will have to."

She and I lay down on the couch to watch television. She fell asleep almost instantly, her face buried in my neck.

That night, I slept between them. They stayed on far sides of the bed, me in the middle drifting from one side to another in all their empty space. In the morning, my mother woke first. I could see her in the dark, reaching for her clothes. When I waved goodbye, she hovered above me, planting a kiss on my forehead. Then she kissed my father. By the time he opened his eyes, she was already dressed and gone.

I have lived in Vancouver all my life. I seldom pass through the old alleys and neighbourhoods where I grew up, but when I do my memory astonishes me. How can it be that this street is exactly the way I remember it? I look for the passage of twenty years, find it only in the height of the trees. But the street itself is the same, the crosswalk and stop sign, the broken pavement, *step on a crack, break your mother's back*, the glass storefronts.

When I was twenty-one, the familiarity of this city comforted me. I was waitressing then, working odd jobs. Every night my girlfriends and I stayed late at the bar, lighting cigarettes, throwing shots of vodka straight back. Men came and went; it was nothing. Some nights, we dropped our clothes on the sand and swam in the ocean. Bitterly cold, it shocked us sober. Other times, I drove along the coast, the sky blacked out. I'd park and watch the big green trees rolling back and forth in the wind and the sight would make me fleetingly happy. Legs stretched out, I would lie back onto the roof of my car and listen to the sound of my clothes flapping.

It was around this time that I met Will. He lived in an apartment down the alley from me, and I used to sit on my back porch watching him come and go. I liked his grey eyes, which seemed dignified on such a boyish face. He had a tall, stooped body and thin, wavy hair. Will has a straightforward sort of face, an open book. It's the face of an innocent, no secrets in it. Everything laid out, plain and simple.

One day I saw him coming down the alley on his motorcycle, a beautifully beat-up old thing. I walked out into his path and stood in front of him. I said I'd seen him coming and going, heard his motorcycle late at night when I couldn't sleep.

He looked at me, confused and a little embarrassed.

"I just have this feeling," I said, swaying back and forth on my feet, "that we are meant to be."

He looked at me searchingly. A surprised smile. "Who am I to argue?" he said, when he finally spoke. That was good enough for me.

That night, he brought me a helmet and fastened the straps under my chin. "Through this hoop and then back again, just like a backpack. Put your feet there," he nodded at two pedals, "and watch the pipe, it could melt your boots. It gets pretty hot. You'll find that sometimes I'll put the brakes on and our heads will collide. Don't worry, it doesn't throw me off. You can hold on here. Lean right back."

We lunged forward. I held onto his waist. The wind knocked every thought from my head. On every straight piece of road, he hit the accelerator and we seemed to lift.

At a stop light, he turned around, flipping up his visor. "I can't breathe."

"No," I said. "Me neither."

"I can't breathe when you squeeze my stomach. Can you hold me here?" He lifted my arms to his chest.

Oncoming cars drilled past us. We leaned into a curve, highway veering up. I held on for dear life. He turned around, mouthing, "Okay?"

"Okay."

The palms of my hands were flat overtop of his heart. I worried

I would stop his breathing, give him a heart attack. Sometimes I could see his face in the side mirror. The back of his body, his white shirt flapping in the wind, was touchingly vulnerable. One wrong move and we'd be flying. Me, him and the bike coming apart in the sky.

When we stopped I was out of breath. "More?" he asked.

I nodded.

"What does it feel like?"

"Like I can't get enough of it."

On the way back to the city, the moon was low and full, a bright orange round above the skyline. The mountains bloomed against sky, one after the other like an abundance of shadows. I remember watching one silent tanker floating on the water. We sped over the Lions Gate Bridge, a chain of lights. I grasped his chest, kept my eyes wide open and thought, *Things should always come this easy.*

That night I dreamed that I would never wake up. When I did, startled, exhilarated, Will was half on top of me, one bare arm reaching across my stomach, still sleeping.

Some facts seem, at first, to explain a person. Will's mother died of cancer when he was young. His father died not long after, an electrical accident at the plant where he worked. When I first walked into Will's apartment, I thought it was an elegy, a place of grief. But no, Will said he just liked to keep things simple. The walls bare, the furniture non-existent. Will slept on a mat on the floor. The living room housed his books, stacked in pyramids. He taught art history at one of the nearby colleges.

I admired his restraint. To me, his apartment was the embodiment of his uncluttered life, exactly the kind of life I aspired to — both feet planted, eyes on the future. The present tripped me up. I was forever sorting out my bearings. Will, on the other hand, was tuned toward a distant point. It seemed to me, then, that the troubles of day-to-day life would never burden him as they did ordinary people. Will was also fearless and I loved this in him. He jumped headlong into our relationship, throwing caution to the wind.

The wedding was fast, the kind that's over in half an hour and then you're outside, pictures flashing, thinking, *What just happened?*, but overcome by happiness the whole time. During the ceremony we couldn't stop laughing. Even saying our vows. Will's face was lit up like a kid's and I started laughing so hard I had to bend over, holding my stomach. A bit of hair was sticking up at the side of his head and I reached out to smooth it down. We were all laughing inside the church and even my mom, hair full of grey now, couldn't find a moment to cry.

We had rushed into marriage. I always joked it was the motorcycle that did it, swept me off my feet, and he would say, "I know it." I had no words to describe how exhausted I was that night when I walked into the alley in front of him. Afraid of everything. I thought I'd give it one last go, talk to him. At that time, something in my life was eating away at me. I couldn't shake it. And there was Will, always on the move. I should just grab hold.

My father was not present at our wedding. He called in the early morning, his voice weak and sorry. "A cold," he said, "has knocked me down."

It did not surprise me, my father's last-minute decision. At that time, he was living alone. When he left my mother, some years earlier, he had stepped away into a different kind of life, one where family obligations no longer weighed so heavily. In some ways, by leaving, he gave my mother and I our freedom. We moved on with our lives while he remained in the background, the one we had never understood. Who took his own failures so much to heart, he could no longer see past them, and obliged them by leaving.

My father rarely tried to contact me. I believed, then, that he had chosen his own circumstances and imposed solitude on himself. In some ways, this came as a relief to me. It forgave whatever obligations I owed him as his only child. When Will and I married, I was twenty-one years old and I didn't want to take my eyes off the future.

Years ago, it was a different story. My parents and I would drive across the city, going nowhere in particular, all of us bundled into the Buick. Through downtown and Chinatown — those narrow streets flooded with people — then out to the suburbs. On the highway, we caught glimpses of ocean, blue and sudden.

I was the only one of us born in Canada, and so I prided myself on knowing Vancouver better than my parents did — the streets, Rupert, Renfrew, Nanaimo, Victoria. Ticking them off as we passed each set of lights, *go, go, go. Stop.*

But nothing in Vancouver had the ring of Irian Jaya, where my parents lived in the first years of their marriage. In 1963, the country was annexed by Indonesia. They outlawed the Papuan flag, named the territory Irian Jaya, and flooded their own people onto the island. My parents, Chinese-Indonesians, arrived during this wave and lived there through the 1960s. "There were no roads," my father said, on one of our long Sunday drives. "Nothing."

My mother nodded her head. "The aborigines came into Jayapura looking for work. It was a rough town. Like a frontier. And the fighting. Do you remember the stories?" She shivered, one hand floating down to rest on my father's knee.

"People thrown from helicopters. The Indonesian army threw resistance fighters into their own valleys. There were many rumours."

Despite the violence and the political tension, my parents missed Indonesia. It came out in small ways, their English interrupted by a word of Chinese, a word of Indonesian. The exotic exclamations at the end of their sentences, *ah yah!*, or calling me to dinner, *makan, makan*. My mother told me that *irian*, a Biak word, means "place of the volcano" and that *jaya*, an Indonesian word, means "success." But those were the only Indonesian words I learned. At home, they spoke Indonesian and Chinese only to each other, never to me. My mother would stand on the porch watching kids race their bikes up and down the back lane, and say, out of the blue, "But isn't it so much cleaner here?"

In 1969, the United Nations led a vote, the "Act of Free Choice," to allow the Irianese to determine their future. The

Irianese voted to become part of Indonesia. "Rigged," my mother told me, her eyes clouding. "And everyone knew it."

My parents said the resistance attacked the gold and copper mines. The Indonesian army, unable to penetrate the jungle, swept through villages. They burned them to the ground and people disappeared. My parents decided it was time to leave. They gave up their Indonesian citizenships for good.

"In Irian Jaya," my father told me, "the road stops dead at the jungle. If you want to reach the next town, you must go by boat or plane. You can't just get in your car and drive there." My father was suspicious of Canadian highways, the very ease of crossing such a country.

Perhaps he drove to test them. On those Sunday drives, we piled into the car, my father losing us in side streets, winding us along highways. In winter, the roads were icy with rain but we hurtled through the dark roads anyway, gutters of water shooting sky high.

On Sundays, the furniture store was closed. Month after month, the old sofas and chairs remained unsold, and my parents fell further behind on their mortgage payments. All the savings they had brought with them from Indonesia seemed to trickle in a thin river out the door, down the street, to some place from which we would never recover it. My family's luck, if a family could have luck, was running dry. This was the high point, the three of us packed in the car, my mother's voice wavering thin and high over the words on the radio. We didn't know how peaceful we were. Only years later, when my father lay in the Intensive Care Unit at Vancouver General Hospital, a thick tube in his throat to carry his breathing, did it strike me just how much the intervening years had changed us and how far away this time had gone.

There is my mother, the navigator, a map of the city unfurled on her lap. Me in the back seat, watching my father's eyes as they glance in the rearview mirror, the way he searches for what might appear. Now, with the distance of time, I look back at my parents differently — I try to reread their gestures, the trajectory of these events. If I change the way shadow and light play on them, will I find one more detail? Some small piece that I could not see before.

In the first years of my own marriage, I could not look beyond Will. Our day-to-day routine was calming to me. He brought a certain contentment to my life, a settled happiness that I had not yet experienced.

When he read late at night, I fell asleep to the scratching of his pencil, the sound of a page turning. Sometimes he would nudge me awake, show me a photograph. The spires of the Angkor Wat, or a rock painting unearthed on the Tulare River. Will has an open heart, he can see the mystery in anything. When he tapped a photo with his index finger, I allowed myself to move with him, swept up in one idea and then another, losing myself in Will's generous imagination. I opened myself up to it, letting this ancient history settle over my own small past.

By the time I was seven, the furniture store had fallen on hard times. I still accompanied my father after school or on weekends.

More and more, I caught him resting. He would be sitting on a couch, looking out the window, just waiting. He had always been a restrained man, and whatever emotions he carried he kept well hidden. Looking around at the couches and the chairs, my father simply waited in silence, turning his head at the sound of the door opening.

One night at dinner, my mother bowed her head. "We better sell now," she said, her voice low.

Beside me, my father ate quietly, bowl held in one hand, his chopsticks lifting slowly.

"There is nothing else we can do. We can't afford it any more."

I pretended I wasn't listening, the polite thing to do. I kept eating, with my legs swinging quietly under the table.

"What about the mortgage?" she asked, shaking her head. "We can't pay the mortgage or the car payments. At this rate we will lose the house, not just the store. Please, don't be so stubborn."

My father pushed his plate away, then stood up and left the table. Beside me, my mother sighed and continued eating. When she was done, she pushed her chair back and went upstairs. I was always the last one. Sitting on my own, I'd forget all about dinner and let my mind wander. Sometimes I was still there at nine or ten at night, lost in thought, my bowl still half full. All the light in the kitchen gone so I would curl my legs up on the chair and rest my face on the table. Small bits of rice stuck to my cheek. Eventually my mother would come and take the bowl away.

That night, my parents went into the bedroom to argue. Their voices were faint through the house like a distant television.

Someone slammed a door hard. Eventually I got up and tipped my own bowl of food over the garbage. When I went upstairs to bed, all the doors were closed and the house was quiet.

The next morning, my parents started up again. I was already sitting at the table, eating breakfast.

My father came out of the bedroom and circled the kitchen table. "What do you want me to do? What do I do when the store is sold?"

"Go back to school. Do something for yourself, make yourself employable."

"I am employed. I'm working as hard as I can. Is it so disappointing to you, everything that I have done?"

She shook her head impatiently. "Don't be ridiculous."

I stared from one to the other. My father laughed suddenly. It was a harsh sound, sad and bitter. He smiled, one hand waving up into the air then falling slowly. "Who is it?" he asked.

"What do you mean?"

"The one at work, the one who promoted you."

"I don't know what you're talking about."

"What did he do that for, promote you? In Indonesia you couldn't hold down a job. Here, a promotion. I can't understand it."

My mother looked at him in disbelief. "I was miserable there. You know that."

"You tell me," he said, his voice even. "How is this possible? Remember, you are the one who wanted to leave Irian Jaya. It is because of you that we are in this situation."

My mother burst into tears. "This has nothing to do with who you are and who I am. I am only trying to do what is best for us."

I stood then, picking up my plate. My hands were shaking and the dish tipped, spilling milk and cereal. My father looked at me, then turned toward the sink. He picked up a cloth and ran it, end to end, across the table. Then he turned back to my mother. "I do not think so," he said. "And it is not your decision."

My mother picked up her purse and walked out the back door, the screen swinging behind her.

"I'm doing the best I can," my father said. "Your mother, she wants everything. Do you see that? She wants everything."

I tried hard to behave as I'd been brought up, to ignore what I was not involved in and to hold my tongue and pretend I was deaf and blind. Eyes lowered, I stared at the table.

Afterward, when he bundled me up and walked me to school, he said nothing. He let go of me and I ran into the schoolyard, immersed myself in hopscotch and California kickball. I would adapt. He knew I would grow up and do well here. My father turned around, he started walking home again.

For six more months, the store pushed on. Whenever my father thought he might have to give in, somebody came along and bought a couch. A sofa here, a love seat there — this somehow kept us going from week to week.

Now, looking back, I see that the store had an impoverished look to it, that the couches were old and worn, and that my father, once so patient a salesman, had begun to speak to his customers with an air of quiet desperation. At home, my parents had fallen into a deep silence, speaking to each other only when necessary. "Tell your mother that —" my father said, and I was thrown out like a line between them.

On the weekends, I kept my father company in the store. Sometimes, during the afternoon lulls, I fell asleep on the lawn chair. Once, just waking, I sat up and listened for my father's movements, the creak of his chair, his shoes on the polished floor. There were no sounds at all. Thinking he had disappeared, I pulled the curtain open and ran out. I can see myself, a small girl in blue sweatpants and a faded T-shirt, my John Denver ears, all keyed up. He was sitting at his desk. I looked at his face, his furrowed brows, and asked, "Is there something wrong?"

He looked at me for a long time, his expression melancholy. Then he said, "No. There is nothing to worry about."

Not long after, the bank sent my father a letter saying they were foreclosing on our mortgage. When we moved out of our house on Curtis Street, my father would be the one who packed. While my mother kept me occupied on the back lawn, he would go from room to room, throwing everything into bags, my mother's good dresses and shoes, my toys and socks. Driving away to our new apartment, we would turn back to the house, catch a glimpse of our excess furniture lined up on the sidewalk, the line of boxes and Glad bags stretching down the block. Years later, my father would tell me that when he looked over at my mother in the passenger seat, he had felt only despair.

But that day in the furniture store, my father was calm. He stood up from his desk and walked to the door. He turned the sign over and said to me, "I don't think anyone else is coming today." My father gathered my crayons and drawings and I started telling him about the book I was reading, Dumbo and the crows and how at the end he flies and his mother who cradles him in his trunk. My father just looked at me. This was the last business he would ever own.

That was the end of it. I don't recall stepping inside the store again. When I saw it next, the windows were papered over so that I could no longer see the interior from the road.

The other day, my father telephoned to give me the news. "Fighting in Aceh," he says. "And another ferry has gone down."

I tell him about Will's new teaching position.

He says, "That's very good news."

This new relationship we have is tentative, like moving in the dark. A step forward, then back, feeling for the perimeter of the room.

"Are you free?" I ask. "We can have coffee."

"I can't drink coffee," he says. "It gives me heartburn."

I file this information away, then I suggest tea.

Silence, as he considers this. "Will you come in the car? I'm having some problems with my knees."

"Of course."

When I hang up the phone, I feel a surge of hope, of fierce protectiveness over him. Perhaps, knowing everything that has brought us here, I would redraw this map, make the distance from A to B a straight line. I would bypass those difficult years and bring my father up to this moment, healthy, unharmed.

But to do so would remove all we glimpsed in passing, heights and depths I never guessed at. That straight line would erase our efforts, the necessary ones as well as the misguided ones, that finally allowed us to arrive here.

NOTES ON CONTRIBUTORS

George Bowering has written more than forty books. He has won the Governor General's Award twice: once in 1969 for poetry, for the books *Rocky Mountain Foot* and *The Gangs of Kosmos*; and again in 1980 for fiction, for *Burning Water*. In 2003, he was appointed Canada's first Poet Laureate. His short-story collection *Standing on Richards* was published in 2004.

Wayson Choy's first novel, *The Jade Peony*, won the Vancouver Book Award in 1996. He shared the Trillium Award that year with Margaret Atwood. His bestselling memoir, *Paper Shadows*, was shortlisted for the Governor General's Award and won the Edna Stabler Award for Creative Non-Fiction. Choy lives in Toronto. His most recent novel, *All That Matters*, was shortlisted for the Giller Prize in 2004.

Douglas Coupland is the author of *Generation X, Microserfs, All Families Are Psychotic, Hey Nostradamus!, Eleanor Rigby* and *jPod*, among other novels. He is also the author of the non-fiction titles *City of Glass, Souvenir of Canada, Souvenir of Canada 2* and *Terry: The Life of Canadian Terry Fox*. In 2004, Coupland's art and sculpture installation "Canada House" was exhibited at Toronto's Design Exchange. In the same year, he performed his one-man play, *September Ten*, at the Royal Shakespeare Society in Stratford-upon-Avon. He lives and works in Vancouver.

Zsuzsi Gartner is the author of the story collection *All the Anxious Girls on Earth*, which includes "City of My Dreams" and was published in Canada and the United States. She is also an award-winning journalist and has worked as a senior editor at *Saturday Night*. Her fiction has been published widely in magazines, including *The Malahat Review, Geist, Saturday Night* and *Toronto Life*, and has been nominated for national awards. She is on the faculty of The Banff Centre's Wired Writing Studio. She lives in Vancouver.

William Gibson lives in Vancouver, British Columbia, with his wife and their two children. His first novel, *Neuromancer*, won the Hugo Award, the Philip K. Dick Memorial Award, and the Nebula Award in 1984. Gibson is credited with having coined the term "cyberspace," and having envisioned both the Internet and virtual reality before either existed. He is also the author of *Count Zero, Mona Lisa Overdrive, Virtual Light, Idoru,*

All Tomorrow's Parties, *Pattern Recognition* and *Burning Chrome*, which contains the story "The Winter Market."

Pauline Johnson was born March 10, 1861, at Six Nations Indian Reserve, Canada West. She later adopted the native name Tekahionwake, meaning "double wampum." Johnson was popular in her day as an entertainer, reading poems about her native heritage in tours that crossed Canada, the United States and England. Her first poetry collection, *White Wampum*, was published in 1895. She later wrote *Legends of Vancouver*, a collection of tales that includes the story "The Two Sisters." Johnson died in 1913 in Vancouver.

Malcolm Lowry was born in 1909 in New Brighton England. He was educated at the Leys School, Cambridge, and St. Catharine's College. Between school and university he went to sea, working as a deckhand and trimmer for about six months. His first novel, *Ultramarine*, was published in 1933. He went to Paris and wrote several short stories there before going to New York. He then left for Mexico. By 1940, the ever-wandering Lowry had settled in British Columbia. During the period 1941–4, when he was living in a squatter's shack in Dollarton, B.C., he worked on the final version of *Under the Volcano*, his most famous work. Lowry died in England in 1957. "The Bravest Boat" appeared in the posthumously released book *Hear Us O Lord from Heaven Thy Dwelling Place* (1961).

Lee Maracle's critically acclaimed books include *Sojourners and Sundogs, Ravensong, Bobbie Lee, Daughters Are Forever, Will's Garden, Bent Box* and *I Am Woman*. She has contributed to and co-edited several anthologies, including the award-winning *My Home As I Remember*. She is currently the Distinguished Visiting Professor of Canadian Culture at Western Washington University. A member of the Sto:lo Nation, Lee Maracle is of Salish and Cree ancestry.

Shani Mootoo was born in Ireland and grew up in Trinidad. She is the author of a book of short stories, *Out on Main Street*, and a novel, *Cereus Blooms at Night*, which was shortlisted for the Chapters/Books in Canada First Novel Award and the Giller Prize. She is also the author of a collection of poetry, *The Predicament of Or*. A filmmaker and visual artist, she has written and directed several videos, and her paintings and photo-based works have been exhibited internationally.

Alice Munro's fame abroad is matched by the admiration she enjoys in Canada, where she has won the Governor General's Award three times. Her most recent collection, *Runaway*, won the 2004 Giller Prize. Awards for her past collections include the W. H. Smith Prize in the United Kingdom; the National Book Circle Critics Award in the United States; the PEN/Malamud Award for Excellence in Short Fiction; the Rea Award for the Short Story; the Giller Prize, the Trillium Prize and the Libris Award. She lives in Ontario and British Columbia. Her other books include: *Lives of Girls and Women, Dance of the Happy Shades, Something I've Been Meaning to Tell You, Who Do You Think You Are?, The Moons of Jupiter, The Progress of Love, Friend of My Youth, Open Secrets, The Love of a Good Woman* and *Hateship, Friendship, Courtship, Loveship, Marriage*, which includes the story "What Is Remembered."

Stephen Osborne is the editor-in-chief of *Geist* magazine and one of the founders of Arsenal Pulp Press. His regular column in *Geist* has won the Western Magazine Award for Best Column and has been a finalist two other times. He has also won a B.C. Writers Federation Creative Non-Fiction Prize, the 2004 Vancouver Arts Award for Writing and Publishing, the 2004 CBC Literary Award for travel writing and a Maclean Hunter Arts Journalism Residency at the Banff Centre for the Arts. Osborne is the author of *Ice & Fire: Dispatches from the New World*, published in 1999. His first novel, *For You Who Grow Pale at the Mention of Vancouver*, will be published in 2005.

Timothy Taylor is a recipient of a National Magazine Award, winner of the Journey Prize, and the only writer ever to have three stories published in a single edition of the *Journey Prize Anthology*, as he did in the fall of 2000. He is the co-author of *The Internet Handbook for Canadian Lawyers;* his short fiction has appeared in Canada's leading literary magazines and has been anthologized in such publications as *Best Canadian Stories* and *Coming Attractions*. His travel, humour, arts and business pieces have been published in various magazines and periodicals, including *Saturday Night.* He was born in Venezuela and now lives in Vancouver.

Madeleine Thien's short stories have been published in the *Journey Prize Anthology* and *Best Canadian Stories.* Her first collection of fiction, *Simple Recipes,* was published in 2001. A children's book, *The Chinese Violin,* was published the same year and accompanies a National Film Board animation short of the same title by artist and illustrator Joe Cheng. Thien is the winner of the Asian Canadian Writers' Workshop Emerging Writer Award for Fiction. Her work has been shortlisted for such prizes as the Bronwen Wallace Award, a Western Magazine Award and the CBC Literary Award.

Ethel Wilson's small but impressive output has earned her an important place in Canadian literature. The only child of an English Wesleyan minister missioned in South Africa, Wilson was orphaned at ten and sent to Vancouver to live with her maternal grandmother and several aunts. Wilson's fascination with her adopted homeland is the core feature of most of her work. Her books include: *Hetty Dorval, The Innocent Traveller* (which contains the story "Down at English Bay"), *The Equations of Love, Swamp Angel, Love and Salt Water* and *Mrs. Golightly and Other Stories.*

ACKNOWLEDGEMENTS

"Down at English Bay" reprinted from *Innocent Traveller* © 1949. Reprinted by permission.

"The Bravest Boat" reprinted by permission of SLL/Sterling Lord Literistic, Inc. © 1987 The Estate of Malcolm Lowry.

"What Is Remembered" taken from *Hateship, Friendship, Courtship, Loveship, Marriage* by Alice Munro. Used by permission of McClelland & Stewart Ltd.

"Standing on Richards" © George Bowering 2004. First published in *Standing on Richards* by Viking Canada, 2004. Reprinted by permission of the author.

Excerpt from *The Jade Peony* by Wayson Choy. Reprinted by permission of the publisher, Douglas & McIntyre (Vancouver, B.C., 1995).

"Time Zone" excerpted from *For You Who Grow Pale at the Mention of Vancouver* © 2005 Stephen Osborne. Reprinted by permission of the author.